For Jessica. When you're much, much older

1

Freddy parked the car within sprinting distance of the Nine Hills Country Club. I glanced at my watch: six fifteen.

'This guy arrives at six thirty?' I said.

Freddy nodded. 'The past three days, yeah.'

'Cameras?'

'Just one. I did it last night.'

I grabbed a pile of laminated IDs from the glove compartment and flipped through them: SFO Airport Security, Four Seasons Valet Parking, White Arrow Cab Company.

'Be careful with this guy,' said Freddy. 'I don't like the look of him.'

I smiled and clipped the cab company ID to my jacket.

'I'm not kidding,' he said. 'He's a tough looking bastard.'

'It's fine.'

I glanced at the clubhouse – a handful of Range Rovers and Mercedes sat parked in the courtyard. These people weren't tough guys, they were bankers and lawyers. A Harley Davidson sat by the main gates – any money the guy who owned it had 'LOVE' and 'GOLF' tattooed across his knuckles.

'Alright, I'll see you in a few minutes,' I said.

I put on my sunglasses, got out of the car and made my way toward the clubhouse. Its sweeping windows overlooked San Francisco Bay – anyone could be watching. I kept my head down. I crossed the courtyard, pushed open the main door and entered a marble-pillared lobby. A receptionist in a three-pocketed Valentino sports jacket sat at the main desk.

'Cab for Elizabeth Embry,' I said to him.

'Embry?' he replied. He furrowed his brow as he studied the club register. 'Are they visiting the clubhouse or the restaurant?'

I shrugged. 'Nine Hills Country Club, that's all I've got.'

He scanned another register.

'No,' he said. 'There's no Embry. Are you sure you have the right name?'

'Hang on.'

I took out my phone and pretended to dial a number.

'Yeah, the Nine Hills pick-up,' I said into the phone. 'Can you tell the client that I'm waiting in reception.' I paused a moment. 'Alright.'

I put away the phone. 'They're going to call the client,' I said.

The receptionist nodded.

As I waited, I scanned the lobby and thought about what the best play would be. I tried to imagine the guy arriving – pictured him opening the main door and heading toward the reception desk. Chances are he'd be right-handed – I'd stay to his left. If he really was the violent type, then I could use that. Not that I was looking for a fight, but a little physical contact always made my job easier. It was all about distraction.

I heard a car pull to a stop in the courtyard. I checked my watch: six twenty-eight. This would be him. My heart jumped a gear – sent my blood racing around like it was late for something. It didn't matter how good I was at this, the feeling was always the same. I loved it.

I took out my phone like I was receiving a call, and pressed it against my ear. 'Yeah?' I said into the phone. 'You're kidding? I'm at Nine Hills now.'

I addressed the receptionist for a moment. 'The name's Embry,' I said. 'But this isn't the pick-up address, it's the destination.'

As the receptionist rolled his eyes, I heard footsteps approaching the clubhouse. I held the phone back to my ear, and casually stepped away from the desk. The main door then opened – a suntanned hulk in his late thirties entered the lobby. This was our man – head shaved like a bullet, and Jesus, was he huge. A six-foot slab of concrete with no neck. Freddy wasn't kidding. I'm pretty good in a fight, but if this guy caught me he'd snap me like a fucking matchstick.

He headed for the reception desk. I headed for the main door. As we approached each other, I spoke into my phone again.

'This is the second time you've given me the wrong address, Carrie,' I said. 'You've got to start getting it together.'

The guy was thirty feet away. His jeans were 501s. His jacket, Armani – the spring collection. I knew it well. No external pockets – two internal, both in the left panel. As he walked, the left jacket panel creased differently to the right. He had a gym bag in his left hand. An iPhone in the other. He was fifteen feet away.

I continued into my phone. 'That's not what I'm saying, Carrie.'

I was nearly on the guy. Engrossed in my phone call, not looking where I was going. Three feet. Two feet. One. I passed him and gently nudged into his shoulder. He swung a heavy arm and pushed me out of the way.

'Watch where you're going!' he said.

I feigned losing balance – my left hand brushed against the silk lining of his jacket.

'Sorry,' I said to him. 'My fault.'

He didn't even look at me. He just walked to the main desk, signed in and headed out the rear door toward the tennis courts.

I continued into my phone. 'What? Nothing, doesn't matter. Look, we'll talk about it later.'

I exited the clubhouse and lowered the phone from my ear. I raised my other hand – in it was an electronic car key hanging from a fob. My heart slowed to a gentle beat. It really was too easy – fucking Armani jacket, he might as well have just mailed me the key. I glanced around the courtyard. There it was parked next to the Harley – a matte black Ferrari 458. Low-profile tires, eight cylinders, and the best part of three hundred grand. I beeped the car open, slid inside and started it up. In my jacket was a GPS jamming device about the size of a cigarette pack. I switched it on. If Armani man realized any time soon that his car was gone, this would drown out its tracker signal.

I eased down the pedal, quietly swung the car out into the street and headed for Tamlin Auto.

Tamlin was a half-hour drive away – a tiny steel-shuttered garage tucked between fire escapes in The Mission. Just south of the financial center, it was a really shitty part of town. There was a doctor who worked down there – his details were written across his front door in marker pen.

I weaved down the backstreet and pulled the car into the garage bay. The sign above the entrance read, 'Tamlin Auto. Mercedes. Aston Martin. Ferrari.' Freddy was just behind me. He parked outside, hopped into the bay and clattered the shutter down behind him.

I got out of the Ferrari and threw the keys to Miguel. Miguel didn't look like much – a dopey-eyed surfer-dude – but the kid was a wizard. He immediately began clambering all over the car with his scanners and laptops – diving into the engine, sliding under the chassis, he was like a high-tech baboon at a safari park. In a couple of minutes he'd have all the car's alarms, trackers and immobilizers disabled. Untraceable.

Freddy headed over to me. 'Everything OK?' he asked.

I nodded. 'You weren't kidding. He was a big fucker.'

'Yeah, better you than me.'

He grabbed a couple of beers from the fridge and handed me one.

'Anyhow, good work,' he said.

We toasted the Ferrari's good health – we'd been waiting weeks to find one like it. Freddy downed his beer in one shot, his huge hairy knuckles wrapped around the bottle like a drooling gorilla.

'So are you coming over tonight?' he asked.

'I haven't been home in three days, Freddy, I'm wiped out.'

'Why, where did you go after the bar last night?'

I sighed wearily.

'You're kidding?' he said. 'You went home with that Judy? She had to be forty, man.'

I laughed – she was probably closer to fifty. She had these pumped-up collagen lips – I swear, she kissed me, it was like being beaten to death with a rubber dinghy. Judy, last night. Some Portuguese student on Wednesday. I couldn't remember Tuesday. I was twenty-nine, but ached like I was close to fifty myself.

'Anyhow, Linda's in town,' I said. 'I think she's coming over.'

'Oh, come on, Linda?' said Freddy.

As he threw me a look, I caught sight of Bill Tamlin grinning at the Ferrari from behind his nicotine-stained office window at the end of the garage. Bill ran the whole operation. Late forties. Constantly wired. He was speeding through a massive midlife crisis using coffee, cigarettes and cocaine as fuel. I'd worked for him for nearly two years, and in all that time I don't remember having seen him blink once.

He nodded for me to join him. Friday – it was time to settle up.

I glanced at Freddy. 'Alright, business calls.' I squeezed past the Ferrari and headed into Bill's office.

Bill twitched as he lit another cigarette. 'That's good, Michael,' he said. 'That's good, that's good, OK.'

He reached into his desk and pulled out a scratched metal box full of cash.

'The two Astons, the SLS, and this,' he said. 'That's eight grand'.

I nodded. Four cars – it had been an OK week for me. I usually managed four or five. On my best week I'd stolen eleven.

Bill started counting out cash onto his desk, mumbling numbers to himself. I didn't pay much attention, but I didn't need to. There's a hundred different ways to steal a car, but the safest and most reliable is to get hold of the key – it was also the most difficult. Bill knew the value of a good pickpocket and had never short-changed me once.

He finished counting out the cash, tucked it into an envelope and sealed it. I reached for the envelope, but he kept hold of it and started tossing it between his hands. He could be really annoying when he wanted to, and he wanted to most of the time.

He smiled at me, and I shook my head – I already knew what was coming.

'I've got a special order for you,' he said.

I laughed.

'It's not what you think,' he said. 'It's Sally's sixteenth birthday. She wants a Jeep.'

I shot him a look. 'I'm not stealing her a car, Bill.'

'There's a beautiful one parked on 25th Street. Can't be more than six months old, the right color, everything. I'll give you three grand for it.'

'It's your daughter, Bill, you really want her driving around in a stolen car? Buy her one, for Christ's sake, it's not like you can't afford it.'

'Three and a half,' he said.

I stayed silent.

'Four,' he said.

'I'm not negotiating, Bill.'

'If you think I'm going any higher than four...'

'I'm not doing it.'

'Listen, you work for me.'

'No, I work for me. If you don't want the cars any more, just say so.'

He eyed me petulantly for a moment. 'Have you any idea what a pain in the ass you can be?'

'I don't know, which answer's going to get me out of this conversation the quickest?'

He gave up. 'Alright, alright,' he said. He tossed me the envelope. 'But you're costing me a fortune here, you know that?'

'Your own daughter, Bill. You're such a cheap bastard.'

He laughed to himself. I buttoned the envelope into the inside pocket of my jacket, then headed for the door.

'Yeah, yeah, before you go,' he said. 'Yeah, some guy called yesterday, looking for you. Said he was your brother?'

I stopped dead at the door and stared back at him.

'Jon?' I said.

‘Yeah, Jon, that’s right.’

‘What did he say?’

‘Nothing. I said you weren’t here. That was it.’

I felt lost for a second. Couldn’t believe that he’d called – and here, of all places. I hadn’t been home, there was probably a message for me there.

‘I didn’t know you had a brother,’ said Bill.

I nodded.

‘I’ve got to go,’ I said.

I zipped up my jacket and headed out.

Home was a fourth-floor apartment overlooking The Embarcadero. Normally the rent would have been out of my league, but the landlord was some Japanese artist who’d decorated the apartment in his own inimitable style – black carpets, black ceilings and deep red marble walls. Etched into marble were golden images of running bulls, all hooves and glittering horns. I guess it was art, but I was the only prospective tenant who ever made an offer to live in it. Every person I’d ever brought back here said the place was a hell-hole that would drive them out of their minds in less than twenty minutes. But I actually found the place quite peaceful.

I got in and headed straight for the phone. Its display was flashing – two new messages. I picked up the receiver and hit play.

‘Message received today at four seventeen p.m.’

‘Hey, it’s me,’ came a woman’s voice. It was Linda. ‘I’m going to be a little late tonight. Around nine. Don’t do anything without me. Bye.’

The machine beeped. I listened carefully.

'Message received yesterday at six twenty three p.m.'

'Michael. It's Jon.'

I smiled. It was great to hear his voice. I hadn't heard it for over a year now.

'I hope you're well,' he said. He paused a moment. 'I need to speak to you, Michael, it's important. I don't have a cell number for you. I don't know if you're still at that Tamlin place. I'll give it a try. Call when you get this. Bye.'

The message clicked off. I eagerly thumbed through the phone's contact list, found Jon's number and hit the dial key. I waited as the number rang.

It went to voicemail.

'Hi, you're through to Jonathan Violet. Leave a message. Thanks.'

'Jon, it's me,' I said. 'I got your message. It's…it's really good to hear from you, Jon. Look, I'm home. Call me here when you get this. Or my cell, it's 415 555 397. I hope you're well. Speak soon.'

I hung up, then nodded to myself. He'd finally called.

I headed into the kitchen and opened the fridge. Three bottles of champagne – it wouldn't be nearly enough. I grabbed my keys and darted over to Plum's mini-market across the street.

'Give me six bottles of Dom Perignon, will you, Danny?' I said.

Danny threw me a disapproving look over the rims of his half-moon reading glasses.

'Six?' he said.

'Yeah, it's been a good day.'

'Been a good day a lot for you recently,' he replied. 'You keep drinking like this, you're going to end up dead, you know that?'

I sighed. 'Come on, Danny, I'm in a hurry.'

'In a hurry. Mr Big Shot, where are you hurrying to with six bottles of champagne?'

He took out his keys and unlocked a glass cabinet beneath the counter. As he started counting out bottles, I stepped over to the newsstand and grabbed the papers – the *New York Times* and the *World Review*. I quickly browsed the *Review*, looking to see if Jon was in it. As I flipped the pages, a set of footsteps stopped behind me.

'Michael,' came a woman's voice.

It was Polly, a friend of mine. She was a waitress at The Butterfly, a few blocks away. In her thirties. Skinny as a rake. Not what you'd call pretty, but sweet.

I smiled at her.

'How are you?' she asked.

'Good. And you?'

She nodded, but she looked tired. She had an eleven-year-old son, Dominic. His dad died four years ago. Polly was raising him on her own now and having a hard time of it.

'I haven't seen you in a while,' she said.

'I actually dropped by last Saturday, but there was no one home.'

'Yeah, I took Dominic down to see his grandparents. He's spending the week there.'

'How's he doing?' I asked. 'How did the magic act go?'

Polly laughed to herself. 'He messed up one of the tricks. He was really disappointed.'

'Which one?'

'With the four cards.'

'King's Castle, yeah, it's a hard one. Tell him not to worry about it.'

I'd shown Dominic a few tricks for his spot in the school show. Magic – it was one of the few things that I knew anything about.

'He was looking for you,' she said.

'Yeah, I'm sorry. I've been all over the place the past few weeks.'

I looked around, then reached into my jacket and took out the envelope full of cash that Bill had given me. I plucked out two grand.

'So listen,' I said.

'Michael…that's not why I said hello.'

'I know.'

'Really, you don't have to.'

'Don't worry, business is good.'

Like most people, Polly thought I was in the export business – luxury cars. It wasn't a million miles from the truth.

I offered her the money. 'It's fine,' I said.

There was a moment of silence. It was the usual routine – Polly maintaining that she couldn't take it, and me knowing that she would. But it was quicker today. She stared uncomfortably at the cash, then sighed.

'Thank you,' she said.

She took the money and placed it in her handbag. Danny peered down the aisle from behind the counter.

'Six bottles,' he said. 'Anything else?'

'Just the newspapers,' I replied. I turned back to Polly. 'I've got to go. Say hi to Dominic for me, will you?'

I headed back toward the counter.

'Why don't you stop by this weekend,' she said. 'I'll make you something to eat. Home-cooked meal.'

I glanced back at her. She smiled awkwardly.

'Thanks,' I said. 'But...I'm kind of busy this weekend.'

'Are you sure? Dominic won't be back until Sunday night.'

I stared carefully at her. There was definitely something attractive about her, but that's not what this was about. Polly was one of three single mothers that I was regularly helping financially these days. They were just local people who I'd go talking to – moms who were struggling, who had kids that I understood. I might have been helping them, but the truth was I needed them more than they needed me. I wasn't about to mess with that.

'I can't,' I said. 'But thanks.'

I paid for the champagne and headed home.

Saturday morning hit me with bright sunshine and a burning hangover. I ached like I'd been hit by a brick, but that was par for the course these days. I hauled myself up in bed and glanced at the phone. Jon hadn't called yet, but he was always busy, always everywhere. I can't remember the last time he'd spent more than two weeks in the city.

I grabbed a near-empty champagne bottle off the floor, took a mouthful, and glanced at Linda lying naked beside me. I smiled. She was all woman – soft hips, full breasts and thick brown hair. She looked like she belonged in a Renaissance painting. I kept my eyes on her, and for a moment felt bad that she was engaged. She was my oldest friend and one of the few people who knew anything about me. We'd always slept together, on and off, but she wanted kids now. In April she was marrying some dermatologist in LA named Kirk. I was just a last fling before she settled down to family life.

She stretched out in the bed and smiled coyly at me.

'Tell me how much you love me,' she said.

I laughed.

'Good morning,' I replied.

She rolled over and threw her arms around me. 'Come on, tell me,' she said. 'Would you climb the highest mountain for me?'

I rolled my eyes. 'Yeah.'

'What about swim the deepest ocean?'

'I don't know, is it near the mountain?'

She kissed me on the neck. 'And would you steal the most beautiful little Mercedes for me?'

'Why don't I just steal that first and you can drive up the mountain yourself.'

She smiled, then took the champagne bottle from me and raised it to her lips. She looked me up and down like I was the sexiest fucking thing on the planet. And, for her, maybe I was.

She lay back on the pillow.

'Come on,' she said. 'Just once. Tell me.'

'Fine. I love you.'

She stared blankly at me. 'That's the best you've got?'

I laughed. I leaned in to kiss her, but she stopped me.

'Don't you even come near me, dragon breath,' she said.

She pushed me away, grabbed the newspapers from the bedside table and started browsing the headlines.

'So what do you want to do today?' I asked.

She glanced distastefully at the red marble walls of the bedroom. 'Whatever, just so long as we're out of this place.'

She continued browsing the headlines. A story in the *Times* then caught her eye. Its headline read, 'Berghoff Family Executed.'

She shook her head to herself.

'They found the bodies,' she said. 'That's fucked.'

'Yeah, well...I think everyone knew they were dead.'

I glanced at the story – it made for some hard reading. David Berghoff was the chairman of the Charter Berghoff Bank in Chicago. Two months ago his family were kidnapped by an armed gang. Holding the family hostage, the gang forced Berghoff to disable the security at the bank and open the vault. The gang got inside, but the safe deposit boxes were all triple-keyed – Berghoff couldn't open them. They shot him dead and got out. However, Berghoff had managed to set off an alarm, and the gang ran into a firefight outside the bank. Four police officers died. Three of the gang burned to death in a car, but another two got away. Now Berghoff's wife and kids had been found shot in the back of the head. I swear, whenever I had any guilt about stealing for a living, all I had to do was read a story like that, and I felt like a fucking saint.

I took a mouthful of champagne and stared back at the phone. Linda smiled at me.

'Don't worry, he'll call,' she said.

I nodded. My door intercom then buzzed.

Linda glanced at me. 'Expecting someone?'

I shrugged. It had just gone nine – probably the neighbors wanting something. I pulled on some clothes and headed for the door. I hit the intercom button.

'Hello?' I said.

'Can I speak to Mr Violet, please?' came a man's voice. I didn't recognize it.

'Speaking,' I said. 'Who's this?'

'I'm Officer Philip Reed, San Francisco PD. I'm with Officer Ray Meron. We'd like speak to you.'

I froze.

Fuck.

I glanced at the living room window. It opened onto a tiny balcony that overlooked the street four floors below. About ten feet from the balcony were the upper branches of an oak. I'd jumped into the oak once before, but that was for a drunken bet – nearly broke my fucking leg.

I gathered myself. They may not be here for me. If they weren't, then not letting them in was going to raise some eyebrows. If they were, I'd jump.

I hit the intercom button again. 'Fourth floor,' I said, and buzzed them in.

The elevator was broken – eight flights of stairs would take them a minute or so.

'It's the police,' I said to Linda.

'You're kidding!'

'I might have to get out of here.'

Linda scrambled into her clothes.

'Fuck! Fuck! Kirk can't know I'm here!' she said.

I opened the apartment door. I could hear them coming up the stairs, about five flights below. Linda hopped toward the door, pulling on her shoes and zipping up her dress. I glanced up the stairs.

'Wait at the top,' I said. 'The moment they're in the apartment, get out of here.'

Linda scurried up the stairs. I quietly closed the door behind her, darted into the living room and pulled the sofa away from the wall. The sofa's rear upholstery was Velcroed in one corner. I ripped it open. Inside were neatly stacked blocks of cash in zip-lock bags. About a hundred and fifty grand. I threw the cash into a black shoulder bag and headed over to the balcony window. I opened the window slightly – left the bag beside it.

I couldn't believe this. Jon wouldn't have tipped-off the police. He might have hated that I was a thief – hated it enough not speak to me. But he wouldn't have told the police.

But maybe that's why he'd called. Fuck.

There was a knock at the door. I pushed the sofa back against the wall, then checked the window one more time. Everything was set.

I headed to the door and opened it. Two uniformed cops in their thirties stood in the hallway.

'Mr Violet?' said one of them.

'Yeah.'

'I'm Officer Reed. This is Officer Meron.'

Meron nodded politely.

'Can we come in, please?' said Reed.

I showed them into the living room and invited them to sit on the sofa. I kept myself as close to the window as I could without making it look obvious.

'Would you like to sit down, Mr. Violet?' said Reed.

'I'm fine.'

Reed and Meron glanced at each other for a moment.

'You're the brother of Jonathan Violet, the journalist?' said Reed.

'That's right,' I said.

He took a deep breath. 'It's my unfortunate duty to have to tell you that your brother was killed two days ago in a burglary at his home.'

I stared blankly at him.

'We're sorry, Mr Violet,' said Meron.

Time slowed to a halt. I couldn't believe it. This had to be a mistake.

'But...but there was nothing in the paper,' I said.

'No,' said Reed. 'We spoke to his editor at the *World Review*. They didn't want to run the story until we'd spoken to you. I understand there's no other immediate family?'

I took a deep breath. 'No,' I said.

I felt myself fading away. Like it was me who was gone – like I'd just disappeared.

I gazed at the shoulder bag resting beside the living room window. I wouldn't have jumped. I'd have told them everything. They could have locked me up and thrown away the key. Just not this.

2

Gold's Hour is an old colonial house about forty miles south of Monterey. It sits on its own down a sandy road overlooking the Pacific. The beach there is mainly rocks, but the house is beautiful. White pillars and wood. Cypress trees hiding it from the road.

It belongs to a woman named Miriam Reece – it was a gift from a grateful client that she used to look after. Miriam had lived there for about eight years, but she was moving to Seattle in the spring, and the house would soon be closed. The windows on the ocean side all had mattresses hanging from them as they aired, like the rooms were sticking their tongues out.

I lay on a bare bed in an upstairs room, and gazed at the tiny pink flowers in the wallpaper. I'd been lying there for maybe two days now. Petunias, I think. Yeah, they were definitely petunias.

A breeze blew in through the open sea-view window, and Solange padded barefoot into the room. A glossy redhead in a deep blue silk robe, she held a carved wooden pipe in her hand. Four thousand dollars a day for her.

She knelt by the bed and smiled. I nodded. She held a tiny blue flame to the pipe, and the heroin began to bubble. A rancid vinegary smell, but that was OK. Everything was OK now. I put my lips to the pipe, then laid back on the bed and just drifted – a lone pleasure boat heading out to sea.

Solange took off her robe. She eyed me for a moment, then slowly began to dance. Naked curves and sways. The sound of her feet brushing against the floorboards.

I watched as she rolled and arced – as she painted shapes in front of me. The beauty of it all. The setting sun burning gold behind her. The sea glittering to the horizon. And I began to laugh at how meaningless it all was – and those poor bastards who believe anything else. The priest who'd visited me, his eyes warm with sympathy as he'd talked about Jon and finding meaning in God's great universe. There was none.

The universe. It's like Solange. You can read whatever you want into her smile, but the truth is she doesn't give a solitary shit about you.

I closed my eyes and drifted. The pain sinking beneath the waves once again.

Olivet Memorial Park shimmered a warm green in the Tuesday morning light. I stood at the outer edge of the mourners around Jon's grave – maybe a hundred of them. A halo of crisp black suits and dresses. They were mostly colleagues of Jon's – media people – I didn't know any of them. Aside from my Uncle Harry and a couple of faces from the old neighborhood, I kept myself distant.

As we waited for Jon's editor to address us, I gazed at my parents' graves lying just beyond Jon's. They'd died in a hotel fire in Santa Cruz when I was thirteen. Jon was fifteen. I rarely visited their graves. The fire hadn't left much, and the coffins were empty aside from a few personal belongings. Whenever I wanted to feel close to them, I usually drove to Bodega Bay. It had been their favorite place.

Jon's editor, Simon Faro, emerged through the crowd. In his sixties. Manicured hands. Patek Philippe chronograph. Probably spent his life in old school ties and wood-paneled rooms.

He took his place at the graveside.

'Jon was a crusader,' he said. 'Fearless. A man who fought corruption and criminality at every turn. Who wrote with power and insight. That he should have been taken so early is not merely a tragedy for those of us who knew him, and who have lost a dear friend…but to the entire nation, which has lost a valuable voice. In an often questionable world, Jon was a haven of strength. He was the best of us. He will be missed.'

It felt like he was talking to me. Like the world would be a better place if I'd been lying there instead of Jon. And I think I'd have been alright with that trade.

Not that Simon Faro knew the first thing about me. As far as he and everyone else here were concerned, I was simply a brother that Jon had grown apart from. There was only one mourner who looked like they might have known the reason why.

She stood alone, way back from everyone. In her early thirties. Raven black hair, deathly white skin – she looked like the ghost of a woman who'd been beautiful once. I didn't know her name, but from the way she was looking at me – a harsh unwavering stare

– it was a good bet that Jon had told her something. I guessed that she must have been his girlfriend.

I felt uneasy and turned away – caught sight of Uncle Harry weaving toward me. He looked every inch like the high school math teacher he was. Ill-fitting suit. Straggly gray hair. He was my dad's brother and about the only family I had left now. Jon and I went to live with him in Oakland after Mom and Dad died. A stickler for rules and regulations, he'd tried his best, I'll give him that.

He ushered me away from the mourners, then took a folded note from his coat pocket and offered it to me.

'Simon's address,' he said.

The wake was going to be held at Simon Faro's house in Hillsborough.

'I can't go,' I replied.

'You need to be there, Michael.'

'Come on, I don't know these people.'

'Linda's going to be there.'

Linda couldn't get into town until the afternoon. But seeing her was just going to make me feel worse – she reminded me of better days, and I couldn't think about them now.

I gazed at the memorial garden just beyond us – at the tiny white envelopes resting against the rose stems. Messages from the lonely to the lost. I remembered seeing similar envelopes after my parents died – how I'd just wanted to gather them all up and throw them into the wind.

I took a deep breath and rubbed some life into my face.

'I'm thinking of getting away for a while,' I said.

Harry eyed me for a moment, then nodded. 'That might be a good idea.'

'Europe maybe, I don't know.'

I reached into my jacket pocket and took out my wallet.

'You need anything?' I said. 'Any money?'

He shook his head. I grabbed a thick wad of bills from the wallet.

'Michael, don't,' he said.

'It's fine.'

'It's not,' he said. A harsh tinge to his voice.

I stared curiously at him. I'd helped him out plenty of times in the past. After all he'd been through looking after me and Jon, I figured it was the least I could do.

As he headed back to rejoin the mourners, I took hold of his arm.

'Harry?'

He stopped and gazed into the distance.

'I had lunch with Jon a couple of months ago,' he said. 'He told me why you and he weren't speaking. I don't want your help any more, Michael, do you understand.'

I closed my eyes. Shit.

'No, wait, Harry, listen…'

'I can't have this conversation with you now.'

He released himself from my grip and headed away.

There was nothing I could say anyhow. Any way I cut it, I was a thief – part of the same business that had killed Jon. As Harry rejoined the mourners, I stared back at Jon's grave. The raven-haired girl was still there – still had her eyes on me like some vengeful spirit.

I wasn't wanted here.

I trudged back toward the cemetery gates and my Aston parked just beyond them. I cleared the gates and found Freddy leaning against the car – his lumbering frame crammed into a black suit and tie. I was surprised to see him. I hadn't told him about Jon – they'd never met. But it felt good to see a friendly face.

'I'm sorry about your brother,' he said.

I raised a smile. 'Thanks.'

'Linda told me. No one heard from you in days, I ended up calling her.'

'I'm sorry, I should have told you.'

'Look, if you'd rather be on your own…'

'No,' I said. 'No, let's get out of here.'

Freddy and I climbed the stairs of my apartment building. I tugged my tie undone – I just wanted to get out of this suit and pack a bag.

'You know where you should go?' said Freddy. 'Switzerland. I visited Mary's folks there a few years back. Just mountains and trees, it's beautiful.'

But I wasn't looking for any kind of spiritual experience. I needed bustling crowds, strange women and limitless alcohol. Losing myself in the abyss – it had always worked for me.

'I don't know,' I said. 'I was thinking about heading down to the south of France. Monte Carlo, maybe.'

'Yeah? Why not? All the cars you could want, cash, jewelry. It's like the place was built for you.'

I climbed the final flight of stairs, then glanced at my apartment door on the upper landing – I went still. The door was open. The lock, drilled.

'What?' said Freddy.

I hushed him and nodded toward the door. I listened. A knocking sound was coming from inside the apartment. I couldn't hear any voices, couldn't tell how many guys were in there. My blood started pumping. I glanced at Freddy – he nodded. A small single-handed fire extinguisher was attached to the landing wall beside me. I grabbed it and felt its weight – about ten pounds of pressurized steel – it would fucking hurt. I pressed my back against the wall and edged up the stairs, Freddy behind me. The noise inside the apartment continued. I reached the top of the stairs and gripped the extinguisher firmly in my hand. I quietly pushed open the apartment door. The black carpets had been completely pulled away, every floorboard taken up. Broken furniture piled against the cracked red marble walls. It must have made a huge noise. Not that anyone would have heard – my neighbors were at work. Midweek the building was deserted.

I took a step into my hallway and peered into the kitchen. It was trashed – cupboards ripped from the walls, broken glass like frost on the floor. The knocking sound was coming from the living room. The door was only half open, I couldn't see the entire room. Freddy and I stepped forward on the loose floorboards – they creaked. The knocking stopped. I froze and held tight to the extinguisher. But no footsteps approached the door.

The noise started again. Definitely from the living room. I signaled to Freddy – he nodded that he was ready. I gritted my teeth and charged through the door. I span around the room, wielding the heavy steel, searching the corners. But no movement anywhere – the room was empty. As Freddy quickly checked the rest of the apartment, I heard the knocking sound again. The balcony window was knocking against its frame in the breeze. I let the extinguisher swing lifelessly to my side.

Freddy reappeared in the living room. 'Motherfuckers,' he said.

I stared at the sofa. The rear upholstery was torn away. I ran over to it and peered inside – the money was gone. I stared at Freddy and tried to make some sense of it.

'How much did they take?' he said.

'A hundred and fifty.'

But I didn't give a shit about the money, nor the apartment. My mind started to race. Jon and I both burgled in less than a week? This was no fucking coincidence.

I capped the anger in me and tried to think. I took a careful look around the apartment. Absolutely everything lay in pieces. TVs and table lamps, cabinets and chairs. They'd even dismantled the tiny LED clock on the kitchen table – they'd thought there was cash in it?

'They took the money,' I said. 'But they came looking for something else.'

'Like what?' said Freddy.

'I don't know.' I thought carefully to myself for a moment. 'Something that they couldn't find at Jon's.'

My heart faded as I thought about his message.

'He was probably trying to warn me,' I said.

Fuck. This was something to do with his work, I was sure of it. I'd told the police that he'd called a few hours before he'd died – that he'd said it was important. They'd dismissed it. Jon's computers had gone, some cash, a couple of watches – it was a burglary that had gone wrong, simple as that. Bullshit.

'What do you want to do?' said Freddy. 'Go to the police?'

I shook my head. I didn't want them looking into me at all.

'Whatever these fuckers came looking for, I know I didn't have it,' I said. 'Maybe Jon still does.'

***

Freddy and I reached Jon's apartment in Chinatown twenty minutes later. It was on the third floor of an old Victorian walk-up, all dusty staircases and mahogany shadows.

Police tape sealed the edges of Jon's door. I took out the key. Before Jon and I had fallen out, he'd given me a copy. It had always served me with a glimmer of hope that he'd never asked for it back. Unless, of course, he'd changed the lock. I glanced around the corridor, then peeled away the police tape.

I slid the key into the lock. The door clicked open.

It looked like someone had driven a combine harvester through his apartment. The whole place had been shredded just like mine. Glass cabinets, smashed and torn from the walls. The hi-fi in pieces – plugs dismantled. Rotting food on the kitchen floor – every jar from every cupboard had been emptied. No way had this just been a burglary. They'd been looking for something specific. I didn't know what – documents maybe, photographs. Whatever it was, I knew that Jon kept copies of everything he was working on, on a flash drive. The drive looked like a cheap plastic cigarette lighter – it even produced a flame. Someone might take it by accident, but no one was going to steal it deliberately. We needed to find it.

'You take the bedroom,' I said. 'I'll start here.'

Jon's desk lay on its side in the far corner of the room. It was as good a place to begin as anywhere. I picked a path through the debris toward the desk. As I did, I caught sight of the bathroom. I wasn't ready for it. A near-black, dried pool of blood on the floor tiles. A mist of black droplets on the walls. I closed my eyes.

'Fuck,' I said. I kept breathing as the tears welled up in me. 'Oh, Jesus-fuck.'

Freddy stepped over to the bathroom door and quietly swung it shut.

'Let's just find this thing and get out of here,' he said. 'It's no good you being here.'

I wiped my eyes dry, then nodded. I took a deep breath and stepped toward Jon's desk.

I tried to keep myself focused, but the remnants of Jon's life lay discarded all around me. Letters, photographs and keepsakes – things I hadn't seen in years. The antique fountain pen that my mother had given him. The poem that he'd written for my dad's fortieth birthday. Beneath the broken shelves in the living room, I found the lion that he'd carved out of a piece of driftwood when we were kids. I picked it up and gazed at it.

I remembered that day. Dad had taken us all to Bodega Bay for the weekend. As Jon and I played in the sand, we came across this strange-looking piece of twisted wood in the surf. We picked it out of the water and tried to imagine how far it had traveled – what distant oceans it might have crossed. As I got ready to throw it back into the sea, Jon stopped me – he wanted to keep it. I remember telling him that it was just junk, but he took it home. A few weeks later he showed me the lion. He'd turned that lost piece of driftwood into something good. He'd given it new life.

I gazed at the lion, then carefully placed it on his desk.

Freddy and I went through everything. Bags, suitcases and clothes. Freddy even went through the bathroom, but we couldn't find the drive anywhere. It was early evening by the time we gave up.

I sat on the living room floor and stared miserably around the apartment.

'It's got to be here,' I said. 'Jon never took it out of the apartment.'

Freddy shrugged. 'Maybe they found it.'

'Then why come to my place?'

'Maybe he gave it to someone. I mean, if it was that important.'

I sighed – maybe.

Freddy leaned down and picked up a handful of photographs lying on the floor. They were pictures of my mom and dad standing outside the little bookstore they'd owned. My dad's green eyes shining away. My mom holding his hand, her cherubic little face bright red from the sun.

Freddy sat down beside me. 'Is that your parents?' he said.

I nodded.

'You look like your dad,' he said.

I said nothing.

Freddy straightened out a fold in the photograph, then glanced at another – the four of us at a music festival. Mom and dad wearing the African print caftans that they'd bought at one of the festival stands.

Freddy smiled. 'They look like real hippies here.'

'They were,' I said. I gazed emptily at the picture for a moment. 'They used to smoke grass in the house.'

'You're kidding?'

I shook my head.

Freddy eyed the photo more carefully – in the background was an open-air stage full of brightly dressed musicians.

'Were you at a rock concert?' he said.

I nodded. 'England. Glastonbury.'

'How old were you?'

'I don't know, ten, eleven maybe. They took us every year.'

'To England?'

'Uh-huh. My dad was into the whole medieval thing, he loved it out there. He'd show us these ancient sites...tell us stories about what happened.'

And for a moment I remembered how much those stories had meant to me. As a kid, magic had been a passion of mine, and the time of King Arthur, Avalon – for me it was the time when magic felt its closest to being real. They may have been myths, but there'd been hope in them. Not like today when there's nothing. No magic. No mystery. No wonder in anything.

'We'd go to these old cathedrals,' I said. 'I'd take brass rubbings from the floor. Knights with swords. Then I'd draw in these backgrounds. Armies fighting under dark skies. Maidens and dragons.'

Freddy raised his eyebrows at me. 'Maidens and dragons?'

I shot him a smile. A nerd I may have been once upon a time – but no more. I was a player now. Burning the candle at both ends, in the middle, and a couple of other places that only Charlie Sheen knows about. I'd run down that nerd years ago, and he wasn't getting up again.

I gazed at myself in the photograph – that stupid kid with his romantic dreams.

Freddy nodded to himself, then slid the photographs onto Jon's desk. 'They sound like cool people,' he said. 'I can't even imagine my parents smoking grass. They freaked out enough when they found my cigarettes.'

I eyed him for a second, then went still.

He stared curiously at me. 'What?'

‘They found them?’ I said.

He shrugged. ‘Yeah.’

I kept my eyes on him and tried to think.

When we’d lived with Uncle Harry, Jon and I used to smoke a little grass ourselves. After Harry would go to bed, we’d open the bedroom window, roll a joint and talk into the early hours. Harry always suspected that we were smoking, but could never find it. He went through our bedrooms a couple of times, but Jon used to hide it in a small tin – tacked to the underside of the fridge with modeling clay.

I got up and headed into Jon’s kitchen. Freddy followed me. The fridge was pulled away from the wall – they’d definitely looked behind it. I kneeled down and ran my fingers under the front edge of the base. Nothing. I tried the left side edge. Again nothing. I pulled the fridge further away from the wall, bent down and tried the right side edge. My fingertips ran across a familiar rubbery texture.

I smiled at Freddy. ‘I found it,’ I said.

I prized it away from the base. A wad of modeling clay about the size of a flattened golf ball. I turned it over – and felt confused for a moment. There was no cigarette lighter, no flash drive.

Pressed into the clay was a necklace. Tiny. Delicate.

I carefully peeled it out of the clay. It had a small pendant – a thin gold disc, about an inch in diameter. One side depicted the sun – a tiny diamond, no more than half a carat in size, sat in the middle of embossed gold rays that emanated out to the edge. The back was thumb smooth apart from an inscription: ‘For Miranda’. It hung from a slender gold chain. It may not have been worthless, but it wasn't far off – it couldn't have been worth more than a couple of grand. I watched the pendant twist as it dangled between my fingers.

'You think this is what they were looking for?' asked Freddy. He stared curiously at it. 'It doesn't look like anything worth dying for.'

'Yeah. But Jon hid it.'

Freddy studied the inscription on the pendant. 'Who's Miranda?'

I shrugged – I had no idea. Maybe Jon's boss would know.

I tucked the necklace into my jacket pocket. 'Come on, let's get out of here.' We exited the main entrance of Jon's building and headed for my car parked at the end of the street. I reached for my phone – Jon's boss was hosting the wake, Harry would have his number. As I dialed Harry, Freddy grabbed my arm and slowed me down. He nodded toward a silver Mercedes S600 parked in front of my car. Inside sat two men. Through the glare on the windshield I couldn't see whether they were looking at us or not. The driver raised a phone to his ear. Freddy and I slowed even further – the guys reacted. The car doors opened and both of them stepped out. Well-built. Gray hooded shirts. In the shadow of the street lights I couldn't make out their faces.

Freddy glared at them. 'What the fuck are you looking at?' he said.

I grabbed Freddy – I already knew these guys were bad news. One of them reached inside his shirt.

'Run!' I yelled.

The guy produced a silenced pistol. Freddy and I sprinted for the backstreet next to Jon's building – a bullet zipped past us and splintered into the brickwork. I ducked and sped for the corner just ahead. Another silenced gunshot, then a stumble. I glanced back – Freddy was lying on the sidewalk, his head split wide open. I slowed as I gazed at him, his blood pouring in thick surges across the paving stones. I couldn't breathe. Screams from people across the street. I tore around the corner, trying to shake myself awake as I hurtled down the backstreet. I could hear the guys approaching the corner behind me. The other end of the backstreet was a hundred feet away – another Mercedes pulled up beside it, tires screaming. Two more guys in hooded shirts leaped from the car and ran for me. The guys behind me swung round the corner. I scanned the buildings beside me – steel shutters and fire escapes. A guy in a white baseball cap was smoking a cigarette beside an open fire door – he darted back inside.

'Call the police!' I yelled at him.

I ran for the fire door as it swung closed. I caught it with the ends of my fingers and pulled it back open – bullets ringing into it as I slammed the door shut behind me. I tumbled down a tight staircase, dance music blazing in the darkness ahead – gunfire shattering the door lock behind me. I reached the bottom of the stairs and ran into the murky catacombs of a nightclub. I heard the two guys behind me yell for the others to cover the main entrance. I ran deeper into the club – a small dance floor with a labyrinth of ghostly lit corridors and rooms leading off it. It was still early – no crowds that I could lose myself in – just a couple of dozen people. My blood raced as I tore down the maze of corridors looking for another exit. There was nothing – just black walls decorated in chaotic patterns of shattered glass. A sign at the end of the corridor read: 'The Apocalypse. The end of time. Where we come to dance.' I ducked through a doorway and into a small dimly lit room. A couple of stoned-looking girls were slumped on a red sofa. A second corridor ran past a tiny brick archway just beyond them. This second corridor must have led up to the club's main entrance – I could hear voices, commotion, footsteps running down stairs.

'What's going on?' asked one of the girls beside me.

I hushed her – listening as the footsteps reached the bottom of the stairs by the archway. I edged back out of the room and hid in the first corridor. The pounding music in the club then stopped. Raised voices from the dance floor, then a scream. I kept my eyes on the corridor that led up to the entrance. I ducked back as a guy in a hooded shirt appeared in the archway.

'You cover the main door,' he said to another.

He had an accent – European – French maybe. He pulled the slide on his pistol, then started walking. I pressed myself against the corridor wall and prayed that he wouldn't head through the room where the girls were sitting. I listened carefully – as he headed deeper into the club. One of them covering the main door, the other three inside – I stared up the corridor at the corners and doorways, the panic buzzing though my head. I could hear people crying, then more footsteps approaching – I couldn't tell whether they were coming from the corridor or the room. I glanced around – nowhere to hide. I unscrewed the light in the ceiling just above me – my end of the corridor went black. I froze as a silhouette appeared in the orange glow at the far end of the corridor. He stared toward me, gun in hand. I kept absolutely still. He looked around then spoke to someone behind him.

'Wait,' he said. The same voice – the French guy.

He produced a phone, then dialed a number. He held the phone away from himself and listened.

My phone rang. Fuck! I switched it off. The bastard turned toward me and fired. I dived back through the room where the girls were sitting – could hear the guy covering the main entrance racing for the archway. I saw his shadow stretching down the corridor wall. He was two seconds away, steadying himself with his right hand – the gun would be in his left. I leaped onto the sofa and launched myself toward the left-side pillar of the archway. The guy appeared, raised his gun, but I was airborne – I grabbed his left arm as I crashed into him, the weight of my body smashing his arm against the pillar's edge. I felt his arm snap – the guy yelling as we crumpled to the floor. I could hear the French guy just around the corner behind me, the other two pounding through the club. I scrambled to my feet and pulled myself around the archway, bullets from French tearing into the wall behind me. I clambered up the stairs, sprinted out of the main entrance and immediately found myself faced with two gun-wielding cops.

'On the ground now!' one of them shouted at me.

I dropped to my knees and raised my hands. The street was empty – crowds of people cordoned off way up at the junction. I heard someone in the distance yell at the cops, 'That's him, that was the guy!'

'They're in the club!' I said.

The hooded guys ran out onto the street behind me.

'Don't fucking move!' the other cop yelled at them.

The cops took aim. The hoods ground to a halt.

'Drop the fucking guns!' said the cop.

Three police cars tore around the corner and headed for us. The cops in front of me then collapsed as the hoods opened fire. I dived for cover between the police cars screeching to a halt. Their doors swung open, but with two dead officers on the street, no one was asking any questions – the cops started shooting. I leaped to my feet, bullets zipping past me as I crashed through the main door of a bar on the other side of the street. I glanced back – four cops were chasing the guys from the club down the backstreet, another two coming after me. I pushed my way through the bar crowds toward the rear exit – blurred glimpses of panicked eyes gazing at me. A barman grabbed me and tried to stop me. We struggled a moment – I lifted his keys, pushed him out of the way, then slammed though a heavy rear door out into a staff parking lot. Five cars – I hit the beeper. A black Chevrolet Malibu lit up. I jumped inside and started it up. As I reversed hard out of the lot, the cops burst out of the rear door – bullets thudding into the bodywork of the Malibu. The passenger window exploded across me as I swung the car around. I ducked, slammed down the pedal and swerved around the first corner I could find.

I had to get out of town, had to hide. I didn't know who the hell those guys in the club were, but they were professionals – well-armed and coordinated. They had my fucking phone number? As I swerved around another corner, I took the phone from my pocket. They could probably locate it, but I needed to make one call before I threw it. I switched it on and dialed Harry's number. I got his voicemail.

'Harry, it's me,' I said. 'Look, something… something's happened, OK, I don't know what, something to do with Jon. Stay away from my place. Get out of town. Please, just go!'

I ended the call and opened the window. As I got ready to throw the phone, it rang. I answered it.

'Harry?' I said.

There was pause at the other end of the line.

'Do you have the necklace, Michael?' came a man's voice. Gentle-sounding. Foreign accent – I couldn't place it.

I went cold. 'Who is this?' I said.

He laughed softly. 'You have it, don't you,' he said. 'For Miranda?'

'Did you do that? Did you kill Freddy?'

'We just want the necklace, Michael. Leave it for us somewhere. Just walk away. We'll leave you alone.'

'You did that to Jon, didn't you?' I said. 'I'm going to fucking kill you.'

'Yes, that's very touching, but you need to be smart now. I'm going to give you one chance to get out of this alive.'

'I'm going to fucking kill you!'

He laughed. 'You know it's actually very nice to speak to you, Michael.'

'Fuck you!' I said.

I threw the phone out of the window, the blood coursing through my veins like broken glass. Whoever that fucker was, I wanted him dead.

I heard police sirens approaching the junction ahead of me. I swung a hard left and sped toward Russian Hill. I needed to dump the Malibu and fast – every cop in the city was going to be looking for it. I pulled the car to a stop on a deserted street near a park. I jumped out, then scurried down Bay Street looking for another car.

I watched the traffic and tried to figure out where I was going to hide once I was out of the city. Hotels were out – they could track my credit card, and I had next to no cash. I could lift it, but that would take too long. I thought about my parents' old farmhouse. It was all the way up in Sonoma – I just didn't know how safe it was going to be. Jon and I could never face selling it, but the house was no secret – plenty of people knew about it. And if those fuckers had my phone number, God knows what else they knew. It was a risk, but I had ten grand stashed there, and I wasn't going to survive without cash.

A silver VW Golf pulled up beside an apartment building just ahead of me. A woman in her thirties got out. I hated stealing from women, but I had no time to be noble – I could hear more police sirens in the distance. I watched as she dropped the car key in her handbag. Magnetic clasp. She was carrying a bottle of wine – visiting friends – she wouldn't know the car was gone for hours.

I eyed her carefully for a second – she was wearing gold earrings. I straightened myself up, then headed toward her.

'Excuse me,' I said as calmly as I could.

She stared warily at me. I stood away from her – no threat.

I smiled. 'This is going to sound like an odd question, but would you mind telling me where you got your earrings?'

'My earrings?' she replied.

'I couldn't help noticing them. My girlfriend has the same ones, and I've lost one of them. She doesn't know yet and you'd be saving my neck if you told me where you got them.'

She relaxed a little and smiled. I felt my heart sink – I hated doing this to her, but I needed the car. I stepped toward her.

'Would you mind…could I just check they're the same ones?' I said.

She swept her hair away from her left ear and turned her head to one side – she couldn't see my hands now. As I leaned in to take a look at the earrings, I pried open the clasp of her handbag and slid my hand inside. Handbags were tricky – easy to get into, but there's phones, compacts, all kinds of plastic casings that can rattle against each other. I secured three casings tightly between my fingers, then snaked my thumb around the satin depths of the bag. I felt the key, hooked it by the ring, then released the casings.

I could hear the police sirens getting closer. 'Yeah, they're the ones,' I said to her.

'Macy's,' she replied.

As she turned back to me, I ran my key-loaded fingers through my hair and let the key slip down the rear collar of my jacket.

'Thank you,' I said. 'Really. You've saved my neck.'

'I'm glad I could help.'

She smiled again and headed into the apartment building. I waited until the main door closed behind her, then grabbed the key and slid inside the Golf. Sirens approaching – I ducked low in the seat. Three police units then tore down the street in front of me and pulled to a stop by the park. Six cops jumped out and started covering the area around the street where I'd dumped the Malibu.

I watched as they headed into the shadows, and prayed that they'd find a witness – security camera footage – anything that told them that I had nothing to do with the shootings. Not that it would help me now. They'd still be looking for me, and those fuckers from the club would be right on their tail. I didn't know what I was going to do – I just needed to get to the house. The moment the cops were out of sight, I started up the Golf, pulled out onto Bay Street and headed north.

3

It was one in the morning when I pulled the car to a stop on a deserted farm road just outside Sonoma. There was no moon – no light this far out in the hills. Just a haze of scrub that covered the fields like a black fog. I scanned the car's interior one final time, making sure there were no satnavs or phones that might give away my location. I doubted the car had a tracker, but I wasn't going to take the risk. I stared out of the windshield. The farmhouse couldn't be more than two or three miles – I'd walk the rest of the way. I rolled the car into the bushes, then headed across the dark fields.

Blurred images from the nightclub filled my head. The hooded figure racing through the archway toward me. The French guy aiming his gun. I tried to capture any details – a glimpse of a profile or hair color – but the pictures were a haze. Not that those fuckers mattered to me now. It was the guy who'd called me in the car. He was the one I wanted.

I heard thunder ahead, the hills around me taking sudden form as lightning flickered across the horizon. I reached the southern slope of Cava's Hill and made my way toward its thick wooded peak. The hill rose two hundred feet above the scrub, and would give me a bird's eye view of the farmhouse that sat just beyond it.

I reached the top of the hill and waited within the trees. I could see the house below me – its pointed tin roof cutting a black triangle above the oaks that circled it. It looked just as I'd remembered.

My parents bought the house the year before they died. They were going to renovate it and move the family out to a better life in the country, but they never finished it. In the years since, it had become Jon's and my retreat away from the city. At least it had until that June night last year when Jon found out about me. I hadn't returned since.

I eyed the house carefully. It looked dark. Quiet. If those bastards from the club knew about this place, they'd have been here already – turned the place over, looking for the necklace. But there were no cars parked nearby, no lights, no movement anywhere. The house looked untouched.

I crept down the hill, jumped the brook that ran past the yard, and sneaked up to the windows. I peered inside. No signs of intrusion. The old carved-wood furniture sat where it always had. The cabinets unopened. Jon's books resting neatly on the shelves.

The spare door key was underneath the white stone rabbit in the yard. I unlocked the rear door and slinked inside. I kept the lights off – didn't know who might be watching. I darted though the shadows, checking the ground floor rooms. The kitchen. Living room. Study. I made sure the windows and doors were all locked, then headed upstairs and checked the bedrooms. The house was empty – a dusty shell. It didn't look like anyone had been here for months.

I entered my old bedroom by the stairs. It felt cold. Stark. A bare mattress on the black iron bed frame. I pulled the drawer out from the bedside table and felt around underneath it. Taped to the underside was the plastic bag full of cash. I'd hidden it there a couple of years ago in case I ever got into trouble – I never thought I'd actually need it. I grabbed the bag, tossed it onto the bed, then opened the oak wardrobe in the corner. Inside were a couple of old sweatshirts, sneakers and a pair of jeans. I needed to get ready to move quickly if I had to. I climbed into some fresh clothes, then headed into the bathroom and studied myself in the mirror. With these bastards trying to find me, I needed to look as different as I could. Medium length brown hair. I rummaged around in the bathroom drawer and found an electric clipper. I leaned my head over the sink and shaved my hair – a ragged, sixty-second buzz cut. I brushed the loose strands away from my neck, then put on my aviators and studied myself again. It wasn't pretty, but it would do.

Rain started to drum against the tin roof. The storm was approaching. I headed back into my room and took a careful look out of the window. The hills looked empty and still – just the trees trembling in the wind. I was safe for the moment at least.

I took a deep breath, the adrenaline in me dropping a gear. I sat on the bed and plucked the necklace from my jacket pocket. The pendant glistened in my palm as lightning flashed across the hills. I eyed it curiously – the inscription, 'For Miranda'.

I tried to imagine why it might be worth killing for. I hung it from my fingers and watched it twist in the dark, its faces flickering. But, for all the secrets it may have held, my thoughts drifted away from it.

Being back at the house. Back in these old rooms.

All I could think about was Jon.

I closed my eyes and listened to the tin roof creaking in the wind. The brook bubbling outside. The familiar chorus of the house just kept pulling at me. Kept taking me back to that weekend of last year.

The last time that I'd seen him.

The June sun was burning high above the house as Jon and I heaved white chalk rocks into the front yard. Jon laid one of the rocks by the kitchen wall, then slapped the dust from his delicate hands. It made me smile. The rest of him was built like a trooper, but he had the fingers of an artist. It was like his arms had wanted to join Special Forces, but his hands wouldn't give up the piano lessons.

He stared up the road, then rolled his eyes. 'Oh, Jesus,' he said.

I turned and saw it – the sunlight glinting off the roof of an orange pick-up crawling up the road. Randal Hap's pick-up. I glanced back at Jon's lifeless old BMW blocking the road just outside the house. It had died that morning, and we were clearing away the rocks that lined the yard before pushing it onto the grass. Its rear wheels had locked up, and there was no way we were going to push it all the way into the driveway. Randal lived half a mile up the road, and with the brook on one side, and the rocks on the other, he wasn't getting around the car.

He pulled to a stop and poked his withered, ninety-year-old face out of the pick-up window.

'You can't park your cars in the road!' he said.

Jon nodded. 'We're aware of that, Randal, thank you. Unfortunately, it's not parked, it's broken.'

'Just get the goddamn thing out of my way!'

'We're trying, but it might take another few minutes, OK? Unless you want to take the barrel road.'

'I ain't heading back.'

'OK, so we're waiting, five or ten minutes.'

'Which is it? Five or ten?'

'Well if we're going to stand here discussing it...'

'Just get!' said Randal, and he spat in the dirt.

I stared at him and laughed. Old people. Evolution had to come up with death just to stop the constant whining.

Randal eyed us as we hauled another couple of rocks.

He then nodded at Jon. 'I saw you on TV this morning.'

Jon grinned back at him. 'Yeah, what did you think?'

Jon had hammered Vice-President Howard over his involvement in the Bara investment fund. They'd broadcast the interview that morning.

'You got no respect,' said Randal. 'Man's in the White House, for Chrissake. What, you think you're smarter than him?'

Jon smiled. 'Don't confuse being smart with being right, Randal. They're not the same thing.'

'Is that so?'

'Yep. The greatest innovators in human history...all surrounded by smart people who did nothing but tell them that they were wrong. Statistically speaking, if you're smart, chances are you're an idiot.'

'Yeah, what does that make you then?' said Randal.

Jon nodded to himself. 'You know, that's a good question.' He glanced at me. 'What do you think?'

I picked up another rock. 'I think the sooner we get Randal home, the better.'

I hauled the rock toward the house. But Jon kept his eyes on me. He just stood there.

'Come on, let's get this done,' I said.

He nodded. 'Yeah.'

We managed to push the car off the road, and Randal was thankfully inflicting some other part of the world. As Jon called a tow truck, I grabbed a beer from the kitchen and gazed out of the window at Suki and Danielle. They were walking together on Cava's Hill, taking photographs in the sunshine.

Danielle had been seeing Jon for about six months. I liked her a lot. A producer at NBC, she was this effortlessly elegant creature. She could sneeze and it looked like ballet. Then again, when you're as rich as she was, grace comes easy. Her dad was some high-flying financier – not that she ever made a big deal about it.

As for Suki? I'd been with her for a few weeks, and to be honest, she wasn't for me. Early twenties. Actress. Pretty, but a little upwardly mobile for my taste. I hadn't really wanted to bring her to the house that weekend, but she wanted to meet Danielle, what with NBC and everything.

Jon strolled into the kitchen. 'The guy says it sounds like a busted axle.'

I nodded. 'It was on its last legs when you bought it anyhow.'

He grabbed a beer from the fridge, then gazed out at the girls on the hill. He smiled.

'They seem to be getting along,' he said.

I shrugged apathetically. He threw me a look, then shook his head to himself.

'You're ending it?' he said.

'Don't worry, I'll wait until we get back to the city.'

'Why, what's wrong this time?'

'Ah, just time to move on.'

'All you ever do is move on. Don't you want something meaningful?'

'That's how you find it. Looking for love's like looking for oil, you've got to drill a few holes before you hit a gusher.'

He laughed. He took another sip of beer, then sighed wearily as he stared at his sorry-looking BMW perched on the edge of the lawn.

'So I might be in the market for a new car,' he said.

'I'll sort you out. Find you something a little more suitable.'

He raised his eyebrows at me.

'You're not the BMW type,' I said. 'You're more...I don't know...Italian. Quick, colorful.'

'That's me, is it?'

'Lime green Lamborghini.'

'A BMW will be fine, thanks.'

I smiled.

He nodded to himself, then leaned back against the kitchen counter.

'So work's good then, huh?' he said.

'Uh-huh.'

'OK. OK, good.'

'Why?'

'Just asking.'

I laughed. Jon never 'just' asked anything.

'Still think I'm being followed, huh?' I said.

He took a deep breath. 'I'm seeing the same faces around you, Michael, I swear.'

'Same faces. You've been covering Washington for too long, you know that.'

'Yeah, maybe.'

But the truth was I'd noticed those same faces too. At the ball park. At the airport. Distant eyes that were gone the moment I tried to get a look at them. I was worried that the police were tailing me. I'd kept a low profile over the past few months just in case. Either way, it wasn't something that I could discuss with Jon.

He eyed me carefully. 'If there were any problems, you'd tell me, right?'

I held his look. 'Everything's fine.'

We all had dinner at the house that night. We talked about the interview with the Vice-President – Jon's first at his new job. He'd quit the *Washington Post* that April and moved to the *World Review* in San Francisco. It felt like he'd returned home.

'This is where you belong,' I said. 'I mean Capitol Hill's fine, but let's face it, you weren't making any friends up there.'

Jon laughed to himself.

Suki stared curiously at him. 'Does it ever bother you?' she said. 'That you've pissed-off so many people. Powerful people.'

'Capitol Hill?' he replied. 'Ah, they're a bunch of lackeys, the lot of them. It's the money men I want. The guys who stay in the shadows, they're the ones you've got to watch out for.'

Danielle's graceful demeanor tightened a little.

'I don't know,' she said. 'You knew Washington. You should have stayed. The only time you've ever been in trouble was when you were following the money.'

Jon sighed. 'Come on, that was different.'

'No,' she said.

'You think Capitol Hill isn't about money?'

She went quiet.

Suki glanced at him. 'Something happened to you?'

He shrugged like it was nothing. 'I followed a money trail down to Mexico a few years ago,' he said. 'I was getting coffee one morning, and these two guys dragged me out the back of the shop. They held a gun in my face and told me the story stops here.'

'You're kidding,' said Suki.

I laughed. 'That's not the best part.'

'Yeah,' said Jon. 'They're holding me in this alley behind the shop. And these guys are high as clouds, faces sweating. This police unit drives past, then pulls to a stop. These guys just start shooting at the police...it was insane. Next thing I know, these two idiots have dragged me into an office building down the alley...police units everywhere. These guys start demanding passage to the border, where they say they're going to release me. Seventeen hours they had me tied up in this building.'

'Jesus,' said Suki.

Danielle glanced at him. 'You still don't know who they were working for?'

'Best guess, Tico Hernandez,' he replied. 'But it could have been any of them.'

'So what happened?' asked Suki.

'A friend of mine I was working with down there,' said Jon. 'He got me out.'

'He pulled some strings?'

'Not exactly,' said Jon. 'He sneaked into the building and shot them both dead.'

Silence at the table.

Danielle shook her head to herself. 'If he hadn't been there, Jon...'

'He killed them?' said Suki. 'Who was he?'

I eyed Jon curiously. He'd never told me who this friend of his was. I'd only ever heard him refer to him once as 'T'.

'It doesn't matter,' said Jon.

He was still being cagey about it, but fair enough – I wasn't going to push it. I raised a glass of Scotch. 'Well, here's to a good friend.'

Jon smiled.

'If something like that happened to me,' said Suki. 'I'm not sure I'd have the nerve to keep going.'

'It happens,' said Jon.

'But it doesn't though, does it?' said Danielle. 'Not to most people.'

Jon shot her a look. 'Well, I can't stop.'

As Danielle looked away from him, Jon's manner softened. He thought to himself a moment, then took hold of her hand.

'You know, my parents ran the same little bookstore all their lives,' he said. 'Books about the environment, education. It was never going to make them any money, but they believed in what they were doing...the message. No matter what hardship fell their way, they never changed course. They stood for something, you know? I can't ignore that. I won't.'

Danielle nodded, but she stayed quiet. We all did. But then Jon glanced at me, and it felt like there it was – the question in the air. How my parents could have inspired him to take such a noble path, but not me – the drunken 'used car' dealer.

It was time to change the subject. I took a deep breath. 'Come on, let's do something.'

'Like what?' said Jon.

'I don't know, let's go out. They're showing a Lord of the Rings marathon in town if anyone's interested.'

'Yeah, I think I'd rather hang out with Tico Hernandez,' said Jon.

He leaned back in his chair, then smiled at me.

'You know what I'm in the mood for?' he said. 'A little magic.'

Changing the subject suddenly didn't feel like it had been such a good idea.

He winked at me. 'Come on, astound us.'

Suki threw me a curious look.

Jon nodded at her. 'He was a little wizard when he was a kid, he didn't tell you? The Amazing Michael Violet.'

'A long time ago,' I said.

'But you were good,' said Jon. 'Really good. He used to perform for us and everything.'

'Really?' said Danielle. 'Show us something.'

'I haven't done it in years.'

'Card tricks and mind-reading,' said Jon. He nodded thoughtfully to himself a moment. 'But there was this one trick that I could never figure out.'

He reached into his pocket and produced a dime.

'Show them the trick with the coin,' he said.

He slid the dime across the table toward me.

I stared uncomfortably at it. I didn't do magic any more, certainly never in front of Jon. It would have felt like I was sailing too close to the wind.

'Come on,' he said.

'I'm drunk,' I replied.

'Please,' he said. 'It's the greatest trick.'

It was. Bare hand, sleeves rolled up high. You held a coin between the tips of your fore and middle fingers. You then very slowly curled your fingers into a fist – but real slow – no movement enough to flick the coin anywhere. At the same measured pace you then uncurled your fingers wide like a starfish. And the coin was gone. It was an illusion created by a Serbian magician named Branco Dugme. In his notes on the trick, he warned people how hard it was to master – that it had taken him over a year to get it right. It took me three weeks.

'Please,' said Danielle. 'I'd like to see it.'

I shook my head.

Jon smiled. 'Not The Amazing Michael Violet any more, huh? Dad's little Merlin.'

The vaguest hint of provocation in his tone. It was strange. I didn't know if I was just being paranoid or not, but I didn't like it.

I glanced back at the coin. Maybe he should see it.

I picked up the dime, then rolled my shirt sleeve up to my elbow. I held the coin between my fingertips, and slowly turned it around so everyone could see both sides of my hand. As I gradually made a fist, Jon kept his eyes fixed on me. I held the coin lightly against my palm.

The coin then clattered onto the table as I let it slip from my fingers. Danielle and Suki laughed.

I stared at the coin, and shrugged. 'The magic's gone, what can I tell you.'

Jon nodded. As he reached for his wine glass, his cell phone rang.

Danielle threw him a look. 'We said no phones this weekend.'

Jon glanced at the caller ID. 'I'm sorry, I've got to take this.'

He left the table, then headed upstairs to take the call.

We waited. We drank a little Scotch. Even started watching a movie. But it was nearly an hour before Jon came back down. His whole demeanor had changed when he did. He looked empty.

'Everything OK?' I asked.

He didn't reply – didn't even look at me. He just walked over to Danielle and kissed her.

‘I’m going to bed,’ he said to her.

‘What happened?’ she asked.

He shook his head. ‘It’s fine.’

‘Are you sure?’

He nodded. ‘I’m just tired. I’ll see you in the morning.’

‘You want a hit of this Scotch before you go?’ I said.

But he just turned and headed back upstairs. It was cold, but Jon got like that sometimes – whenever any shit happened, he was always the first to know about it. It was best just to leave him to it. The moment he was gone, Suki glanced at me.

‘He’ll be fine,’ I said. ‘It’s just work.’

‘I’d better go up,’ said Danielle. ‘Make sure he’s OK.’

As she followed Jon up, I took a mouthful of Scotch. And I stared uneasily at the coin on the table.

I didn’t sleep well that night. I was woken by a bad dream – the same one that I’d had since I was a kid. Fevered images of a knight riding into battle, sword in hand. Grey, crow-swept skies above him. As he rides, he becomes engulfed by flames. He topples from his horse, disintegrating as he hits the ground. Then quiet. Soft flakes of ash skittering in the wind. The crows circling above.

I felt sick when I woke. I watched Suki breathing for a moment, then got out of bed. I headed over to the window, and tried to clear my head.

I gazed out at Cava’s Hill. As I did, I caught sight of a tiny orange glow down by the brook. It was Jon. He was sitting alone on the bank, smoking a cigarette. He hadn't smoked in years.

I pulled on some clothes and headed downstairs. I opened the kitchen door, crossed the road and joined him by the brook.

'You're smoking again?' I said.

He didn't reply.

I sat down next to him on the bank. 'So are you going to tell me what happened?'

He stayed silent.

'Come on, I'm worried,' I said.

He laughed. 'You're worried!'

'I am.'

He gazed at his cigarette.

'What's going on?' I asked.

He eyed me for a moment, then smiled acerbically.

'You know I've never seen your office,' he said.

'My office?'

'I've never been there.'

'You can visit any time you like. It's not exactly spectacular.'

I kept a small office on Columbus Avenue, but it was just for show in case the tax man ever needed to see where my business was based. I hadn't been there for months – there was nothing in it apart from a desk and chair.

'I'd like to see it,' he said.

'Fine. Drop by this week.'

'Let's go now,' he said.

'Now?' I said. I eyed him carefully. 'What's going on?'

He blew a cloud of smoke into the night air, then nodded to himself.

'Darren Tavener called me,' he said.

'Tonight? That was the call?' I was surprised – Darren was just a friend of ours from the old neighborhood.

'He saw the interview and wanted to wish me congratulations,' said Jon.

'Yeah?'

'He lives in San Diego now. About to set up his own practice. He doesn't have many clients yet, but…it's funny, he told me how well you were doing though.'

'Darren? I haven't spoken to him in years.'

'I know,' said Jon. 'He was driving through Pac Heights three weeks ago. He saw you come out of some fancy house there. He was going to stop, but you jumped into a Bentley and sped off before he got a chance to say hi.'

I stayed quiet.

'You know, I told him you didn't live in Pac Heights,' said Jon. 'That you didn't drive a Bentley. That it probably belonged to some client of yours, and you were selling it for them.'

'That's right,' I said.

'Did you get a good price for it?'

'What is this, Jon?'

He eyed me carefully for a moment, then shook his head.

'I was always so proud that you turned yourself around, Michael, you know that? That you made something of yourself. And I always felt so terrible whenever I doubted you, because I knew you'd never lie to me, would you?'

My heartbeat faded.

'I spoke to another friend of mine tonight,' he said. 'Did you know that a Bentley Continental was reported stolen from a house in Pac Heights three weeks ago?'

Jesus.

I couldn't believe this was happening now.

'Tell me you're not a thief, Michael,' he said. 'I need to hear you say it.'

For a second I considered explaining away the Bentley somehow – but it was pointless. This moment had always been coming. When you smash your toe on a door frame, there's a half-second gap before the pain hits when you think you might have gotten away with it. From the moment I started stealing, my life felt like that gap – hoping the pain wasn't to going to hit. But it was here now.

I stared down at my hands. The words just came.

'I'm not hurting anyone, Jon,' I said. 'I take Ferraris from bankers. I'm not stealing the family Subaru, OK.'

The hurt in his eyes as he gazed at me.

'How long?' he asked.

I knew this was the part that was really going to hit him.

'How…long?' he said, his voice trembling.

'Seven, eight years.'

He stared at me as if the words were alien to him.

'I'm sorry,' I said.

'All this time?'

'I didn't want to burden you with it.'

He grabbed me and raised his fist. He wavered for a moment, but the anger in him was too much – his fist thudded against my cheek. I slipped on the bank and tumbled into the brook.

He glared down at me as I picked myself out of the water.

'I never felt alone until today, you know that?' he said.

I nodded. 'I've felt it a lot longer, believe me.'

'Fuck you!'

'How could I tell you?'

'You're my brother!'

'Yeah, what part of you would have understood?' I wiped the blood from my mouth. 'In your ivory tower. Did you give a shit what was going on with me? Really? Just you and your fucking crusade.'

He shook his head. 'I don't want you coming back here.'

'Don't worry, I won't.'

I pulled myself out of the brook.

He eyed me bitterly. 'If mom and dad...'

'Don't!' I said. 'Really. You don't know what you're talking about.'

I headed for the house, the sickness welling up inside me.

I spend the next few days in a drunken twilight. Hating myself for having lied to him – for being that weak.

When I eventually summoned up the strength to call him, he didn't answer. I left him messages at home, at work, telling him that I was sorry, but I got nothing back.

I had the key to his apartment, but using it would have made things worse – and so I just waited for him outside. In the end, some neighbor of his told me that he'd gone to New York. He didn't know how long for.

I managed to get through to Danielle at NBC a few days later. Although she was polite, she refused to give me Jon's details in New York. She wouldn't tell me why he was there or for how long – but what worried me more, was that even though she knew something had happened, she didn't know what. Jon couldn't even talk to her about it. Jesus.

I didn't know what to do next. Emails were no good if you had anything serious to write. I doubt the Constitution would have carried so much weight if there'd been a bunch of Viagra ads flashing all over it. But I was out of options – even Harry was keeping quiet.

I spent two days drafting an email. I wrote that I wanted to put things right between us. That I'd stopped stealing. That I wanted to make a fresh start – be the brother that he'd always hoped I'd be.

I sent the email, and I got nothing back from that either. I did my best to stop stealing anyhow – I wanted to be good to my word. I stayed off the street, kept my itching hands in check, and tried to think what else I could do with myself. But the will in me began to fade. Jon's silence spread across the year, and I found myself slipping back. The old habits. The old thrills.

I figured I'd find the strength, once I'd heard from him.

That night at the house turned out to be the last time that I saw him.

There was a crash of thunder. I clenched my fingers around the necklace. The storm was raging over the house – thunder I could feel in my bones. I checked my watch: four a.m. I'd been asleep for an hour, but felt no better for it. I sat up in the bed and listened to the rain hammering against the windows. I felt uneasy – something wasn't right. I could hear a noise through the rain. Shuffling.

Someone was in the house.

I spun out of the bed. As I edged over to the window, I stayed light-footed – I didn't want to give myself away. I carefully glanced outside. A black Audi A5 was parked by the house. It didn't belong to anyone that I knew. Through the streaming rain I couldn't see if anyone was waiting inside it. If there was, I'd be an easy target if I climbed out of the window. I grabbed the bronze lamp stand from the bedside table and pulled the wire out from its base. I held the stand firmly in my hand, then crept over to the bedroom door and listened. More shuffling. Doors opening. It was coming from downstairs. No voices. One set of footsteps. Probably one of those fuckers from the nightclub.

I grabbed the bedroom door handle and slowly twisted it – tried to lift the weight of the whole door on the handle to stop the hinges creaking. I pulled the door open a little. Whoever was downstairs was going through the drawers of Jon's desk in the study – I recognized the smooth sound of the runners. The study door was about fifteen feet from the bottom of the staircase. I could cover that in a second.

I edged out onto the upper landing. The glow of a flashlight arced across the bottom of the stairwell. I tightened my grip on the lamp stand, and slowly stepped down the stairs. I could hear him opening the filing cabinet by Jon's desk. If he was going through the files then his back would be to the study door – he wouldn't know what hit him. I reached the bottom step – the study door to my right, just beyond the corner of the stairwell.

The flashlight then went out. I stopped dead. Listened.

No sound now. I slowly leaned my head around the corner. The study door was shut – a thin line of light illuminating the gap between the door and the floorboards. He was inside. I stepped off the stairs and crept over to the study. I leaned my head close to the door and listened carefully.

I froze as I felt a blade against my throat.

I could hear someone breathing just behind me to my right. A flash of lightning lit the room. The blade pinched against my skin as its owner slowly stepped round in front of me. Another lightning flash and I saw her – the raven-haired girl from the cemetery. The ghost. She held the knife firmly against my neck.

'What are you doing here?' she said.

'I could ask you the same thing.'

She eyed me coldly.

'You need to leave,' she said.

She slowly lowered the blade and tucked it away in a leather sheath on her belt.

I kept my eyes on her as she opened the study door and headed back to the filing cabinet. She looked like a rag doll – a no-frills street kid. Old jeans, baggy sweater. Her long black hair hanging limp. No make-up.

She opened another cabinet drawer.

'What are you looking for?' I asked.

'This doesn't concern you,' she said.

She started emptying folders and envelopes. Pouring their contents across the desk.

'OK, who are you then?' I asked.

'I was a friend of your brother's.'

'Journalist?'

She shook her head.

I glanced at her pale green snorkel jacket lying across the study chair. One of its pockets hung open. Inside was a plastic cigarette lighter – Jon's flash drive. I stared intently at her. I didn't know who she was, but Jon wouldn't have given that to just anybody.

'You have Jon's flash drive,' I said.

She grabbed her jacket and threw it over the desk so it was out of my reach. 'You were his girlfriend?' I said.

'Just leave me alone.'

I kept my eyes on her, then nodded.

'Fine,' I said. 'But if you're looking for a necklace inscribed to Miranda, you're not going to find it there.'

She shot me a look. 'What do you know about it?'

'I know they killed Jon because of it.'

I took the necklace from my pocket and held it up between my fingers. She looked taken aback at the sight of it.

'Where did you get that?' she asked.

'I found it hidden in his apartment.'

She stepped toward me. 'You need to give that to me,' she said.

I shook my head, then wrapped the necklace around my fist. 'I've got my own score to settle here.'

'I'm going to make sure whoever killed Jon pays for it, don't worry about that.'

'Then we've got something in common.'

She laughed scornfully.

I nodded toward her snorkel jacket. 'What's on the flash drive?' I asked.

She eyed me a moment – realized that she wasn't going to get the necklace that easily. She leaned back against the wall and looked me up and down, trying to get the measure of me. She produced a pack of cigarettes and lit one with the flash drive. A tiny blue flame.

'Jon told me about you,' she said. 'You think I'm going to trust you?'

'If you know anything about me, you'll know that I didn't have to mention the drive. I could have just taken it.'

'Then why didn't you?'

'Because this is Jon we're talking about,' I said. 'And if he gave you the drive, then you must have been important to him.'

'I was,' she said.

She leaned away from the wall and stepped toward me.

'You hurt him,' she said.

I wasn't going to deny it. 'I lied to him, yeah.'

'You were all the family he had,' she said. She studied me like I was a curiosity under a microscope. 'How do you live with yourself?'

'I go out a lot.'

She kept her eyes on me, then stepped away.

'What are you planning to do?' she asked.

'Find whoever killed Jon and blow his fucking brains out.'

'Really?' She laughed to herself.

'Why, you got any better ideas?'

She rolled the flash drive around between her fingers.

'Jon was killed because of a story he was working on,' she said. 'I'm going to finish it for him.'

'Put whoever did this behind bars, huh?'

'It's what he would have wanted.'

She was probably right, but I was in no mood for civilized justice. You can build all the prisons you like – some people you just have to kill before they'll listen.

'Whatever you might think of me,' I said, 'Jon was my brother. If you know anything, you need to tell me. Either way, the necklace is staying with me.'

She took a long, thoughtful pull on her cigarette. Gray smoke curled out of her lips as she kept her eyes fixed on me.

She nodded. 'You betray me, you'll regret it. You understand?'

'What's your name?' I said.

'Ella.'

'Then fair enough, Ella.'

Ella plugged the flash drive into an old laptop in the study.

'Jon gave me the drive a couple of days before he died,' she said. 'He said it was just a precaution, but he sounded worried.'

'How did you know him?' I asked.

'We were friends,' she said.

I waited for her to elaborate, but she just opened up a document on the drive. Cascading windows filled the laptop screen – pages of notes, transcribed interviews and photographs.

'Two months ago Jon was given the necklace by a girl named Danielle Fisher,' she said.

'Danielle? Yeah, I know her, she was his girlfriend.'

'The necklace belonged to her father, David Fisher. He was a financier. He died in August during routine surgery. He was worth close to eight hundred million when he died. Apparently he told Danielle that of all the things they own, the necklace was the most important. She asked Jon to help her find out why.'

'Her father never said?'

Ella shook her head. 'He was fifty-two. I don't think he was expecting to die on the table.'

'What about the mom, might she know?'

'He didn't tell his daughter, he certainly wouldn't tell his wife. They got divorced years ago, Fisher had an affair with some housekeeper. They don't speak.'

I held the necklace up to the light.

'So, what, there's something hidden in it?' I said. 'A microdot or something?'

Ella shook her head again. She scrolled through the pages on the laptop and started reading out a lab report.

'Jon had the necklace analyzed,' she said. 'There's nothing hidden in it. Nothing engraved or etched apart from the inscription. They put every single link under the microscope. The diamond is medium grade, just over half a carat. The gold in the pendant is eighteen-carat, standard zinc copper alloy. The gold in the chain and clasp is nine-carat. It's one of two hundred similar necklaces that were manufactured by Halls and Webb Jewelers of Chicago in 1993.'

'One of two hundred?' I said.

'Some limited edition. Jon found a couple of others for sale on the net. Two thousand five hundred dollars a piece.'

I gazed at the necklace. It wasn't even unique – why the hell did they want this one?

'We need to speak to Danielle,' I said.

'She disappeared three days ago,' said Ella. 'They found a body yesterday. They think it's her, they're testing it. It was heavily burned.'

Jesus. I pictured her, that evening at the house. I felt sick just thinking about it.

I glanced back at the screen. 'What about Miranda?' I said. 'Did Jon have any ideas who she might be?

'Nothing that he put on the drive,' said Ella. 'But he received a call six days before he died. From a woman. She didn't say who she was. She said that Fisher had a business partner, Philip Swan…that she'd heard them argue about a necklace on two occasions.'

Ella scrolled down to a photo of Swan. In his fifties. A real fat bastard. Looked like he was ninety-percent sweat.

'Is this the fucker we're looking for?' I said.

'I doubt it,' said Ella. 'Jon asked around about him. Swan's scared. Since Fisher's death, he hasn't set foot outside his home without at least three bodyguards.'

'You think he'll to talk to us?' I said.

'He's not talking to anybody,' Ella replied. 'But during one of these arguments, this woman overheard Swan mention the name Gatsby.'

'Gatsby?' I said. 'As in The Great?'

Ella nodded. 'Swan has a huge library in his home. Thousands of books apparently. From the way they were talking, this woman thinks the book might have something to do with it.'

'Then we need to get hold of it,' I said.

'Jon tried. He couldn't even get near the place. Swan owns the Howardson Building on Market Street. The whole top floor is his private residence. Massive security.'

'Whatever,' I said. 'It's a home. It has a door. It'll have a key.'

She took a pull on her cigarette. 'And keys are your business, aren't they, Michael.'

I nodded.

She thought to herself for a moment, then pulled the flash drive out of the laptop and grabbed her jacket.

'There's a hotel opposite the Howardson called The Bluebird,' she said. 'We'll stake out Swan's place from there.'

‘Wait, take it easy for a second,’ I said. ‘If we’re doing this, I’m going to need to know who you are.’

She stayed silent.

‘How do you know Jon?’ I asked.

‘It would be better for both of us if you stopped asking me questions.’

‘Yeah, why’s that?’

She said nothing and just headed for the door. I got to my feet, then realized that I’d missed something obvious here. I glanced back at the open filing cabinet that she’d been emptying. You needed a key to open it – Jon always kept it locked. The cabinet didn’t look damaged at all. A thought then hit me.

‘How did you get into the house?’ I asked her. ‘Did Jon give you a key?’

Ella nodded.

‘Show it to me,’ I said.

She eyed me warily, but didn’t produce any key.

‘You broke in?’ I said.

‘You’re going to call the police?’

I headed into the living room and took a look around.

‘You didn’t break any windows,’ I said. ‘You came in through the door.’

‘It’s not exactly Fort Knox.’

‘True. But you’d still need to know how to pick a lock...the door...the filing cabinet.’ I eyed her suspiciously. ‘I heard you rifling around in the study, but I didn’t hear you break in. You know what you’re doing, don’t you?’

I could feel the anger rising in her – the electricity in the air around her.

'Don't think that you and I are the same, Michael. We're not.'

I couldn't believe this.

'You're a thief?' I said.

She eyed me coldly, then headed out for her car.

4

With all that Jon and I had been through, I found it hard to imagine that he'd ever get close to another thief. Admittedly, what had hurt him was that I'd lied about it, but even then, he wouldn't have had any time for Ella unless she was on the right side of the fight somehow. I'd known at least one thief who'd turned legit – who now used his talents 'obtaining' hard-to-get evidence for law firms. I think his official job title was 'consultant'. Ella had to be something like that – it was the only thing that added up.

Either way, she wasn't talking to me. As she drove us back to San Francisco, she hardly looked at me, let alone said anything. She kept her eyes fixed on the road.

I nodded to myself. 'When you said Jon couldn't get into Swan's apartment…you mean, you couldn't. You worked for Jon, didn't you? Getting hold of information for the paper.'

She stayed quiet, but I figured I was on the right track.

I shook my head. 'I can't believe he asked you to do that.'

'He didn't. I offered.'

'So what happened?'

'Like I said, I couldn't get near the place. But from what I hear, you think you're God's gift, so we'll see how that works out.'

'God's gift?' I replied. 'I mean, I'm not denying it, but where did you hear that?'

'Jesus, just listen to yourself.'

'You know, this doesn't need to be as hard as you're making it.'

She shot me that judgmental look of hers. 'Sure it does.'

I held her look, then sighed wearily. 'Look, I don't know what you call yourself...consultant, morally challenged house guest, whatever…you're still just a thief, OK.'

'Don't think you know me, Michael.'

'Whatever.'

I shook my head – I didn't need her holier-than-thou bullshit on top of everything else. Fucking thieves, I can't stand them. I stared out of the window and tried to concentrate on the task at hand.

I might have thought I was God's gift, but the truth was I didn't have the first idea how I was going to get hold of Swan's key. If he was moving around with three bodyguards, I didn't know if I was even going to get near him. I'd dealt with bodyguards before, but never so many. Swan was paranoid, which meant that any kind of approach on the street was going to be tricky, if not impossible. And even if I did get the key, it was a good bet that he had live-in staff – most of the apartments in the Howardson did. I actually knew the building quite well – in the past year I'd stolen two cars from its underground parking lot. It was all high-end apartments except for a private restaurant club on the ground floor. The main entrance of the building regularly had a doorman and two plain clothes security guards, but they were the least of my worries. Bodyguards – there had to be another way.

We reached the city, bought a couple of new phones, then checked into The Bluebird Hotel. Ella used a fake ID and credit card in the name of Celia Jones. At least I assumed they were fake – there didn't seem much point in asking her about it.

The bellhop showed us into a small fifth floor room that was decked out like a seventies nightmare. Orange patterned walls and chrome spheres. A lava lamp glowed on the bedside table – it looked like an alien had taken a dump in a bottle of Gatorade. As Ella transferred the numbers between the new phones, I tipped the bellhop a twenty.

'We don't want to be disturbed today,' I said to him. I winked at Ella. 'It's our first anniversary, isn't it, sweetie?'

She threw me that look of hers. 'It feels much longer,' she said.

'Of course, sir,' said the bellhop. He nodded politely, then left the room.

Ella tossed me one of the phones.

'I need to make a call,' she said.

She headed into the corridor outside the room and closed the door behind her. She was playing her cards close to her chest. I didn't like it, but I wasn't going to push it – she was helping me and right now that's all that mattered.

I headed over to the hotel room window and gazed at the Howardson Building across the street. It was nine floors of brown stone – a real monument to old money. I stared up at Swan's penthouse. Towering windows. Finely carved masonry. Ceilings that had to be twenty-five feet high. I couldn't make out much detail through the windows, but none of the rooms facing the street looked like they were a library. It had to be deeper inside.

As I thought about the best way to lift Swan's key, I took a dime from my pocket and started my exercises. I spun it and let it dance across my fingertips – the coin twirling from ring to thumb, then index to middle. This wasn't some poker player lazily rolling a coin across his knuckles. This was speed. Accuracy. Magic. Faster and faster until the coin and my fingers were nothing but a blur. Not that I even glanced at it – I kept my eyes on Swan's apartment.

I grabbed the dime to a halt as I saw a figure in one of the rooms. Probably the maid. Blonde hair tied straight back, white blouse. She was opening windows – airing the place. The upside to live-in staff was that the place wouldn't be alarmed. The downside was there'd be someone there when I broke in.

Ella entered the room and got off her phone.

'OK, Swan's definitely in town,' she said. 'He's attending some charity fundraiser this afternoon.'

'Where are you getting this from?' I asked.

'A friend.'

'What friend?'

She walked to the window and stared at the Howardson.

'He's in town, that's all that matters,' she said. 'How do you want to do this?'

'He's taking three bodyguards with him?'

'At least.'

I sighed and glanced back at Swan's apartment. The maid was still at the windows. She had linen with her now – was changing a bed by the look of it. She was going to be our best bet.

'We'll do the maid,' I said. 'She's got to have a key, right?'

Ella eyed her carefully.

'How are you going to get her down from the apartment?' she said.

'You still have Jon's lighter?'

'The fire alarm?'

I nodded. 'They'll empty the building. There's a restaurant on the ground floor. I'll set off the alarm from there.'

Ella stared down at the restaurant.

'I'll do it,' she said.

I glanced dubiously at her. The restaurant was smart and exclusive. It might be easier for a woman to get in than it would be for me, but Ella looked like she lived on the street.

'You got anything else to wear?' I asked.

She laughed to herself.

'Fine,' I said. I wasn't going to worry about offending a woman who'd held a knife to my throat.

'We'll set it off after Swan leaves,' I said. 'While everyone's milling about outside, I'll take the maid's key. Plus it'll clear the apartment long enough for me to find the book.'

Ella toyed pensively with a tiny silver cross hanging around her neck. It was meant to ward off evil. Me probably.

'You're sure you can do this?' she said.

'Don't worry. Once I'm close, I can take pretty much anything from anybody.'

'Show me,' she said.

I shot her a look.

'I'm putting a lot of faith in you here,' she said. 'Show me. Take my watch.'

She held out her wrist – a black plastic digital watch strapped around it.

I rolled my eyes. 'I can't take it, you're expecting it. It's all about distraction. Plus, that's a rubber clasp...'

I grabbed her wrist and turned it over so she could see the clasp of the watch. 'They're really tricky to open,' I said.

She glanced at the clasp. 'You're making excuses.'

'I am,' I replied.

I let go of her wrist and held up my other hand. In it I had her cross hanging from its chain. She gazed at it, and instinctively placed her palm to her neck.

'Not bad,' she said.

'Not bad?' I replied. 'Come on, you were expecting something. That was great.'

She smiled to herself, then reached for a bottle of water and took a sip.

She eyed me carefully.

'You're very sure of yourself, aren't you?' she said.

'You've got to be in this business.'

'A little too sure of yourself, maybe.'

'What's that supposed to mean?'

‘It’s a thrill for you, isn’t it? You’d do it even if you didn’t have to, wouldn’t you?’

I stayed quiet. She may have been right, but I wasn’t going to give her the satisfaction of admitting it. I stepped toward her, reaching around her neck as I put the cross back on her. She went still like an animal – kept her eyes on me. My face was right beside hers as I carefully tied the clasp. I could smell her hair – natural and warm. Could sense her breasts gently rising and falling beneath me as she breathed. I turned and gazed at her lips only a few inches from mine. She stared defiantly back at me, like I’d regret it if I even thought about making a move on her. I held her look for a moment, then let the cross hang.

As I stepped away from her, she smiled like she’d just won some kind of stand-off. Like I was weak.

I wasn’t.

‘And here’s your watch,’ I said.

I tossed her digital watch back to her. She looked more than a little taken aback as she caught it.

‘A little too sure of myself?’ I said. ‘Don’t worry, I know what I’m doing.’

I returned to the window and continued watching Swan’s apartment.

***

At three thirty a black Bentley Silver Spur with license plate ‘PS1’ disappeared down into the Howardson’s underground parking lot. I stood by our hotel room window watching it – I’d been waiting there since noon. ‘He’s about to leave,’ I said.

Ella emerged from the bathroom wearing a short black shift dress and high heels – and I just stared at her. I couldn't believe it, she looked sexy as fuck. Still no make-up, but it didn't look like she needed it. Not that she was looking for my approval – she didn't even glance at me. She just tied her hair up with a clip and joined me at the window. I kept my eyes on her, and for a moment wished that I'd kissed her instead of taking her watch.

She stared at the Howardson. 'There.'

I looked back at the building. PS1 was exiting the parking lot on the side street. The car was now full – four people all in black tie. I could just about make out Swan's bulbous head sitting in the rear seat next to one of his bodyguards. As the car sped off, I glanced at Ella – she flicked the lighter to make sure it was working. A tiny blue flame.

'Five minutes,' she said.

She placed the lighter in her handbag and headed out of the room.

I watched from the hotel window as she made her way across the street toward the Howardson. She was going to set off the sprinkler system in the ladies' room of the restaurant.

As she reached the main entrance, the doorman stopped her. They spoke a moment, but Ella looked calm and poised – smiling easily like some lunch crowd princess. As the doorman ushered her inside, I glanced up at the other apartments in the building. I caught sight of a few people in the upper floors – a few TVs blazing blue in the lower ones. That was good. When they cleared the building, there'd be a small crowd of residents milling about. It wouldn't be too difficult to get close to the maid.

I checked my watch – two minutes to go. I slipped the new phone into my pocket, put on my aviators, and headed out of the hotel.

I crossed Market Street, stopped outside the pillared entrance of the Howardson and pretended to look for a cab. As I searched the traffic, I heard the alarm go off – a muffled ringing from deep inside the building. I calmly glanced at the upper floors like I was looking for a fire.

The alarm continued. Residents then slowly began to emerge from the building. No fuss, they just drifted out – some of them even had plates of food. It was a truly cosmopolitan panic. As the building's security guards ushered more people out, Ella emerged with them. I kept my eyes on the doors, waiting for Swan's maid to appear.

More residents drifted out – a small group. Swan's maid then emerged from the door behind them. I eyed her carefully. White blouse. Black denim jeans – Diesels. As she glanced up at the building, I kept my eyes on the upper floors and slowly edged toward her. I'd bump into her – apologize. I took another quick look at her. A key chain disappeared into the front left pocket of her jeans. The other end of the chain was attached to one of her belt loops.

Fuck. It had a security clasp – a combination lock. You needed to line up a four digit code to release it. Fuck.

Ella glanced at me – could tell that something was wrong. She drifted over to me.

'I can't get it,' I whispered.

'What do you mean?'

'She's wearing a combination lock.'

Ella stared at the maid's key chain. 'There's nothing you can do? We may not get another chance like this.'

I glanced around and tried to figure a new plan.

The Howardson's porter appeared at the main door and told us this would only take a few minutes to straighten out. I glanced up at the building, then stepped out into the street to get a better view. I remembered the maid had been opening windows. I looked up – one of Swan's windows at the front of the building was open, but it was too exposed. It overlooked everyone waiting outside the main entrance. I headed over to the side street where it was quieter. Down the left-hand side of the building, I could see another small open window in his apartment. I studied it for a moment. Below it was a thick stone ledge. Below the ledge was the window of another apartment – one that belonged to someone here in the crowd. I didn't know who. I thought to myself a moment – no choice. Shit.

I walked over to Ella. 'I need a paper bag,' I said to her.

'What?'

'A paper bag.'

I looked around. There was a convenience store on the next block.

'Go get one. Give it to me when I ask for it,' I said.

Ella eyed me curiously, then headed for the store. As she did, I casually drifted toward a small group of residents. They'd been among the last ones to come out of the building – probably from the upper floors.

I waited until Ella emerged from the store. I watched as she folded a small brown paper bag into her handbag, then I slipped off my sunglasses and started breathing heavily – noisily.

'Shit,' I said. I grabbed my forehead. 'Fuck.'

I crouched down and closed my eyes. One of the residents approached me – a man in his forties.

'Are you alright?' he asked. He placed a hand on my back.

'Panic attack,' I said.

I stood up and tried to catch my breath.

'It's fine,' he said.

I started hyperventilating – rocking around uneasily on the sidewalk.

'Just take it slow,' he said.

'I need a bag,' I replied.

Ella appeared beside me. She clicked open her handbag and offered me the brown paper bag. I grabbed it and breathed into it – made a big deal about it. I started swaying and fell to my knees. The residents around me scurried to my aid. They tried to pick me back up, their arms clambering around me.

'It's fine, just breathe,' said one of them.

'Sit him up,' said another.

They grabbed my arms, my back, and tried to get me seated on the sidewalk. But I was fighting for breath – reaching out, grabbing hold of anyone near me with my one free hand. Holding the bag to my mouth with the other.

'I need to get inside,' I said.

Ella offered to help.

'There's a sofa in the lobby,' said one woman. 'Lay him down there. I'll call an ambulance.'

'No ambulance,' I panted. 'Just...I need to lie down.'

Ella took me by the arm and led me inside the deserted marble lobby of the Howardson.

'What the hell was that?' she said.

I quickly tore open the paper bag. Inside were five of the residents' apartment keys. I grabbed them and shoved them into my pockets.

'There's an open window at Swan's,' I said. 'I can probably climb in from the downstairs apartment. Go back to the hotel room, let me know if the maid comes back up.'

She nodded approvingly at me, but I didn't give a shit now – I just wanted this over with.

I got into the elevator and headed up to seven, the floor below Swan's.

The elevator doors slid open onto a tiny landing with a black and white mosaic floor. There were only two apartment doors. I got my bearings – the apartment on my right would be the one below the open window. I took out the keys and started trying them in the lock. The first key – useless. So was the second. Third – garbage. Fourth. The door clicked open.

I slipped inside the apartment – a wash of Persian carpets and crystal chandeliers. I ran to the far end. A leaded window overlooked the side street. I turned the handle, pushed the window open and stuck my head out. The ledge below Swan's apartment was a good seven or eight feet above the top of the window – it had looked a lot closer from the ground. I'd have to stand full length, balancing on the top of the window frame to reach it. I tugged at the window to make sure it was sturdy, then glanced down at the tiny side street, a hundred and fifty feet below. There were a few people walking by, but they weren't looking up. There was an office block on the other side of the street. The offices on my level looked empty, but there were a few suits milling around on the floors above. Someone would see me for sure if I wasn't quick about this.

I climbed up onto the window sill, then paused a moment. This was alien territory for me. Scaling buildings? I was a hundred and fifty feet up and way out of my league. I stared down at the sidewalk and tried to summon up the strength. When it came to scary shit like this, common sense was the enemy. Don't think. Just do it.

I grabbed the top of the open window with both hands and hauled my body over it. I felt the frame dig into my stomach as my legs dangled in the air – two fucking hinges were all that were holding me up now. I steadied myself against the stone wall of the building with one hand, then pulled a leg up onto the top of the window. The hinges creaked – something snapped. Fuck – I clung to the window. The panic in me as I stared down at the frame. I tried to keep calm – don't think, just do it. I raised my leg again, placed the sole of my foot on the frame and pushed myself up into a standing position. I balanced precariously on the top of the window, my fingers grasping to any edges in the building's masonry that I could find. The ledge above me was just out of reach – I'd have to launch myself at it. As I readied myself, the hinges creaked again. Jesus. I felt myself losing balance. The window snapped – I jumped and grabbed at the ledge with my fingertips. The window buckled below me, a single twisted hinge stopping it from crashing to the street below. I dangled from the ledge, my fingers clinging to the rough stone. I pulled my chin above the ledge, shot an arm out across the stone, then dragged my body onto the ledge.

My heart raced as I gathered myself a moment. I glanced at the open window of Swan's apartment just a few feet to my right. I crawled along the ledge, pulled open the window, then tumbled in, head first. I landed on a polished mahogany desk, smashing a china lamp in the process. This wasn't elegant cat-burglary, but I didn't give a shit how it looked. I was just happy to be back inside.

I got to my feet in a wood paneled room – a cramped study full of leather armchairs and stuffed animals. Peacocks and lizards. I opened the study door and headed out into a long winding hallway. Glass display cabinets full of swords and muskets lined the walls. Another full of violins. In between them, white marble busts of composers and writers – their heads sitting on columns like a bunch of Pre-Raphaelite Pez dispensers. The place looked like a museum.

My phone vibrated – it was Ella.

'I'm in,' I said.

'Good,' she replied. 'They're still outside.'

'I'll be as quick as I can. Call me the moment they start heading in.'

I hung up and ran down the hallway. A dining room to my right – tapestry chairs and pewter candlesticks. Beyond that, a wood-paneled reception with shields hanging from the walls. I headed further down. A huge stone archway then appeared to my left. Rows of book shelves on the other side – this was it.

I headed into the vast, galleried library. Polished wooden book shelves twenty feet high covered the walls. Rolling ladders. Suspended walkways. There had to be a hundred thousand books in here, easy. I ran to the nearest shelf and studied a leather-bound volume – *A History of Egyptian Agriculture*. Reference books. I glanced around – the books on the upper level looked smaller, more like novels. I clambered up a wrought iron spiral staircase and started scanning the books on the next level. I found Charles Dickens' *Our Mutual Friend*. This level was novels. Gatsby would be here somewhere.

I paused a moment. The novels were ordered by author. My mind went blank – who wrote The Great Gatsby? I couldn't remember. I grabbed my phone and called Ella. There was no answer. I hung up and tried the internet on my phone. A polite message on the screen informed me that my account wasn't set up for web access. Shit. I tried Ella again. Still no answer. Fuck, where the hell was she? I glanced at the novels. There were thousands of them – I couldn't go through them all. Come on, I knew this. Gatsby. I tried to think. Time was against me. Come on…The Great Gatsby. It felt like I was trying to win a car.

F. Scott Fitzgerald!

I laughed. I couldn't believe it. Something that I'd learned at school was actually of some fucking use. I ran down the suspended walkway and started looking. Faulkner. Ferber. Filliman.

Fitzgerald.

I glanced at the volume titles and found it. The Great Gatsby. It was a paperback – it looked new, this was no first edition. I quickly checked to make sure there were no other copies on the shelf. Just the one. I grabbed it, then went still. I could hear voices in the apartment. A door closing. Shit. I laid face down on the suspended walkway and kept my eyes on the entrance to the library.

The maid walked past the archway. She was with a security guard – a huge Middle Eastern guy in a dark gray suit. They were checking the rooms.

Why the hell hadn't Ella called?

Fuck. I couldn't get back out the way I'd come in – the downstairs window was trashed. The only way out was the main door.

I heard the maid's voice. 'I'm sure it's fine,' she said.

'I need to check,' replied the guard.

I could hear them inspecting the other rooms – doors opening. Silence for a moment, then heavy footsteps approaching the library. I pressed myself as flat against the walkway as I could. The edge of the walkway had a raised lip – six inches – it wouldn't give me much cover. The security guard entered the library. He glanced around the lower book cases, then disappeared underneath the walkway where I was lying. I stopped breathing – stayed deathly still. He reappeared below me, then headed for the bookcases on the other side of the room. From there he'd be able to see me on the walkway for sure. Shit, I was going to have to fight my way out of this. I slid the book into my jacket pocket, and lifted my head slightly. I could see him on the other side of the library, looking around. He'd see me any moment. Fuck.

'Hasani!' came the maid's voice. 'The study!'

The guard turned and ran out of the library. The maid must have found the smashed china lamp. This was my chance. I swung my legs off the walkway and lowered myself to the floor. I crept over to the archway and took a quick look down the hallway. I couldn't see them. They were in the study, but they wouldn't be there for long. The main door was a hundred feet down the hallway to my left. The elevator had to be just outside. I crept down the hallway as quickly and quietly as I could. I reached the main door and opened it.

'What the fuck!' yelled the security guard from the other end of the hallway.

I slammed the door shut behind me and ran for the elevator. I hit the call button – could hear the guard running inside the apartment.

'Come on, come on!' I yelled at the elevator.

The elevator opened. I jumped inside, hit the button – but nothing moved. The apartment door then burst open in front of me and the guard ran out. As he sprinted across the landing, the elevator door lazily began to slide shut. I raised my fists as he leaped for the door – but too late – his hands slammed against the steel as the elevator closed. I was on my way down, but not clear yet. The guard didn't look like he had a radio mic, but he'd call the foyer guards from his phone, no question. I needed to get out quick. I reached the ground floor and exited the elevator.

The lobby was full of people. Chaos. Residents complaining to the porter that they couldn't find their keys. The lunch crowd returning to the restaurant. I calmly headed for the main doors. Three security guards were standing by them – one was on his phone. He started looking around. I changed direction and veered across the lobby toward the restaurant. I glanced back – the guard on the phone was looking at me.

'Stop him!' he yelled.

The guards ran for me. I sprinted through the restaurant, looking for another exit – the kitchen, anything – all I could see were walls and windows. The diners looked startled as the security guards ran into the restaurant. A couple in their sixties were sitting at a window table at the far end. It was my only way out now. I ran for them, leaped up onto their table and launched myself back first through the window. The glass billowed out with a splintering crash as I landed on the sidewalk. I picked myself up and sprinted down the backstreets.

I could hear the guards giving chase – their voices in the afternoon air behind me. I kept running, weaving through the streets. I darted around a busy corner, then slowed to a stroll. A large crowd was crossing the main junction ahead of me on Market Street. I slipped into the crowd, crossed the street with them, then casually stepped onto a streetcar.

As the car rolled up Market Street, I slumped into a seat and caught my breath. I peered out of the window at the Howardson – the police were pulling up by the main entrance. I shook my head – I couldn't believe that Ella had hung me out to dry like that. This book had better have been worth the trouble.

I grabbed it from my pocket and quickly flipped through the pages, looking for anything out of the ordinary. Regular paper, regular text. No handwritten notes in the margins. I ran my fingertips across the covers and tried to feel if there was anything hidden inside them. It looked and felt like a run-of-the-mill store-bought copy. Fuck it – I stuck the book back in my jacket, then took another quick look out of the window. The Howardson was disappearing out of sight. I put my sunglasses back on, stepped off the car, then carefully made my way back to The Bluebird via the side streets.

I reached our hotel room, cursing Ella's name as I opened the door.

'What the fuck was that?' I said.

I halted in the doorway. The room was dark – the curtains drawn. In the shadows I could see Ella kneeling on the floor by the bed, her hands clasped behind her head. I felt the cold touch of metal against my cheek. I turned – a guy in his thirties was holding a silenced pistol on me. Shaved blond hair. Slavic-looking. His hands in surgical gloves.

'Not a sound,' he said. He dragged me inside the room and swung the door shut behind me. A second guy then emerged from the far corner of the room.

Same pistol and gloves. He smiled at me – his face a gnarled scaffold of cheekbones and jaw.

'Glad you could join us,' he said. 'On your knees.'

I recognized his voice. French accent. It was the guy from the nightclub.

5

The Slav kept his pistol firmly aimed at me as I clasped my hands behind my head and knelt down on the floor opposite Ella. She stared at me – a thick stream of blood flowing from her mouth.

I kept my eyes on the French guy as the Slav started searching through my jacket pockets. These were the fuckers who'd killed Freddy, and were probably the ones who'd killed Jon too. I felt like going for their throats.

The Slav found the book in my jacket and tossed it to French. French studied it a moment, nodding to himself as he stepped behind me. I rocked forward as he pushed the barrel of his gun against the back of my head.

'The necklace,' he said.

'Fuck you,' I replied.

He smashed the butt of his gun against my skull. I toppled to one side with the pain.

'The necklace,' he repeated.

I eyed the motherfucker.

'I don't have it,' I said.

'Take off your jacket,' he said. 'Slowly.'

I lowered my hands and slipped my arms out of the sleeves. As I placed my hands back behind my head, he grabbed the jacket and started searching every fold in the material. He wasn't going to find the necklace in my jacket, but he'd find it soon enough – I was wearing it around my neck. I'd put it on while I took a shower, in case Ella decided to take it and leave me behind. It lay just underneath the collar of my shirt. A few centimeters of cotton were all that were keeping me and Ella alive right now. I kept my hands behind my head – could feel the necklace's clasp between my fingers. French produced a glinting crescent-shaped blade, ripped open the jacket lining and started pulling it inside out.

I cooled my anger and tried to think. The book had meant something to these guys. They must have been looking for it too – had probably been watching Swan's apartment all day and stumbled into us in the process. They'd been holding Ella for at least fifteen minutes – chances are, their other guys would be here any moment. I needed to hide the necklace – it would be our only bargaining chip. I glanced at Ella, then nodded subtly down toward the collar of my shirt. She stared at me for a moment, then understood. It was all about distraction.

She shifted around on her knees. In a second both guys had their guns on her. 'You don't fucking move!' said French.

Ella went still. I undid the clasp – one end of the chain swung down beneath my shirt. I held the other end between two fingers, circled my fingertips against each other, and wound the necklace up into my right hand.

Silence. French lowered his gun and finished searching my jacket. He threw it, stepped over to me and pointed the gun at the side of my head.

'You move, you're dead,' he said.

He carefully reached into the right front pocket of my jeans. He found some cash, threw it across the floor, then checked my other pockets. I eyed him venomously.

'Are you the one who killed Jon?' I said.

He smiled to himself.

'Are you?' I said

'Take off the shirt,' he replied.

'It's not here…'

He cocked his gun.

'The shirt. Now!'

I lowered my hands, the necklace tucked between the flesh of my thumb and the palm of my right hand. As I reached down to the lowest button of my shirt, I slipped the necklace into the front pocket of my jeans. I undid my shirt and took it off. French grabbed it. He ran every inch of the material through his fist, then threw it.

'Shoes, socks,' he said.

I did what I was told. I took them off. He searched them, then threw them to one side.

'Stand up,' he said. 'Jeans, take them off.'

This had to be done faultlessly – one glimpse of the necklace and Ella and I were gone. I slowly got to my feet and undid my belt. As I slipped off my jeans, I lifted the necklace out of the pocket and back into my right palm. I was a mass of nerves. I'd never had to pickpocket myself before – it was the most intense fucking gig of my life. As I placed my hands back behind my head, French grabbed the jeans and crushed every inch of the denim between his hands.

'Underwear,' he said.

I reached down, pulled off my boxers and threw them to one side. As I stood naked in front of Ella, French crushed my underwear through his hand. He pointed his gun at Ella.

'You,' he said. 'Up!'

Ella got to her feet.

'Take it all off,' he said.

The Slav winked at her – she stared coldly back at him. She unzipped her dress and let it fall to her ankles. She was wearing a black bra and briefs. I gazed at her body and felt shaken for a second. Her back and stomach were covered in a mess of red scars like someone had whipped her repeatedly.

The Slav raised an eyebrow at her. 'You like it rough, huh?' he said.

He waved his gun for her to continue. If she was uncomfortable doing this, she didn't want this fucker to know about it. She mechanically unclasped her bra and let it fall from her shoulders. Her breasts swung free – also scarred. She slipped off her heels, pulled down her briefs, then stood there naked. Broad shoulders like a swimmer. Sleek breasts. Delicate black pubic hair. Her beauty stained by the wounds that swept across her.

As French searched Ella's discarded clothes, the Slav leered at her – staring at her vagina like some creep in a strip joint.

'That pussy of yours work?' he said. 'Or is it as fucked as the rest of you?'

Ella stayed silent.

French tossed her clothes to one side, then pointed his gun at us.

'Both of you,' he said. 'Hands against the wall. Legs apart.'

Fuck, they were going to cavity search us.

'I don't have it,' I said. 'I gave it to a friend of mine. If he doesn't hear from me in the next hour, your necklace is going to wind up on the front page of every fucking newspaper in the country!'

French glanced at the Slav, and they both smiled.

'You're a very bad liar,' said French. 'Hands against the wall.'

As Ella and I headed for the far side wall, French's phone rang.

'Nobody move,' he said.

He answered the phone.

'We have him, sir,' he said. 'We're checking now. We have the book.'

I listened carefully. Sir – it was probably the guy who'd called me last night. This was the fucker I wanted. There was more talk from the other end of the line.

'Yes, sir,' said French. 'Three minutes.' He hung up.

'Get dressed,' he said. 'We're leaving.'

He turned to the Slav. 'They're in the parking lot,' he said. 'I'll make sure the elevator is clear. You bring them out.'

The Slav nodded, then gestured for us to get dressed.

Ella's bag had been emptied across the bed, her clothes strewn across the floor. She left the dress and climbed into her jeans and sweater. As I pulled on my clothes, I looked around for a place to hide the necklace.

'Keep it,' Ella whispered as she put her heels back on.

I glanced at her – she didn't look back at me.

I hoped she knew what she was doing. I slipped the necklace back into the pocket of my jeans. French opened the room door, and checked that the hallway was clear. As French headed out, the Slav took off his jacket and casually draped it over his gun. He kept his eyes on me as he gestured toward Ella.

'We're going for a ride,' he said. 'One sound and I'll kill your bitch where she stands.' He glanced at Ella. 'Same applies. We only need one of you.'

He grabbed the book, tucked it into his shirt, then kept his gun on us as he backed toward the door. He quickly glanced down the corridor, then beckoned us out of the room. Ella and I headed out into the corridor – French waiting by the elevator at the far end. We started walking toward him, the Slav right behind us. I glanced nervously at Ella. The elevator went straight down to the parking lot – we'd be as good as dead the moment we set foot in it. For a second Ella eyed a door just ahead of us in the corridor marked 'Laundry' – she was then a sudden a blur of movement. She kicked her leg back, caught the Slav in his face with her heel. Her shoe came off, embedded deep in his eye. Bullets down the corridor from French. I ducked. Ella swung open the laundry room door – it gave us a moment of cover from French as he ran toward us.

'The book!' yelled Ella.

I reached out. Bullets splintered the door around me – I ducked back behind it. The book was too far. Ella opened the room's laundry chute. We wouldn't both get down there in time, French was only a few feet away. I heard his pistol click empty – now was my chance.

'Go!' I yelled at Ella.

I dived out into the corridor and reached for the Slav's gun. French ran at me and kicked my hand – the gun skittered down the corridor. He kicked at my face. I dodged it, swung my fist and caught him full in the jaw. The fucker hardly moved. He smashed me against the corridor wall, whipped out the crescent blade and jabbed at me. He caught the lower side of my neck – a deep cut – blood pouring down my chest. Ella ran out from the laundry room, looking for the Slav's gun. French swung the blade at her – I grabbed his arm and sank my knee into his stomach. As he buckled onto the floor, I stamped on his face – boot print suntan – he felt it this time, the motherfucker. He lost hold of the blade, leaped up and barged me back against the wall. I head-butted him – heard his nose crack – it dazed him for a second. Ella ran for the book, ducking as the elevator doors opened and two more guys with silenced weapons started shooting. She grabbed the book, dragged me into the laundry room, then dived headlong into the chute. As French ran for me, I leaned over the chute and threw myself down into the darkness.

I fell headfirst – the metal booming as I clattered against the tight steel walls. I couldn't see a thing. I hit a corner with my ribs and slowed for a second. Then free-falling, straight down. Light below me, noise, brightness. I hit an exit ramp and slid out across a tiled floor, a trail of blood in my wake. As Ella dragged me to my feet, a couple of terrified-looking laundry staff cowered to one side of the room. Ella pulled me through a door into a loading bay – white laundry sacks hanging from the ceiling. We tumbled through them, and out into the street at the rear of the hotel, alarms ringing behind us.

I put my hand to my neck and tried to stop the bleeding. My shirt was soaked with blood. Even with my adrenaline pumping, I was starting to feel dizzy – was struggling to walk. Traffic everywhere, cars edging down the street. Ella tried to stop one – they all locked their doors. She hammered at their windows, but they looked too scared.

We stumbled down the street and around a corner. A yellow cab was dropping off a fare. We jumped straight into the back.

The driver stared in alarm at me. 'Jesus!' he said.

'Drive!' said Ella. 'Just drive!'

He pulled out into the thick traffic waiting at the lights. A few more cars pulled up behind us. The cab driver glanced at me in his rear view mirror.

'Maybe you need another cab,' he said.

'Just get us out of here!' said Ella.

I held my hand to my neck, but I couldn't stem the blood. My vision was going gray. The driver looked to see if he could make a U-turn, but cars were stacking up in the other direction too. We were stuck. Ella and I glanced out of the windows, looking for any side streets we could take. We caught sight of French running out into the road ahead of us. Two other guys ran out behind him – they started looking inside the cars waiting at the lights. Ella dragged me down onto the cab floor.

'Don't look back at us,' she said to the driver.

'I don't want any part of this!' he said.

'Are the cab doors locked?' she said. 'Unlock them.'

He released the locks. I reached for the door handle, but my body faded beneath me. I collapsed onto the cab floor. 'Fuck.'

Ella gazed down at me. No way was I going to make it out onto the street.

'You have a phone?' she said to the driver. 'Hold it to your ear. The guys checking the cars ahead. Tell me where they are.'

The driver nervously held a phone to his ear.

'Relax,' she said. 'Just tell me what you see.'

'They're heading down the middle of the road,' he said. 'Four or five cars ahead.'

I took a deep breath and glanced at the cab door.

'They're heading this way,' said the driver.

I reached into my pocket, took hold of Ella's hand and gave her the necklace.

'Go,' I said to her. 'There's no point in you staying.'

She kept hold of my hand and stared at me for a moment – warmth in her eyes for the first time. She kept her eyes on me, then took the necklace.

'They're checking the van ahead of us,' said the driver. 'Get the fuck out of my cab!'

Ella grabbed the door handle, then glanced back at me.

‘Don’t wait,’ I told her.

I felt myself drifting – my head swimming. Through the dizziness I could hear sirens in the distance. Raised voices on the street. The sirens were getting closer – they must have found the Slav’s body.

‘They’ve stopped,’ said the driver.

Ella waited.

‘They’ve stopped, they’re heading back,’ he said. ‘They’re talking to someone in the back of a car.’

‘What car?’ said Ella.

‘A silver Mercedes pulling out of the hotel,’ he said. ‘The lights have changed, we’ll be moving in a second.’

Ella let go of the door handle. She knelt down beside me as the cab began to creep forward. I blinked heavily – blood and sweat in my eyes. As the cab slowed to a halt again, I kept my eyes on the car roofs slowly edging past the cab window. The silver roof of the Mercedes appeared. It stopped in the traffic right beside us. I gazed up at it. The guy I wanted was in the back of that car. I needed to see his face – needed to know who I was up against. I edged toward the door and pulled myself up to the window. Ella grabbed my arm to stop me.

‘No,’ she said.

But he was right there. I slowly raised my head and stared at the tinted rear windows of the Mercedes. I could just about make out a figure in the back seat. I couldn’t see his face – just his arm by the window. Dark suit. A delicate, porcelain white hand. But there was someone sitting next to him – a woman. Embroidered cream dress. Silk gloves. Her face hidden behind some kind of a white veil – like a bride or something. She slowly leaned forward in her seat, then turned and looked at me. Before I could duck down, the cab lurched forward and she disappeared from view. Behind the Mercedes, the doors of a black Lexus then swung open – French and the two other guys jumped out of it and ran for us. The cab slowed to a halt again behind a van waiting to turn at the lights.

'Move!' yelled Ella.

The guys descended on the cab, grabbing at the door handles – the driver locked them. As French reached for his gun, the driver spun the wheel and hit the accelerator. We crunched against the rear corner of the van, mounted the sidewalk and sped out past the lights onto Market Street. Pedestrians scattered around us. But no gun-shots – it was too open, too many people even for these fuckers. I hauled myself up and stared out of the rear window. French and his men were running after us, but we were moving now.

We cleared Market and weaved into the backstreets. The cab's engine whined as we accelerated away, but the sound was fading. Ella said something, but her voice disappeared as well. As she pressed her hand against my neck, I lay back in the cab seat, my arms limp at my sides.

I felt myself falling into the darkness.

I was gone.

6

I could feel hands on me. People dragging me across a room full of shadows. Ella's voice above me.

'He's Jon's brother,' she said.

'I don't care,' replied a man with a southern accent.

'He's going to die,' said Ella.

'One less thief on the planet, big fucking deal.'

'Get Tully.'

'I don't want this guy here, Ella.'

'It's not down to you,' she said. 'Get Tully!'

Pain as I was dumped on a mattress. People shuffling around behind me. I felt my head being turned to one side so I could breathe.

'Michael,' whispered Ella. 'Michael, open your eyes.'

I forced my eyes open. Ella's face was right in front of me, a white blur in the darkness.

'I can't take you to hospital,' she said. 'They'll be looking for us there. A friend of mine's going to fix your neck. He's a medic, OK?'

I nodded weakly – and my eyes started to close again.

'You need to stay awake,' she said.

I tried to focus on her – could see a red stain seeping across the mattress beneath me.

'Come on, Michael, stay awake,' she said. 'Talk to me.'

She took hold of my hand.

'Tell me about Jon,' she said.

I tried to catch some breath.

'He told me about San Diego,' she said. 'The islands. Tell me.'

'The islands,' I said.

'You rented a boat. What kind?'

'Seventy-foot sloop,' I said. 'Sailed it up the coast. Just the two of us.'

'Yeah? Did you swim? He said you met a couple of girls. What were their names?'

I couldn't remember. I just pictured Jon and me on the boat. Jon laughing as he gazed up at the brilliant white sail, his sunglasses flashing against the cobalt sky. The two of us singing when we saw the lantern light on the sea that night. Sharing tequila with the yacht that drifted by.

A perfect postcard of a memory. And it tore me like paper.

'I didn't mean to hurt him, Ella,' I said.

She nodded.

I gazed emptily at her. 'Some roads...you just can't turn around on them, you know.'

And I tried to remember. My brother. I hadn't meant any harm.

I was nineteen when I started stealing. I'd like to say it was desperation that drove me to it, but it wasn't. I did it for the joy of it, pure and simple.

Not that life had been easy going for me up until then. Uncle Harry had kicked me out of the house that year – which was no huge surprise to anyone. We'd been arguing a lot, mostly about what I was doing with myself. Jon had just graduated in law and been offered a job at the *Washington Post* – but me? I'd dropped out of high school, and had done little since except drink, get into fights, and lose one stupid job after another. Car wash. Video store.

Then that March I got arrested. Nothing serious. I got drunk one night, broke into a warehouse and spent two hours driving forklifts around until the police showed up. I don't even know why I did it. Harry gave me hell for it. Jon too. Normally Jon cut me a lot of slack, but after the arrest, all his frustrations with my drinking and my indifference came pouring out.

'You know how heartbroken mom and dad would have been to see you now?' he said.

I nodded and poured myself a glass of whiskey. He slapped it from my hand.

'You're not stupid, Michael! Why are you like this?'

I stared at him. Anything I could have said would have just made things worse.

'I don't know what to do with you,' he said. 'You want me to turn down this job? Is that it? You want me to stay here?'

'Do what you want. Just leave me alone.'

I picked the glass up from the floor and poured myself another drink. He watched me for a moment, then grabbed his jacket and left.

It's hard living in someone's shadow. Harder still, when you love that person – when you want them to achieve the greatness that you know is going to leave you in the dark. And Jon cast a dark shadow. At school, at sports, with girls – he was always the guy who could. I knew it. Mom and dad knew it. It wouldn't have been any surprise to them that Jon was at the *Washington Post*. Straight out of the gate, he'd landed a job at one of the biggest dailies in the country. It was typically Jon. Brilliant.

I moved out of Uncle Harry's that March and got myself a job at a dry cleaners in the city. Found a shitty little apartment in the Mission – a damp basement that looked like it had bruised walls. But it was fine. I worked most days. Got drunk most nights. I hardly knew I was there. I just rolled through the days – no direction, no meaning – in a drip-fed haze of cheap whiskey and dry cleaning fumes. If you'd told me then that I'd be clearing three grand a week in less than a year, I probably wouldn't have even had the energy to laugh at you.

But it was coming sure enough. Life rolls like a truck, but it can turn on a dime. And it turned for me one weekend at work.

Sure Mac's Dry Cleaners was owned by this nervous, buttoned-down guy named Frank McLaren. He was in his forties and a little on the heavy side – not really fat, just kind of soft and doughy-looking. But he was sensitive about it. He'd go to the gym every morning before work, then get so depressed that nothing had changed, he'd pound down a box of donuts. I swear, I heard him cry once. It was a shame. He was a decent guy.

But we had this regular customer – a pug-nosed thug in his thirties named Benny. Silk suit. Black Porsche. About as charming as a broken ankle. He'd peel cash from sweaty rolls of bills, and talk about all the girls he'd fucked like he was Brad Pitt or something. Ugly motherfucker. He could have driven a Ferrari full of Perrier through Ethiopia, he wouldn't get laid. But Frank would listen and smile, be polite – Benny was a paying customer. Then one morning Benny came in wearing a skintight vest, and Frank cracked some joke about his weight and how he could never wear stuff like that. Benny saw this as a green light. From then on, every time he came in, he'd make some stupid joke about Frank. Every time. Not even funny jokes, just nasty. You could see Frank buckling under the weight of this idiot. I just wanted to hit the fucker – and there was one morning when Benny saw that I was close to it. He eyed me for a moment, then started talking about how connected he was. That he knew Sid White, this local hood – like it was meant to scare me. Like I gave a shit. Frank stepped in and told me that it's fine.

After that, Frank would send me out the back whenever he saw Benny's Porsche pull up. I'd do as he asked – I'd stay out of sight. But Benny knew I was there, and he'd just crack his stupid jokes even louder.

I did nothing about it, and had no intention either until Linda came to visit me one Saturday. It was the first time I'd seen her since I'd moved out of Uncle Harry's. We spent the day in bed, then decided to head out to the G-Bar in North Beach. It wasn't really my kind of place – a lot of Swiss watches and over-priced drinks – but some blues band that Linda liked were playing there.

The bar was packed wall to wall that night – and although I didn't see Benny at first, I recognized his self-important howl cutting through the clamor. He was sitting at a table, laughing around with a bunch of meat-heads. On his lap was some blonde wearing the heaviest make-up I'd ever seen – it looked like she'd drawn a cartoon of herself on her own face. I stared coldly at Benny as he took out his wallet and ordered champagne for the table.

Linda glanced at me. 'Who's that?'

I shook my head. 'This client at the store, doesn't matter.'

I grabbed a couple of Jamesons from the bar, then dragged Linda as far from Benny's table as I could. We found a little corner and made ourselves at home.

The band played. Crawling Kingsnake. Heavy blues, but they got the crowd going. I was never much of a blues hound, but Linda loved it. As she got up to dance, I went to get us some more drinks. I squeezed through the crowd, then slowed. Benny and his buddies were propping up the bar ahead of me. I guess I could have waited, gone to some other part of the bar – but I didn't.

I squeezed through and handed the barman a twenty. 'Two Jamesons please.'

Benny turned to me and laughed.

'Laundry boy!' he said. 'Hey, this guy cleans my shirts!'

I nodded.

'How are you?' he asked.

'Good,' I replied.

'Yeah?' he said. 'How's that fat fucking boss of yours?'

'He's fine,' I said.

It was strange – I wanted to make some smart-ass comment, but I just gazed at him. All I could think about was the wallet that I'd seen him take from his jacket. I'd done a lot of magic as a kid, sleight of hand. It fell away from me after Mom and Dad died, but my hands were itching as I stared at Benny. He turned to his friends and cracked some dumb joke about Frank being the size of an elephant. As he did, I glanced at his inside left pocket, and wondered how I'd do it. He was standing close, but not close enough. Better he approached me, than the other way around.

'Elephant?' I said.

He turned to me. 'Yeah. You got a problem with that?'

'It's just there are three-year-olds who could come up with something smarter than that.'

He leaned in close to me. 'Watch yourself,' he said.

His jacket hung open right in front of me. It was almost disappointing how predictable he was.

I smiled. 'I didn't know stupid came in so many flavors.'

He grabbed me by my neck. As his friends restrained him, I slipped my fingers into his jacket pocket. I felt his wallet brush against my fingertips, but I let it go – he was paying for all the drinks that night, he'd miss it in a second. Plus, I could already feel the serrated teeth of his car key.

His friends pulled him off me.

'The guy's not worth it, fuck him,' said one of them.

'You're nothing!' Benny said to me. 'Fucking laundry boy!'

I did my best to look scared – no confidence here.

'Motherfucker!' he said.

He reached into his jacket and took out his wallet. He threw a couple of bills onto the bar, then headed back to the table with his friends. I watched him for a moment, then slipped his car key into my pocket.

I couldn't believe the thrill of it. A rush like I'd never felt. Like I was invisible – standing right in front of him, and he couldn't see me.

I grabbed Linda. 'Want to go for a ride?'

Linda laughed as we raced down Columbus in Benny's Porsche. The turbo growling under my foot.

'You're sure he won't think it was you,' she said.

'Laundry boy? Come on.'

I turned on the radio – dance music filled the car.

Linda smiled. 'So where do you want to go?'

I eyed her for a moment.

'Hunter's Point,' I said. It was a disused dock in the south of the city. 'We'll dump the fucking thing in the bay.'

She clapped excitedly, and I hit the accelerator.

We reached the abandoned warehouses at Hunter's Point, then pulled up by one of the docks. As Linda slipped the car into neutral, I grabbed it by its rear spoiler. It's funny, you'd think that rolling a Porsche off the end of a dock would be a moment to remember – that watching the water swallow it up would be some kind of marker. But it felt strangely muted to me. The car splashed, then bubbled into the bay, but all I could think about was the moment that I'd lifted the key. That invisible second amid the chaos of the bar. The thrill of it.

It changed everything.

A single degree doesn't sound like much, but it's the difference between ice skating and drowning. I felt like I was above the water for the first time in years. Like I could breathe.

Benny turned up with his laundry a few days later. He didn't mention the car – he just cracked his stupid jokes, but I didn't give a shit. I didn't care about him, nor Frank. The only thing I was interested in was getting back out there and finding that thrill.

I started spending my lunch breaks drifting through the crowds in Union Square. Brushing past people and taking their wallet. Asking for the time and lifting their phone. It's amazing how close a stranger will stand when they're giving you directions – like the words 'second turn on the left' don't mean anything unless they're squeezed shoulder to shoulder with you, pointing it out.

Wallets, watches and phones, they just flowed. It was incredible. I hadn't done any sleight of hand in years. Aside from an uncanny ability to make girls happy behind the gym building, I hadn't given the dexterity of my hands much thought at all. But the touch was still there.

I felt like this force on the street. Invisible. Unstoppable. The one rule I set myself was to only lift from people who looked like they could afford it. I wasn't interested in making some struggling guy's day even worse. And so I'd looked for the Rolexes and the Tags. The guys with the expensive shoes and the pretty girlfriends.

It might have been crime, but I'd found something that made me feel alive. It's weird – criminals often say that they fell into a life of crime, but for me, it felt like I rose into it. Like I blossomed. Pickpocketing had all the beauty of magic, but with a twist of danger. A garden on a cliff edge. I was at home there.

On a good day, I'd make more money in one hour that I would in a whole week at the dry cleaners. I handed in my notice to Frank, and two weeks later I stopped working completely. I was a professional thief now.

Needless to say, I didn't mention anything to Jon. His career was moving at the *Washington Post*, and I didn't want to mess around with that. He'd been in DC less than six months, and was already pissing off congressmen and getting the stories into print – he loved it. If I'd told him what was happening with me, he'd have just quit, come home and tried to set me straight – be the responsible big brother that he'd always been. And he'd have resented the hell out of me for it. So I told him that I'd left the dry cleaners like it was nothing. Like I'd lost another stupid job. He'd sounded concerned – but losing jobs was par for the course for me, and he knew it. I'd always seemed lost to him, but for the first time since mom and dad died, I was anything but.

I hadn't intended to lift Benny's car key that night, but the move proved prophetic. A year later and I was regularly stealing luxury cars and selling them to David Kesari, this hood who worked out of Golden Gate Park. My cover story was that I'd got a job selling used cars. But by the end of that year I was making way too much money for some grunt on a used car lot – three or four grand a week, sometimes more. I wasn't spending much, but even so, I needed a better explanation.

I called Jon and told him that I was thinking about starting my own business. That I'd made a few contacts, and had this idea to ship luxury cars to Europe. He'd sounded over the moon to hear it. I'd been in the 'used' car business for about a year at that point – as far as Jon was concerned, I'd found a career. Setting up on my own was the logical next step.

'You'll make a success of it,' he said. 'You've got it in you, Michael, I know it.'

I said nothing.

'Anything I can do to help?' he said. 'I've got twelve grand put aside.'

'Jon...'

'I'm just saying. If you need it, it's yours.'

I stayed quiet. My trusting brother trying to pull me out of his shadow. I felt like shit. Stealing Ferraris from bankers? Who gives a fuck. But deceiving my own brother like that?

Lying to Jon was definitely the worst part of it all. I started distancing myself from him – canceling trips to see him. We always tried to spend at least one weekend a month together, either in San Francisco or DC. But I just found it too hard to face him and answer questions about my new business. Everybody lies – it's the oil that keeps the engine running smoothly – but this was different. This was going to be a whole production that I'd have to maintain for God knows how long. A constant stream of deceit – he wouldn't even know who I was.

And for what reason? Money? I didn't care about it that much. It was the thrill of the steal that I couldn't let go of. But what did that mean? Can criminal life even have any meaning? I've never seen an identikit that's smiling, I'll tell you that. I might have found my feet, but it was as if there was nothing beneath them.

I tried to stop lifting, but I just kept slipping back. I'd see some opportunity, and before my moral compass even began to twitch, I'd have the keys in my hand. That sense of power flowing through me. I kept setting myself targets – I'll stop next week, next month – but they were as useless as new year's resolutions. Even if they'd been UN resolutions, I doubt they'd have worked – a bunch of peacekeepers following me around, I probably would have ended up stealing their jeep. It was an addiction and it wasn't going to let go of me any time soon, I knew that.

I decided to tell Jon the truth and just let the chips fall. I knew it might cost us our relationship – at least for a while – but with no meaning to what I was doing, it just wasn't worth the heartache of lying to him about it.

I decided to tell him after his birthday. Jon's twenty-fifth was just around the corner, and I didn't want to ruin that for him. Birthdays had always been important to us, and that year I was flying us both out to London for the Wimbledon tournament. Jon was a huge tennis fan, and I'd bought us center court seats for the men's final – six thousand dollars a ticket. Ill-gotten gains, but fuck it, they were already paid for. Not that Jon knew we were going to London, let alone Wimbledon – I just told him to pack a bag.

We spent a week in London. Clubs. Restaurants. I rented a '67 Bentley and drove us to Glastonbury for a night. I really laid it on thick – storing away every smile on his face before we returned home and everything turned to shit.

Then the evening before the men's final, we ended up in a pub on Baker Street. I hadn't mentioned the tickets the whole week, I wanted to keep them a surprise – a grand finale.

As we sat drinking, I glanced at the cloudless sky.

'We really lucked out with the weather this week,' I said.

Jon nodded and took a deep mouthful of beer.

'Actually, I was going to ask you,' he said. 'Is there a plan for tomorrow?'

I eyed him carefully. 'Yeah, why?'

'It's the Wimbledon final. They're setting up a screen in the hotel bar. I thought we could watch it before we headed out.'

'Oh man, I wish you'd told me. I've already arranged something.'

'No, that's cool,' he said. He flashed his eyes at me. 'So what have we got lined up?'

I stared back at him for a moment. I hadn't intended on telling him then, but the tickets were burning a hole in my pocket. I couldn't resist it. I reached into my pocket and placed the tickets on the table in front of him.

'Happy Birthday,' I said.

His eyes widened. 'You're kidding.'

'Men's final. Court side.'

He just gazed at the tickets.

'I...I don't know what to say, Michael.'

I smiled.

A kid sitting at the next table then leaned toward us. Neat blond hair, he was maybe twelve years old, sitting with his dad.

He stared at the tickets. 'Are they really for tomorrow?' he asked.

I nodded. 'The real deal.'

'Could I just...?'

'Sure.'

I handed him the tickets, then laughed. He held them in his palms like they were sacred – feathers from angel's wing or something.

His dad nodded gratefully at me. 'He's a big tennis fan.'

Jon smiled at the kid. 'Who are you rooting for?'

'I don't know, I like them both,' the kid replied. 'It's going to be great. I can't wait. I just pray the weather stays good.'

'Ah, no need to pray,' said Jon. 'God's a sports fan too.'

The kid smiled. 'You think?'

Jon winked at him. 'Sure he is. Why do you think stadiums don't have roofs?'

The kid laughed. As he gazed back at the tickets, Jon watched him carefully – the amazement on the kid's face just to be holding them. And I already knew what Jon was thinking. The kid's T-shirt was frayed at the collar. Cheap sneakers. His dad was wearing a Timex. These two were a million miles from center court.

The kid offered me back the tickets. 'Thanks,' he said.

I glanced at the tickets, then stared at Jon.

'It's your present,' I said.

Jon nodded. 'Yeah, but it's your gift.'

I thought to myself a moment – it had been a great week anyhow.

I shrugged at the kid. 'Keep them,' I said. 'Have fun.'

The kid stared blankly back at me.

His father too. 'You're not serious?' he said.

'Yeah,' I replied.

The father looked bemused. 'We can't possibly accept this.'

'Then just leave them on the table,' I said. 'Someone will want them.' I turned to Jon. 'Come on, let's go get some Indian food.'

I got my feet – and I'll never forget the way Jon looked at me. Like I was a man for the first time in my life. Like I was someone that he was truly proud to call his brother.

I knew then that I'd never tell him. That I could never face taking that feeling away from him. And I felt OK with it. Because there it was – the wonder on the kid's face. The only meaning that crime could ever have. Some rich asshole loses a sports car, and this kid gets to live a little. It might have been little more than an excuse for me to continue a life that I loved, but it felt like a good one.

Robin Hood. I could live with that.

7

My neck was numb when I regained consciousness. I felt like I was floating. Painkillers rushing through my veins. I reached a hand to the wound – it was dressed. I slowly hauled myself upright on a cot, and tried to get my bearings.

I was in some kind of storage room. A caged ceiling light cast a dull glow across shelf units full of steel cases and motorcycle helmets. Radio sets and circuit boards. I blinked heavily and brought my wristwatch into focus. Nearly two in the morning.

I could hear blues guitar drifting through the air. B.B. King. I staggered over to the storage room door and opened it. Beyond it lay a dimly lit corridor – dented steel doors all the way down. The smell of dope in the air. I followed the music toward a door at the far end, then carefully pushed it open.

On the other side was a cavernous warehouse full of tattered sofas and tobacco fog. Open crates of whiskey scattered on the floor. A dozen people sat around, drinking. To my right, three muscular guys in their early thirties sat on a couple of sofas, watching me. Big fuckers – arms thicker than my legs. One had a black crucifix tattooed on his neck.

'Where am I?' I asked him.

He turned to the other guys. 'Who gives a fuck where you are, man?' he said.

The guys laughed. One of them, with silver rings on all his fingers, nodded toward a beaten-up sofa in front of them.

'Sit down,' he said.

'Where's Ella?' I asked.

'She's here. Sit down.'

I needed to. I drifted uneasily to the sofa and slumped into it. The guy with the rings turned to another with a V-shaped burn mark on his face.

'Go tell them he's up,' he said.

As the guy with the burn mark headed out of the room, the guy with the rings eyed me.

'You're Jon's brother, huh?' he said. 'We were sorry to hear what happened to him. Jon, well…he was a good guy. Stood for something, you know what I mean?'

'Thanks,' I said. But it didn't sound like he meant it as any kind of compliment to me. I glanced around the warehouse.

'What is this place?' I asked.

The guy with the crucifix tattoo stared at me. 'That's not your fucking business, boy.'

Southern accent. He was the guy I'd heard earlier, and no fan of mine by the sound of it. He nodded toward the sofa I was sitting on.

'You comfortable there?' he asked.

He laughed bitterly to himself and took a mouthful of whiskey.

'Strange how life turns, huh?' he said. 'A friend of ours used to sit there. Ray Harley. He was a good man too. Died in Afghanistan three months ago.'

'I'm sorry,' I replied.

He laughed. 'Listen to him…he's sorry. He was a genuine fucking hero, you got me? And look what we got sitting with us now. A worthless sack of shit thief.'

I sighed wearily.

He leaned forward. 'People fighting. Dying. And why? So you can prowl around stealing cars?'

'Look, you don't like me, I get it, alright.'

'You don't talk to me!'

'Leave him alone, Geary,' Ella said from the doorway.

Geary eyed her bitterly as she headed over to me.

'How are you feeling?' she asked me.

'Better,' I said.

A leather-faced guy in his fifties followed her in. Well-built, but kind of rusty looking, he had a cloud of wiry gray hair under his black beret.

'This is Tully,' said Ella. 'This is his place.'

Tully shook my hand. 'It's a pleasure, Michael,' he said.

Geary laughed.

Tully shot him a look. 'He's Jon's brother. We're going to make him feel welcome, alright?'

Geary kept silent as he stared back at him.

'You need to come with us, Michael,' said Ella.

I nodded. As she led me away, Geary grabbed me by the arm and leaned in toward me.

'You keep your hands off her,' he said.

'I might,' I replied. 'I'll see how I feel.'

He smiled coldly. I pulled my arm from his grip, then followed Ella toward another steel door at the far end of the warehouse. A couple more roughnecks stood guarding it.

'What is this place?' I asked Ella.

'DND Storage,' she replied. 'Underneath the overpass by the airport.'

'Probably the most secret members' bar in town,' said Tully. 'Also the shittiest. You want a drink?'

He grabbed a bottle of water from a packing crate and handed it to me. I glanced at the cases of whiskey sitting nearby.

'Maybe something a little stronger,' I said.

'I wouldn't,' he replied. 'I medicated you pretty good.'

I rubbed the dressing on my neck. 'You did this?'

He nodded. 'Eighteen years in the US army,' he said.

'Then thanks, Tully.'

'Any time.'

We stepped through the steel door and out into the shadow of a bleak industrial unit. It sat between huge concrete columns that supported the highways soaring overhead. Three scrawny-looking dogs running around in the darkness. As Tully pulled up a couple of packing crates for us to sit on, I took a mouthful of water and glanced back at the building.

'They know Jon here,' I said.

Ella nodded.

'How's that?' I asked.

She and Tully exchanged a look.

'How much does he know?' Tully asked her.

'Nothing,' she replied.

Tully nodded to himself. 'You're in good hands, Michael, don't worry.'

'Those guys sounded ex-military too,' I said.

'Yeah, we pretty much all are here,' he replied. 'It's a very private club.'

'Right,' I said. 'So how do they know Jon?'

Tully smiled – I wasn't giving up with the questions. He glanced at Ella.

'You trust him?' he asked her.

I waited with no small amount of curiosity to see how she'd answer.

She eyed me for a moment. 'He's fine,' she replied. It felt like huge praise coming from her.

Tully nodded – then chose his words carefully.

'We're a small group here,' he said. 'We do…freelance work for a number of clients.'

'What kind of work?' I said.

'Unofficial,' he replied. 'The kind they can't risk having on the books.'

I nodded to myself. They sounded like mercenaries, but Jon wouldn't have had anything to do with them if they were. They had to have been government sanctioned – some covert unit.

'How does Jon fit in?' I asked.

'In the course of our work we occasionally stumble across information that's deemed, what…beneficial to the American public? Then we'd go to Jon.'

'Deemed beneficial by whom?' I asked.

'People in big houses,' he said. 'Fountains in the front yard. Not really my kind of folks, but they serve one hell of a cocktail.'

He leaned toward me. 'We all liked Jon here a lot, Michael,' he said. 'Whoever's behind this, I'm going to see them well and truly fucked.'

I believed it. A cold intensity in his eyes now – and it started to add up.

Tully.

T.

I eyed him carefully. 'You're the guy who saved Jon in Mexico, aren't you?'

He nodded.

'Whoever killed him, we're going to find them, don't worry,' he said. He glanced at Ella. 'Tell him what you found.'

'There's a set of GPS coordinates hidden in the book,' she said. 'They were encoded in the text...hidden in spelling mistakes, the book's full of them.'

She handed me a folded sheet of note paper and an iPhone. The note paper had the coordinates written on it – two long lists of numbers.

'It's in Bitterroot National Forest,' said Tully. 'Deep on the Idaho side.'

I stared at the phone. Its screen was displaying a map with a GPS point flashing on it. It was in the middle of nowhere – mountain country – just dense forests.

Tully nodded toward the map. 'Whatever's there, someone's gone to a lot of trouble to make sure no one finds it.'

I nodded. 'Something buried?'

'Probably,' said Ella.

'Miranda?'

She shook her head. 'I doubt it. If you were going to hide a body, why keep the coordinates?'

'Why bury it at all?' Tully added. 'Cut it up. Burn it. Dissolve it.'

He shrugged breezily like he was talking on a cooking show.

'The nearest city to the coordinates is Hamilton, Montana,' said Ella. 'There's a flight out of SFO in the morning.'

'Then we're on it,' I replied.

'Are you sure you're up to this?' she asked.

'Don't worry about me.'

The guy with the rings on his fingers appeared at the shutter door behind us. 'Evan's on the phone,' he said.

'Alright,' said Tully. He turned to Ella. 'We'll see what Evan's got.'

He headed back inside, leaving Ella and me alone in the shadow of the overpass. The gentle rush of cars high above us. I watched as she lit a cigarette. The glow warmed her ghostly face for a moment – and I thought about the hotel. Her scars.

'You're ex-military too?' I asked.

She shook her head. 'I just do recon for them.'

'Recon,' I said. I eyed her curiously. 'So...you go in early, and grab what, laptops, phones?'

She nodded. 'Any information I can find.'

'And these operations are against?'

'Terror groups, drug cartels, whoever's got their sights aimed at the country.'

I nodded – fair enough. 'Stealing from the bad guys,' I said. 'Not the same thing, is it?'

She smiled.

'Did you always do this?' I asked.

She said nothing – just took a pull on her cigarette.

'Come on,' I said. 'Or were you a thief like me once?'

'Would it make you feel better if I was?'

'Sure.'

'Why, are you thinking of a career change?'

'I didn't say that.'

'Because Tully could use someone like you.'

I laughed. 'One of the good guys, huh?'

'Why not?'

I sighed heavily and gazed up at the over pass. 'Because I'm not a good guy, Ella.'

She took the necklace from her pocket. She watched the pendant dangle between her fingers, then stepped over to me. She took hold my hand and placed the necklace in my palm.

'I don't know about that,' she said.

She kept hold of my hand. Her delicate fingertips resting warmly against my skin. A whisper of intimacy – but only for a moment. She stepped away from me as Tully appeared at the warehouse door.

Tully shook his head as he walked over. 'Evan pulled up the traffic cam footage on Market Street,' he said. 'He couldn't make out the license plate on the Mercedes or the Lexus. Probably fakes anyhow.'

The Mercedes. I shot Tully a look as images of the car flashed through me. It felt like I was remembering a bad dream.

'What?' said Ella.

I tried to grasp at the indistinct images in my head – tried to remember what I'd seen.

'The Mercedes,' I said.

'You got a look at him?' said Ella.

I shook my head. 'I didn't see his face. But he was with someone. A woman. It was weird, she was wearing a veil, I think.'

'A veil,' said Ella. 'What do you mean, like a burka?'

'No. White lace, like a wedding veil.'

She kept her eyes on me for a moment, then glanced uneasily at Tully.

She took a long pull on her cigarette. 'Are you sure about this?' she asked me.

I nodded.

'Was she wearing gloves?'

I tried to remember. 'Yeah, I think so.'

'You didn't see her face, how old she might have been? In her forties, maybe?'

Tully glanced at her. 'Why, what are you thinking?'

'Who do we know that wears a veil, Tully?'

He raised his eyebrows. 'Lizzie? Come on, no way, she'd have nothing to do with this.'

'We don't know what this is though.'

'Not a chance. They're strictly global. I wouldn't worry about it.'

'Who's Lizzie?' I asked.

'Elizabeth Brager,' said Tully. 'She and her brother, Marcus, they're arms dealers. A right pair of nasty fuckers.'

Ella stared intently at him. 'She was wearing a veil, Tully.'

‘That don’t mean nothing.’

‘Why the veil?’ I asked.

Tully sighed. ‘Lizzie’s got some skin disease, wears veils or something when she’s out...which is never, by the way.’

But Ella kept her eyes on him.

‘Forget about it,’ he said. ‘Look, they rarely come inland, OK. They stay on the yacht.’

‘Marcus was seen in Kinshasa three months ago.’

‘Marcus comes in maybe, but Lizzie, never. For her to be in the back of a car, throwing bullets at you, it would have to be fucking huge.’

Ella shook her head. ‘I don’t like it, Tully.’

He eyed the necklace for a moment, then produced a hip flask from his jeans and took a deep mouthful.

‘This guy called you, did he?’ he said.

I nodded. ‘Fucker wanted me to leave the necklace for him somewhere.’

‘He have an accent?’

‘Uh-huh. European, I think.’

‘The Bragers are Norwegian.’

I tried to remember the guy’s voice – his gentle tones.

‘Yeah, it could have been,’ I said.

‘Not could have been! Was it a Scandinavian accent or not?’

I gazed into the darkness and replayed the conversation in my head as best I could. He wasn’t French or German, I knew that much. He didn’t have the lilt of Spanish of Italian either. Eastern Europe, maybe. But Scandinavian felt closer.

I stared at Tully and nodded. 'If I had to say, then yeah.'

He stared uneasily at Ella, then took another sip from the flask. He tightened the beret on his head.

'Alright, look,' he said. 'Go to these coordinates and find whatever's there, then I want you to come straight back. I don't care what you find, I mean it, Ella...straight back.'

'What about going to the authorities?' I said.

Ella shook her head. 'If Lizzie's got anything to do with this, we can't trust anyone. Not the police, nobody'

'And you're taking Geary with you,' said Tully.

I shot him a look. 'That tattooed asshole?'

'He may be an asshole, but he's a well-trained one.'

He shouted back to the security guys at the door. 'Get Geary out here!' he said. He turned to Ella. 'I know there's some history between you two. Are you OK with this?'

'I'm fine,' she replied.

I stared at her. Ex-boyfriend?

Geary appeared through the door and headed over to us. I couldn't believe that Ella had been involved with this guy. I paid more attention to him now. He looked like a thick-necked country boy – all rosy cheeks and mean eyes. The kind whose tattoos were less likely to be a military insignia, and more likely to be a present from his grandma.

He arrived in front of Tully.

'You know what's going on here?' Tully asked him.

'A little,' Geary replied.

'You're going to Idaho with these two,' said Tully. 'You keep them safe, you got it?'

As Geary nodded, Tully turned to Ella.

'If it's the necklace they're after, you might want to leave it here,' he said.

'Where is it?' asked Geary.

I opened my hand and held up the necklace.

'It might be Lizzie Brager,' said Tully.

Geary shot him a look.

'Might be,' Tully repeated.

Geary glanced at me. 'You really know how to make a fucking enemy, don't you.' He nodded at the necklace. 'We'll take it with us.'

'Are you sure?' said Tully.

'We don't know what's waiting for us at the coordinates. We might need it.'

Tully went quiet. As he thought to himself, I eyed the necklace.

'I think it's safer if we leave it here,' I said

Geary glared at me. 'If I need the keys to a Chrysler, I'll ask for your opinion. Otherwise, shut up!'

I gazed back at him. I swear, if Shakespeare himself had tried to describe Geary, he'd have struggled to avoid using the words 'fucking asshole'.

Tully nodded to himself. 'Alright,' he said. 'Take it with you. I want you back safe, Ella. Whatever you find, you bring it and the necklace back here, no heroics, you got me? Geary's running this.'

Ella nodded.

Tully turned to me. 'You hear me, Michael?'

I kept my eyes on Geary.

'Michael!' Tully repeated.

'Fine!' I said.

Tully glanced back at the shutter door. 'Cooper! Get this guy some ID!'

Cooper, the guy with all the rings, appeared at the door. As he beckoned me inside, he paused and glanced at a car pulling up in the shadows under the overpass. Tully sighed wearily at the sight of it – a huge, pearl black 7-series BMW. It ground to a halt about eighty feet from us, and just sat there.

Tully rubbed some life into his face.

'They didn't give you a heads-up?' said Geary.

'No, they did.'

'You want me to speak to them?'

'No,' he replied.

Ella stared at the car.

'Are you going to tell them about Lizzie?' she said.

Tully shook his head. 'Not until we're sure.'

'Tully...'

'Not until we're sure!' He took a deep breath, then glanced at Cooper. 'Get this guy some ID.' He nodded at me. 'Go. Now.'

As I made my way back to the warehouse, Tully headed for the BMW. It was a good bet these were the guys that he worked for – the fountains in the front yard. Tully reached the car, glanced back at me, then headed round to the far side. He opened the rear door and got in. I couldn't see who was in the back, but I guess I wasn't supposed to.

'Let's go,' Cooper said to me.

I nodded, then followed him back into the warehouse. As we headed past the other soldiers in

Tully's operation, I could feel the weight of their eyes on me. I was like the new kid at school, a week late and not a friend in the place.

'You know how to use a gun?' Cooper asked me.

I nodded uneasily. I'd fired guns at ranges with friends, but I was no fan of them.

'You're flying civilian, we'll get you sorted out at the other end,' he said. He threw me a vaguely reassuring smile. 'You do what Geary says, you'll be fine.'

As I followed him down an orange lit corridor, I glanced at the stacks of silver bands on his fingers. A charm bracelet around his wrist, the kind that a teenage girl might wear – hearts and crosses hanging from it. Probably belonged to a girlfriend – a good luck gift to ensure his safe return. Still, a guy would need a certain amount of confidence to get away with wearing that. He may have been as threatening to look at as Geary, but there was something a little more considered about Cooper. The kind of soldier who'd tear through Afghanistan with a copy of *The Bridges of Madison County* taped to his flame thrower.

He reached a heavy steel door at the end of the corridor – sleek armored plate and pressure sealed locks. Surveillance cameras above it. He tapped a code into a keypad by the door. The door beeped and clunked open. Beyond it, a dimly lit staircase headed down.

I followed him into a murky sub basement. The thick smell of resin in the air. We passed a long line of padlocked cages, and I slowed for a second. The cages were stacked full of glistening black machine guns and fat caliber pistols. Rocket launchers and cases marked, 'Uranium Shells.' I'd never seen anything like it.

Cooper glanced back at me. 'No mistake. When we turn up, you know the talking's over.'

I had no doubt. Cage after cage of heavy weaponry. These guys arrived with about as much grace as kicking down the Pearly Gates and telling St Peter you're there to fuck his wife.

Cooper yelled at an open door at the end of the corridor. 'Yo, Dixie, we need an ID!'

Dixie appeared in the doorway. A four-hundred pound sack of meat wearing a sleeveless denim jacket the size of a parachute. Long brown hair down to his waist. He flicked the strands away from his face, then nodded at a wall just beyond the door.

'Stand here,' he said to me.

I stepped into a stark office. A computer screen and a bunch of printers sat in the shadow of huge black crucifix hanging on the wall above the desk. Dixie grabbed a camera from a drawer. 'This the pickpocket?' he said.

Cooper nodded.

Dixie pushed me up against the wall like I was a prisoner on orientation.

'Passport?' he said.

Cooper nodded again.

As Dixie dialed the settings in the camera, I stared uneasily at the crucifix. Thick black metal, five feet tall, it looked like it belonged in a cathedral.

Dixie noticed my look and smiled to himself. 'Religious man?'

I eyed him a moment, then shook my head.

He laughed. 'I bet you're not.'

He paused from setting the camera, and closed his eyes like he was savoring fine wine.

'Thou shalt not steal,' he said, as if he was sharing some personal moment of revelation with the world. 'The Lord's words. You should be rightly ashamed of yourself.'

'Uh-huh,' I said.

Cooper threw him a look. 'Just take the photo, Dixie.'

As Dixie pointed the camera, he winked at me. 'Jesus talks about thieves plenty, you know.'

I sighed. 'Yeah? What does he say about making fake IDs? Or is that how he got himself resurrected?'

His expression turned cold. I held his look – I wasn't going to be judged by this guy.

He grunted at me. 'Look at the camera.'

I glanced at the lens – the camera clicked.

He checked the image, then headed over to his desk. He grabbed one of a dozen passports lying by the computer, opened it wide, then fed it into a printer the size of a fridge.

'All good, Dixie?'

I turned to find Geary leaning against the doorway. I eyed him cautiously. I glanced down the corridor to see if Ella was with him – but it was a show of weakness.

He smiled. 'She's busy. A lot to do now.'

He folded his arms, then just eyed me – his testosterone-fueled silence thickening the air in the room.

Cooper toyed impatiently with his rings as Dixie tapped away at the keyboard.

'You want full background on this or just the passport?' said Dixie.

'Just the passport,' said Geary.

Dixie scrolled through lists of names and birth dates on the screen.

'Age?' Dixie asked.

'Twenty-nine,' I said.

He scrolled down the screen, then stopped.

'OK, Caucasian male,' he said. 'You're Daniel Coggin.'

Geary mulled the name over to himself. 'Daniel Coggin. Danny Coggin. Danny C. Yeah, he sounds like a sack of shit too.'

Dixie nodded. 'He does, indeed. Ain't no God-fearing motherfucker either.'

'Boy been shooting his mouth off again, has he?' said Geary.

Dixie turned and stared carefully at him.

'No respect for nothing,' he said. 'Trouble for you.'

Geary nodded wearily to himself. 'Yeah,' he said.

He glanced at me a moment, then took a deep breath. Before I could even react, he slammed me against the wall. I crumpled onto the floor, tried to pick myself up, but he grabbed my right hand and held it locked in his. Pain tearing down my arm. I couldn't move for the sheer power in him.

'There's a chain of command here,' he said. 'You may only be with us for a couple of days, but you're going to learn it.'

He took out a hunting knife. My heart raced as he pressed the point of the blade against the palm of my right hand.

Dixie nodded. 'The righteous path, Mr Coggin.'

The sting as the blade began to pierce my skin. Fuck. I struggled, but Geary held me firm.

'Push the blade right through,' said Geary. 'Rip those nerves...tendons. A thief, no more.'

He toyed the tip of the blade across my palm, carving out a thin bloody trail. He gripped me even harder.

'What's it going to be? he said.

I gazed breathlessly at the blade.

He smiled. 'You know how much I want to do this anyhow?'

'I've got it!' I said. 'Chain of command! I've got it.'

'Yeah?'

I nodded.

'You follow every fucking word I tell you!'

'I've got it!'

'Cos I don't give a shit that you're Jon's brother.'

Dixie strolled over. 'We'll cut that miserable hand right off of you,' he said.

Geary nodded. 'Believe it.'

He twisted my hand a final time, pulled the blade away, then released me. I licked the blood from my palm, and glanced at Cooper.

Cooper smiled. 'Like I said. You do what he says, you'll be fine.'

Motherfuckers.

8

I hate to say it, but Luke Geary was an honest-to-god hero. He single-handedly raided a Taliban fuel dump in Kandahar and saved the lives of two US servicemen who were being held there. He received the Distinguished Service Cross – they'd have given him the Medal of Honor, but he had too long and checkered a history of disobeying orders. It's hard to dislike a guy who could do something like that, but Geary made it easy. He hated the ground I walked upon, and wanted me to know about it at every conceivable opportunity. As far as he was concerned, he and Ella were fighting the good fight, and I was nothing but a self-serving low-life.

I could feel him staring at me as the three of us sat parked in a rented Jeep in Hamilton, Montana. He and Ella were up in front – I was in the back. I adjusted the bandage on my palm, then ran my fingertips against each other in quick succession, checking the movement. It stung, but the action was smooth enough.

I didn't tell Ella what had happened, but she'd taken a good guess. She was pissed as hell at Geary. Not that he gave a shit. He hadn't moved an inch from her side since we'd left Tully's place – not at the airport, nor on the plane. This was an award-winning killer who'd walked into a Taliban fuel dump like it was his local gas station – as ex-boyfriends go, he was a fucking nightmare.

I kept my eyes on Morgan's Gun Store across the street, and tried to get focused. Hamilton was a small mountain town – a quiet hive of pick-up trucks and churches. It was also our last stop before we headed up to the coordinates. According to Geary, we needed a handgun. We'd managed to buy a few rifles around town, but when it came to handguns, the store owners wanted background checks – three days minimum. Tully had a contact who was going to supply us, but the guy couldn't get to Hamilton for another six hours, and we needed to move quickly. And so we waited outside Morgan's. It was late afternoon.

I glanced at the rifles we'd bought lying on the car floor beside me.

'I'm sure these are going to be fine,' I said.

'Really?' said Geary. 'What tactical experience are you basing that genius fucking opinion on?'

I rolled my eyes.

'If you can't do it, just say,' he said.

'I'll get you the gun, don't worry,' I replied.

The main door of Morgan's swung open – a guy in his thirties emerged from the store.

'What about him?' said Ella.

I stared carefully at the guy. He was wearing a blue denim jacket – a stonewashed Wrangler, five buttons, three pockets, no lining. I eyed the jacket's upper left panel. A shoulder holster made a subtle, but characteristic fold in the wearer's jacket. I'd learned to recognize it over the years – you didn't want to be stealing anything from someone carrying a gun. But there was no fold in this guy's jacket.

'He's not carrying,' I said.

Geary sighed like it was my fault that this guy wasn't armed. We carried on waiting, but this was Montana – we didn't have to wait for long. A guy in his forties emerged from the store. Tall, thickset, squeezed into a pair of combat pants like it was a bet. He buried his hands deep in the pockets of a black bomber jacket, and there it was – a subtle ridge in the leather by his left arm.

'He's carrying,' I said.

I grabbed a folded street map off the back seat and got out of the car. As I walked toward the guy, I unfolded the map to its full extent – it fluttered around as it caught the breeze. I felt myself getting tight – nervous – this guy was armed. I kept my eyes on the map as I approached him. The lost tourist – it had always worked for me.

'Excuse me,' I said in my best British accent.

As he stopped, I held up the map.

'I'm looking for Ponderosa Street?'

'Ponderosa?' he said. 'You're way off.'

I offered him the map. He took it and held it in front of himself, as people do.

'You're here,' he said, pointing at the map.

As I stared at it, I moved in so I was standing right beside him. But I was off my game – I got too close, too quick. Personal space is like an alarm zone. He took a slight step away and stared at me. I was making a guy with a gun feel nervous.

'I'm sorry,' I said. 'I'm just…it's my brother-in-law's birthday and I'm two hours late as it is. If you could just show me.'

He nodded toward the Jeep. 'You don't have satnav in that thing?' he said.

'It's a rental. It's broken.'

He nodded, then relaxed a little and stepped back toward me. I grabbed one edge of the map with my right hand, leaving my left hand free, hidden underneath it.

He glanced at me. 'British, huh?'

'Yeah, it's been a long flight.'

He returned to the map. 'OK, we're here…' he said.

I snaked a hand under the map and into his jacket. My fingers brushed imperceptibly against his shirt and jacket lining, figuring the space. I kept my attention on the map – kept him distracted. I felt the butt of the gun between my fingertips. It was secured by a leather strap with a popper. The trick with poppers was not to pull them. You had to keep pressure on them between two fingers and use a third to pry them open silently, quickly – a tenth of a second, a blink of an eye.

'And Ponderosa is…here,' he said.

'Wow, I am a way off, aren't I?'

I took the map back from him. I folded it underneath itself, and around the gun that was now in my left hand. It was heavy – felt like a brick. I wondered whether he'd miss the weight. I nodded at him, the gun safely hidden within the folds of the map.

'Thank you,' I said.

'No problem,' he replied, and headed off down the street. A second later, he slowed – then stopped. Fuck, he was missing the weight. As he turned to face me, I noticed another fold in the right hand panel of his jacket. A double holster – he'd been carrying two guns. Shit. He stared carefully at me. I smiled back politely – casually. If he went for his other gun, I didn't know what the fuck I was going to do – the Jeep was thirty feet behind me. He took a step toward me. I held my breath.

'Are you Tommy Roper's brother-in-law?' he said. 'He's married to a Brit.'

I felt like laughing.

'No,' I said. 'Sorry.'

'Alright,' he nodded. 'You have a good day.'

As he headed off, I sighed heavily to myself.

I got back in the car and unfolded the map – a black pistol inside it. Geary reached back and picked it up. He checked the clip – it was full.

He rolled his eyes. 'Fine,' he said.

'Come on,' Ella said to him. 'He got you the gun.'

He threw her a look, then snapped the clip back into the gun. As he hit the accelerator, I glanced back at the double-holster guy disappearing in the distance. We hadn't even got started yet, and this nobody had already freaked me out. Jesus. For all my bravado, this was going to be deep water for me.

***

We crossed the Idaho state border a few hours later and headed south on Route 93. With the Bragers casting a long shadow on our horizon, no one said a great deal. As Ella studied a map of the area, I gazed at the mountains and thought about that moment with Lizzie – that veiled specter behind the glass. I tried to conjure up some sense of who she and Marcus were.

Tully had given me a file on the Bragers but the information was sketchy. They're in their late forties. Reclusive. They live on a yacht called *The Warren Gate* that spends most of its time in international waters. Although they're rarely seen, Marcus comes inland for business sometimes, and there's a few photographs of him available. The most recent was taken at the Paris Air Show last year. He's six-two. Blond hair slicked straight back. Pale-skinned, but with dark, wide-set eyes. An intelligent air about him, he looks like a Viking lawyer.

Lizzie's appearance is a much grayer area. There are very few descriptions of her, and no photographs – at least not as an adult. There's a few pictures on the net that were taken when she was a kid, but that's about it. She'd been pretty as a kid though. Painfully thin maybe, and with mousy hair chopped like she'd cut it herself – but huge brown eyes and delicate bowed lips.

What photos there are of her were all taken indoors. Lizzie has EPP – erythropoietic protoporphyria. It's an enzyme deficiency that causes the skin to blister in sunlight. Lizzie's had it all her life apparently. She grew up never being able to go outside – probably spent her childhood in some dark little corner. I almost felt sorry for her.

This, and what little else is known about Lizzie for sure, comes largely from one source – press coverage of a court case that took place in Norway when she was twelve. 'The Doll Trial' it was called. It's about the only definitive account in Tully's file, and it makes for some interesting reading. When Lizzie was a child she had a huge collection of china dolls – hundreds of them. They occupied the entire top floor of her parents' house in Oslo. Apparently she'd spend her days sewing these elaborate dresses for them all – finely beaded gowns and embroidered silk suits. She was a talented young seamstress by all accounts. And a keen writer too it seems. As well as their own tailor-made wardrobe, each doll had its own journal in which Lizzie would write entries on their behalf.

Stories about the doll collection spread around the neighborhood where she lived. Plenty of local girls talked about the collection, but their parents had always warned them away from Lizzie. She was considered a damaged child, with one witness describing her as, *'a little shadow at the curtain that we'd occasionally see as we walked past the house.'* However, the daughter of one of Lizzie's neighbors, Kristen Strand, found the prospect of seeing the dolls too tempting.

Unknown to her parents, Kristen decided to pay Lizzie an impromptu visit one afternoon. Lizzie's mother, Helena, answered the door. Lizzie was asleep at the time, however, with her having so few visitors, her mother didn't want to turn Kristen away. She showed the girl up to the top floor where the dolls were, then asked her to wait while she woke up Lizzie. But Kristen didn't wait – she entered one of the rooms that housed the collection.

When Lizzie entered the room, she found Kristen reading one of the doll's journals. Lizzie grabbed it from her. Although Kristen apologized, Lizzie screamed for her to get out. Kristen did what she was told. However, as she left the room, she apparently made some comment about how everyone was right and that Lizzie was strange. In a rage, Lizzie pushed her. Kristen slipped down the stairs, and smacked her head against the floorboards at the bottom. She spent two weeks in hospital. Kristen's parents pressed charges against Lizzie's mother, insisting that Lizzie was mentally unbalanced and needed to be put into care. Lizzie's mother refused to even consider this, and the case ended up going to some tribunal. The dolls' diaries were submitted at the hearing. One entry read:

'Sunday 14th. Elizabeth made me lunch today. Pasta shells in tomato sauce. I didn't like it, but I couldn't tell her. She's angry at me, and I deserve it. I promised to sew up the holes in the night where the morning gets in. Sew them up tight so the day won't hurt her. But the sun was high today. I've let her down. I'm scared.'

The tribunal ordered a psychiatric evaluation of Lizzie, but its findings were inconclusive. Lizzie's mother ended up paying damages to Kristen's parents, and Lizzie remained at home. But I doubt anyone ever visited her again.

Although Kristen wasn't seriously hurt, the story got more than its fair share of local press coverage because of the Brager name. The Bragers are old Norwegian money – a shipping dynasty. They're a long line, and it seems that Lizzie wasn't the only fucked-up member of the clan. Her skin condition might have made her childhood a misery, but by the sound of it, it was her father, Hugo, who screwed her head up. He was a physicist. In 1957 he gave up a promising career at Oslo University, and started writing books about infinity. Lizzie and Marcus' yacht, *The Warren Gate,* is named after his final book, a pseudo-spiritual treatise on the nature of the self. In it he writes that death doesn't exist. How the limitless combinations of subatomic particles just roll on forever – the sequence that signifies the self, randomly and repeatedly coalescing into form. It's eternal life whether you want it or not – it's just numbers – an indifferent universe devoid of morality or meaning. He writes that the greatest gift we have is the absence of a soul. As a result, the identical lives that the individual experiences are eternally fresh and vibrant. The only hell that could ever exist would be to have a memory of it all.

He committed suicide when he was forty-three. Lizzie was six at the time. He left a note saying that he'd see her again, but I doubt it was much consolation to her. Her dad may have continued his eternal journey through the infinite, but her mom moved to Bermuda. Seventy-eight, she lives in a hotel in Mount Pleasant that Lizzie and Marcus own. She's not nearly as reclusive as her kids, but nonetheless refuses to talk about them no matter how many people ask – and plenty do. Marcus is a big player in the arms industry now. He's turned an already sizable family fortune into billions and, according to Tully, has been involved in all kinds of shit in the process. Illegal arms exports to Sudan. Hit squads in Niger. There was even talk that he and Lizzie were responsible for an explosion at a shopping mall in Cape Town. Nine people died, including some diplomat that they were dealing with at the time. With their expanding influence in conflict zones, there are plenty of people who want to know what they're up to. Some journalist turned up in Bermuda a few years back, asking the mother questions about them. She poured boiling coffee over him.

Although there are accounts of Marcus visiting the mother at the hotel, Lizzie's never with him. By the sound of it, she never leaves the yacht. The only time she comes in is when the yacht needs maintenance, and then she remains veiled. The only other noteworthy rumor that's circulating is that she and Marcus are romantically involved with each other, and have been for years – but that sounds more like gossip. That said, it wouldn't surprise me if it were true.

It's hard to know exactly what to believe when it came to the Bragers. They sounded like a horror story that arms dealers tell each other on camping trips.

It was getting dark. Geary turned off Route 93 and onto a small trail that led into Bitterroot Forest. Two thousand square miles of wilderness – the coordinates lying deep within it.

We didn't pass a solitary soul as we weaved into the hills. November, and the forest was still. Just towering pines thickening around us – the Jeep's headlights throwing ghosts through the branches.

With the coordinates not close to any kind of access route, we were going to have to hike once the forest closed in – and that moment didn't seem too far off now. The trees began to interweave above us, turning what was left of the trail into a tunnel – the Jeep jumping around on the broken mud and rocks. Geary fought to keep the car under control as he pushed us forward – weaving past boulders and thumping through low-hanging branches. But soon there was nowhere left to drive. The wild heart of Bitterroot had closed in.

Geary brought the Jeep to a stop in a dry riverbed – nothing but root infested inclines ahead of us.

'Rise and shine,' he said.

He switched off the engine, then checked the GPS locator on his phone.

'It's about twelve miles northwest of here,' he said.

Through the treetops I could see a huge mountain range way ahead of us – maybe two thousand feet high. Gentle slopes, but it was covered in dense forest. It would take us hours to cross it.

We got out of the car, the mountain cold waking me like a slap in the face. We pulled on heavy duty army jackets and gloves, then swung on our backpacks. We had a little food, some water – Tully had given us a satellite phone.

Geary produced the three rifles from the rear seat floor. He checked one – slid the bolt, snapped the magazine – then handed it to Ella. He checked the second and swung it around his shoulder. The third, he just tossed to me.

I stared wearily at him. 'This one's fine, is it?' I said.

'You're baggage,' he said. 'Baggage don't talk.' He stared up at the ridge for a moment, then turned to Ella. 'You good?'

Ella nodded. As she tightened her rifle strap, Geary switched on a flashlight and started walking. I stared awkwardly at the rifle in my hand. I'd never held one before, and Ella could see it – she smiled. She took it from me, checked it and handed it back to me. I nodded gratefully, then followed on after her and Geary.

We slowly made our way through the forest, the hills stretching out ahead of us. Shadows and silence. Just the crunch of thick ferns beneath our boots. A creek bubbling somewhere nearby.

As Geary plowed on ahead, I took off my glove and pulled the bandage away from my palm. I checked the wound. It had sealed – a thin scab running down my lifeline. I grabbed a coin and spun it, checking the movement in my hand again. The coin zipped across my fingertips, flickering in the moonlight like it had a life of its own.

Ella watched it dance. 'You have a real talent,' she said.

I raised a grateful smile.

'You shouldn't be wasting it,' she added.

I grabbed the coin to a halt and sighed. 'Still on this, huh? One of the good guys.'

'Why's that such a bad thing for you?'

I said nothing. I just put away the coin, then pulled the glove back on.

'Are you self-taught?' she asked.

I nodded. But as an answer it wasn't strictly true – nor fair.

'I knew a guy for a while though,' I said. 'He definitely upped my game.'

'Who was that?'

'Patrick, his name was.' I smiled fondly as I thought about him. 'Great pickpocket.'

'Better than you?'

'Oh yeah. ET, people used to call him. Light-fingered. He asked for this starlet's autograph once...before she even finished writing her name, he had her watch and jewelry. The guy was absurd.'

'Is he still working?'

I shook my head. 'No,' I replied. 'No, he died a few years back. Cancer. I mean he was old when I met him, but... the guy was obsessed. I spent those last few weeks with him, and all he did was get me to practice the moves, finger positions, the Hanson Grip. Until his dying breath, I swear.'

'Sounds like you were close.'

I nodded. 'One of my prized possessions is a calf-skin wallet that I lifted from him while he was on his deathbed.' I laughed to myself. 'He wouldn't have wanted it any other way.'

She smiled easily – like she and I were old friends. I wasn't sure that I wanted to bring up the subject of her scars right then, but she noticed me glancing at her body.

'So what happened with you?' I said.

She eyed me carefully. As I waited for her to speak, I went still – a shuffling noise to our right. Geary swung back and pointed the flashlight at the trees. A few insects fluttered around in the beam. More shuffling. Footsteps. I stared nervously into the darkness, then slipped the rifle from my shoulder. Ella gazed at the shadows beyond the trees. We waited. No movement.

'It's an animal,' said Geary.

He was probably right, but I was in no mood to take any chances. I kept looking. Whatever was there couldn't have been more than thirty or forty feet away. If they'd run off, I'd have heard. I kept my eyes on the shadows and searched for any movement.

'Leave it,' said Geary. 'Let's go.'

I gazed at the trees, my finger hovering over the trigger.

Ella nodded at me. 'It's fine,' she said.

'We're wasting time,' said Geary. 'You get freaked by every noise, this is going to take days. Let's go.'

Geary headed back up the hill, his flashlight disappearing into fragments within the trees. As Ella followed him, I heard the shuffling sound behind me again. I turned and stared into the darkness – at the few pools of moonlight that reached the forest floor. A quiet snap came from a black void between the pools. There were eyes in there looking back at me, I could feel it. An iciness in my veins like the darkness itself was watching me.

I gazed into the void, then slowly stepped away – my finger glued to the trigger as I headed on through the trees.

It was two a.m. by the time we reached the crest of the ridge. It might have risen a couple of thousand feet above the forest, but it must have been a good four or five thousand above sea level. I could feel the air thinning. The temperature dropping.

The trees gave way to bare rock as we reached the top. We stopped and surveyed the valleys below us. Thick blankets of forests and grassy plains. Silver rivers that snaked into the distance. It looked like the frontier land – beautiful through one eye, threatening through the other.

Geary checked the GPS locator. 'Another two miles,' he said, pointing west. 'We can probably see it from here.'

I scanned the western valleys. They were darker, more densely wooded. Whatever was down there was well hidden.

'We'll rest for ten minutes,' he said.

As Ella studied the valley with a set of binoculars, I sat down on the bare rock.

Geary grabbed a bottle of water from his backpack. He took a mouthful, then smiled at me.

'So tell me, Mr. Pickpocket,' he said. 'How many cars do you think you've stolen?'

Ella sighed.

'I'm just curious,' he said to her. 'How many?'

'I don't know,' I replied.

'More than a hundred?'

'Uh-huh.'

'A thousand?'

'Maybe.'

'You must have made some money. You keep it all for yourself?'

'Does it matter?'

‘I’m just trying to figure what you stand for. You and Jon were like night and day. I just want to know why.’

I stayed quiet.

‘Leave it,’ said Ella.

‘We’re just talking,’ he said. He turned back to me. ‘You know what I think?’

‘I can’t wait,’ I replied.

‘You couldn’t compete with him, could you.’

I rolled my eyes. ‘You’re a therapist now? I’m not going to get a bill for this, am I?’

‘I mean, he was the talented one, wasn’t he? He could write, play sports, good at school…what was it, UCLA he graduated from? And you couldn’t do any of that, could you? Black sheep.’

‘Come on, Geary,’ said Ella.

I eyed him carefully. ‘Jon and I weren’t as different as you think,’ I said.

‘Yeah? He weren’t no snake in the grass, I’ll tell you that.’

‘That’s what I am, is it?’

‘You’re bad news, boy.’

I laughed – I wasn’t going to listen to this shit any more.

‘Leave him alone,’ said Ella.

‘What, that’s my hour done?’ I said. ‘We didn’t even get to my fear of giraffes.’

Geary threw Ella a long agitated look.

‘Why are you defending him?’ he asked her. ‘You like him now?’

She said nothing.

He nodded thoughtfully to himself, then turned back to me. 'You want to hear something really funny?' he said. 'How do you think Jon found out you're a thief?'

'Geary!' said Ella.

'How do you think?' he said.

She eyed him in disbelief.

'Let me guess,' he said. 'Jon said that some friend of his saw you steal a car.'

I glanced uneasily at Ella.

Geary smiled. 'It's funny, 'cos that ain't even close to what happened.'

Ella closed her eyes. 'You're such a fucking ass, Geary.'

'Truth is the truth, sweetie,' he said. 'Hell, you taught me that.'

'What's he talking about?' I asked Ella.

She didn't look at me – and my blood started to race.

'Are you going to tell him or am I?' Geary asked her.

Ella sighed, then threw me an uneasy look.

'I told Jon about you,' she said. 'He was worried. He thought someone was following you. He didn't know if he was just being paranoid or not. I looked into it.'

I gazed at her for a moment.

'You looked into it,' I said. 'You mean, you looked into me.'

She stayed silent.

'Did he ask you to?' I said.

She took a deep breath, then shook her head.

‘And you told him what you found?’ I said.

‘Why wouldn’t I?’

‘My relationship with Jon was my business! You didn’t think for one moment it might be better if he didn’t know?’

‘Better for who? For you?’

‘Things were fine between me and Jon!’

‘You’re a thief, Michael. He needed to know.’

‘We never spoke again!’

‘That was your doing!’

Geary laughed. ‘Hell, where’s a bag of popcorn when you need one?’

‘Shut up!’ said Ella.

She may have been right, but I didn’t give a shit – I felt betrayed by her. That might have made me a hypocrite, but again, I didn’t give a shit.

A muffled ringing came from inside Ella’s backpack – the satellite phone. She delved around inside the pack and pulled it out. It stopped ringing before she could answer it. She stared nervously at Geary.

‘No caller ID,’ she said.

‘It’s Tully’s phone,’ said Geary. ‘He’s the only one who has the number. Call him back, make sure it was him.’

She dialed his number. No answer.

‘Try the land line,’ he said.

Ella hung up and dialed DND Storage. As she did, I scanned the tree line just below us. Those fuckers had called me in the nightclub – a ringing phone sounded like an alarm bell to me now.

‘Answering machine,’ she said.

I shook my head. 'I don't like this.'

'It's fine,' said Geary.

'We need to move,' I said. 'We need to find whatever's down there and get the fuck out of here.'

I got up and took the lead. I started moving as fast as I could down the broken ground on the western side of the ridge. Ella tried Tully again. No answer.

'Hang up,' I said. 'I mean it. Now!'

She ended the call.

'Try Cooper,' said Geary.

'Switch off the fucking phone!' I said and grabbed it from her.

'They don't know about Tully,' she replied.

'Are you sure?' I said. 'They might have been watching you for weeks.'

I picked up the pace – kept the flashlight off, it would signal our position like a neon sign. We headed down toward the valley system, adrenaline pumping through me. I saw shapes starting to move in the corners of my eyes. I slowed and looked around. Everything was still.

'Relax!' said Geary. 'Give me the phone!'

Something moved to my left, I was sure of it. I stopped dead. I gestured for Ella and Geary to stay quiet. I peered into the dense trees and waited. Just darkness and silence.

The darkness then moved.

Fuck.

'Run!' yelled Geary.

A rippling shadow tumbled though the trees toward us, branches collapsing around it. A brown bear – a grizzly, the size of a car and moving as fast. I turned and ran – Geary in front of me, Ella behind, the ground shaking beneath us. Geary reached for the handgun and span round.

'Get out of the way!' he yelled.

Ella and I leaped to one side. Geary fired – emptied the clip, but the bear pounded on. We threw ourselves down the slope, zigzagging through the trees. The bear roared as it gained ground – twenty feet behind us – rocks flying up around its feet as it hurtled down the slope. Geary freed his rifle. As he glanced back, I heard another roaring sound ahead of us – but it was no animal – it was water. We skidded to a halt at the edge of a ravine. A river tore through the rocks a hundred feet below. Geary raised the rifle – he managed to get out a shot, but it was no use. The bear crashed through the branches behind us – I stared down at the river.

'Don't think about it,' I said.

I grabbed Ella's hand and jumped, Geary leaping out after us. We fell through the air – I closed my eyes and waited for the hit.

We slapped into the water so hard it was like we'd hit rock. I felt numb instantly. I lost hold of Ella's hand as the giant current picked me up and fired me down the ravine. I fought my way to the surface, gasping for breath in the freezing water. I twisted around, but couldn't see Ella. The river sucked me back under. I bounced and toppled – then falling again. Spray all around me as I was thrown down into rapids. Rocks on the river bed tearing against my limbs – the cold washing the feeling out of me. I was fading. Out of breath. I felt myself going limp as the black water carried me on.

The river then went quiet. Moonlight swirling in the water above me – glittering snakes of light. A shadow loomed over me as a pair of hands pulled me out of the water.

'Where is she!' Geary yelled at me.

I spluttered and coughed. Geary let go of me, then stumbled around in the shallows, looking for her.

'Ella!' he shouted.

I got to my feet and stared up and down the river. Large broken branches drifted by. One of them stopped, caught on something in the water way off to our right.

'Ella!' I yelled.

Geary and I splashed our way toward her body lying motionless in the river. We grabbed her and pulled her out onto the bank – her soaking black hair like a shroud across her face. She wasn't breathing. Geary tried to revive her. He started chest compressions – water spilled from her mouth. He pushed repeatedly against her ribcage, opened her mouth and breathed into her lungs. He kept pushing at her chest, but she didn't respond. He glanced at me – it was the first time I'd seen him look scared. He pushed his mouth against hers again.

'Ella! Ella, come on!' he shouted.

She lay limp as Geary kept pushing – kept breathing into her.

'Ella!'

She convulsed. A gush of water erupted from her mouth. She rolled onto her side, coughing up more water as she fought for breath. I leaned down and tried to get a look at her eyes to make sure she was OK. I wiped the hair away from her face.

'Ella?' I said.

She focused – then nodded at me. I dropped my head with relief.

As she dragged herself upright, I caught my breath. I checked my aching ribs, my arms and legs. I felt like I'd fallen down an elevator shaft.

'Who are you?' came a gravely voice from behind us.

Geary and I turned and peered into the trees. A man in a tattered brown leather coat stood in the shadows. The moonlight caught the barrel of a shotgun he was holding.

'Hikers,' I said.

'Uh-huh,' said the man.

'Bear attacked us,' I said.

The guy stepped out of the shadows. In his late forties – long gray hair tied back in a pony tail. Greasy-skinned, he looked like he was made of wax. He turned to someone waiting back within the trees – a Japanese woman, also in her forties. Fragile looking, she was wearing a flower patterned robe and carrying a shotgun that was nearly as big as she was.

'You stay there, Miko,' the man said to her. He carefully looked up and down the river, then walked toward us.

'You got any ID?' he asked.

I nodded. I unzipped my jacket pocket.

'Slowly,' he said.

I delicately reached into my pocket and produced the fake passport that Dixie had put together. I threw it on the ground in front of the man.

'A little late in the year for hiking, don't you think?' he said.

He picked up the passport and checked it. As he did, a small sheet of note paper fell out of the passport – the coordinates that Ella had given me. The man picked it up and studied the numbers. He aimed his shotgun at us.

'Who the fuck are you?' he said.

'Hikers,' said Geary.

'Yeah?' He waved the sheet of paper. 'What the fuck is this?'

'The coordinates where we left our Jeep,' I said.

The man laughed. 'No, they're not.'

I glanced at Geary – our rifles were long gone, the pistol too. Miko stepped forward with her shotgun.

'You get up now, you cocksuckers!' she said.

'You're coming with us,' said the man.

9

Miko and the man kept a safe distance behind us as they marched us through the trees. We might have outnumbered them, but they had pump-action shotguns and a twitchiness that bordered on the crazy – the odds definitely weren't in our favor.

'The knife on your belt,' the man said to Geary. 'Toss it.'

Geary undid the knife and threw it to one side.

'We're not looking for any trouble, OK,' I said.

'Yeah?' laughed the man. 'You're carrying the coordinates to our cabin, and you ain't looking for trouble?'

I shot Ella a look. I didn't know whether she'd decoded the book wrong, but these two couldn't have been who we were looking for. The trees then thinned out as we approached a moss covered wooden cabin in a clearing. Damp black wood. Black door. A generator humming outside. As we neared the cabin, Geary slowed a little and glanced at Miko's gun. She pulled way back from him.

'Cocksucker!' she yelled at him. 'I'll cut your fucking toes off!'

'Yeah, baby,' smiled the man.

'You don't need to do this,' said Ella.

'On the contrary,' said the man.

He pushed open the cabin door, then aimed his shotgun squarely at us.

'Get inside!' he said.

We stepped into a dimly lit room that reeked of fish and alcohol. It didn't look any better than it smelled. Damp bare floorboards. A table and two chairs that looked homemade. The only light in the room came from an old cathode ray TV set that sat next to a DVD player – it was showing a porn movie. Assorted handcuffs hung from nails in the walls. Two huge vibrators sat in a cracked red vase over the fireplace.

'Get in the corner!' said the man. He gestured toward the far wall by the fireplace.

'On your knees!' he said. 'Keep your hands where I can see them!'

We knelt down on the warped floorboards in the corner. As Miko held her shotgun on us, the man grabbed a set of handcuffs from the wall. I could feel the tension rise in Geary – he was going to pounce the moment this guy got near him. The man stepped toward us, then stopped midway across the room. He wasn't going to risk getting close to any of us. He threw the cuffs at Geary, then pointed his gun at him.

'Put them on!' he said.

Geary kept his eyes on him. The shotgun made an ugly crunching sound as the man pumped the slide.

'Fucking put them on!' he said.

Geary stared defiantly at the barrel of the gun, then clicked the cuffs around his wrists.

'Now pull at them,' said the man.

Geary tugged at the cuffs to show that they were secure.

'Harder!' yelled the man.

Geary yanked at them. The cuffs rattled, but didn't loosen an inch.

The man grabbed two more pairs of cuffs from the wall and threw them to Ella and me.

'Same,' he said.

He waved his shotgun at us – the fucking thing looked like it could stop an aircraft carrier in its tracks. Ella and I put the cuffs on, then tugged at them to show they were secure.

'That's good,' said the man. 'We're communicating. I like that. Now, I want you to lie face down by the fireplace, arms out in front of you.'

Ella glanced at Geary. He looked back at her – we had no choice. We laid face down.

'Go get the chain,' the man said to Miko.

Miko smiled and headed outside. We waited. Silence. Just the sound of heavy groaning coming from the porn movie. I glanced at it – some guy was fucking a woman in the ass. The man winked at Ella, then nodded toward the screen.

'You like that, do you, honey?' he asked her.

She eyed him coldly.

'Yeah, I don't go for anal so much either,' he said. 'Hell, why go to McDonald's when there's a sushi bar right next door. Am I right?'

He laughed to himself, then re-aimed his gun as Miko appeared at the door – she was carrying a long steel chain.

'OK,' he said to us. 'Any of you move so much as a fucking hair, I'm going to blow your heads though the floor.' He stepped toward Geary. 'You got me, big boy?'

As Geary nodded, Miko giggled excitedly. The man kept his shotgun on us as Miko threaded the chain through each of our cuffs and padlocked the ends to a steel grill in the fireplace. The grill was bolted into a huge flagstone underneath – we weren't going anywhere. Miko took the key from the padlock, placed it in her gown, then tugged at the lock to make sure it was secure.

'Alright, sit up!' said the man.

As we got to our knees, I stared icily at Miko. Even on my knees, I was nearly as tall as she was. Her left eye twitched as she smiled back at me.

'What are you looking at, cocksucker?' she said.

I continued to stare. The man laughed.

'Are you going to stand for that, baby?' he said.

Miko giggled. She grabbed a poker from the fireplace, and smashed me on the side of the head. I stumbled and fell to the floorboards, the chain tugging Geary and Ella down with me.

'Good girl,' said the man.

As Miko and the man sat down at the table, Geary glanced at me. I subtly eyed my left hand. In it I had the key to the padlock – Miko hadn't felt a thing as she'd hit me. Geary nodded.

The man rested his shotgun on the table in front of him, then leaned back and folded his arms.

'Where did you get the coordinates from?' he said.

'No one,' Geary replied.

'Fuck that.'

'Just kill them,' said Miko.

'Hang on there, baby.'

'Chop them!' she said.

I stared nervously at them. They were a couple of stir crazy, cabin-fevered fuckheads.

'Look, the coordinates are wrong,' I said. 'We're not here because of you.'

'Sure you are,' he said. 'Who gave them to you, Swan?'

I couldn't believe it – we were in the right place?

I took a chance. 'We're looking for someone,' I said. 'Swan said you might be able to help.'

The man laughed. 'Did he really. What's my name?'

'He didn't say, he just gave us the book.'

'I don't fucking think so! Now, you're going to tell me who you're working for, or I'm going to blow holes in all your heads and throw you back in the river.'

Miko threw her arms around him and started rubbing his crotch.

'I know, baby,' he said. 'Later.'

I shifted around uncomfortably on the floor, then came to rest with my left hand on the padlock.

'We're not working for anybody,' said Ella.

The man laughed. 'I ain't playing games here, honey.'

'We're not here for you,' she said.

The guy snapped. He picked up the shotgun and bounded toward us. 'The book! The coordinates! Who gave them to you!'

'I stole it from Swan's apartment,' I said.

'That either makes you a seriously talented thief or full of shit,' he said. He aimed the shotgun at my head. Miko started to clap excitedly.

'We're looking for Miranda,' said Ella.

The man look confused for a second. I twisted the key into the padlock. The shackle made a clicking sound as it sprung open. Miko sat bolt upright – she looked for the padlock.

'Baby!' she shouted.

The chain slipped free.

'Motherfucker!' the man yelled.

I leaped and crashed into him. The gun went off – blew a hole in the cabin wall. We tumbled to the floor, both of us clinging to the shotgun. But my hands were cuffed, I couldn't fight. As Ella and Geary freed themselves from the chain, Miko screamed and ran for her gun. The man let go of the shotgun with one hand and punched me in the jaw – the gun slipped from my hands. He swung it around and pointed the barrels at my face.

'I wouldn't,' said Geary.

The man went still. Geary had Miko's shotgun pointed at the side of his head. The man looked around for Miko – she was lying unconscious by the far wall. Ella was standing over her.

'You don't touch her!' the man screamed. 'You don't lay a fucking finger on her!'

He shook with rage, his finger quivering on the trigger as he pushed the shotgun barrels into my cheek.

Geary winked at him. 'You pull that trigger and you and your little fuck puppy here are gone too,' he said.

The man kept the barrels on me.

'Your call,' said Geary.

The man stared at Miko for a moment. The fear in his eyes then overtook him. He crumbled and let go of the gun. As Geary grabbed it from him, the guy ran over to Miko and held her in his arms.

'Baby?' he said.

Miko groaned and opened her eyes.

'Bitch,' she said. 'She hit me!'

'I know, baby.'

'Rusty-legged whore!'

'The keys to the cuffs,' said Ella.

Miko burst into tears. The man hugged her close to him.

'The keys!' repeated Ella.

'In the vase,' he said.

Ella threw the vase on the floor – it smashed, sending the two vibrators and a set of keys skidding across the floorboards. Ella picked up the keys and unlocked our cuffs.

'Get on the floor,' Geary said to the man.

The man stared venomously at Ella. He picked Miko up in his arms and walked over to the fireplace. Geary held the gun on them as I cuffed and chained them to the grill.

'Let her go,' said the man. 'It's me you want.'

'Just shut up!' I replied.

'It's me you want. Don't hurt her,' he said.

I wiped the blood from my head where Miko had hit me.

'Who are you, what's your name?' I said to him.

He bowed his head and said nothing.

Geary stepped forward with the shotgun. 'We can do this easy or hard. It's up to you.'

'What's your name?' I asked him again.

'Walt Travers,' he replied.

'How do you know Philip Swan?'

'I used to work for his business partner.'

I stared dubiously at him. 'You worked for David Fisher, the financier?'

He nodded. 'Years ago.'

'Doing what?'

'I used to write software for his security company.'

'Why did they hide the coordinates of this place?' asked Ella.

'Because of me!' he replied. 'They needed to be able to get hold of me in case of any problems with the software. You see a phone here? The internet? We don't want anything to do with the outside world. Swan and Fisher didn't want anyone finding me either. Look, it's me you want. Let her go.'

Geary pointed the shotgun at Miko. 'She ain't going anywhere.'

Miko burst into tears again.

'Baby, I promise, it'll be fine,' said Walt. He glanced nervously at me. 'Look, I don't know what's on it, OK. I never did. I just wrote the software, that's all. You've got to believe me.'

I stared curiously at him. 'You don't know what's on what?' I asked.

He looked puzzled for a moment. 'The disk,' he replied.

I didn't know what he was talking about.

'The disk,' he repeated. 'The Charter Berghoff Bank? The robbery?'

This was the news story – the gang who'd kidnapped David Berghoff, tried to open the safe deposit boxes, then shot his wife and kids.

'Berghoff?' I said.

'Yeah,' said Walt. He glanced curiously at us all.

'What do you know about a necklace?' asked Geary.

'What necklace?' said Walt.

'Miranda!' said Geary. 'Who the fuck is Miranda!'

'I...I don't know what you're talking about!'

I unzipped my jacket pocket and took out the necklace.

'This mean anything to you?' I asked.

I turned it around so he could see the inscription. He stared blankly at it.

'Never seen it before,' he said. It sounded like he was telling the truth.

I sighed – fuck.

'What disk?' asked Ella.

'The Berghoff robbery,' Walt replied. 'The DVD in the deposit box.'

'Wait, hang on,' I said. I tried to remember the story. 'The gang didn't take anything…Berghoff couldn't open the boxes.'

'Yeah, they fucking took something!' said Walt. 'You think they went in there looking for cash? They went in for the disk, and they got it by the sound of it. None of this shit would be happening otherwise.'

He stared at us, a bewildered look on his face.

'Who the fuck are you guys?' he said. He eyed me carefully. 'You're not here to kill me, are you?'

'No, but things change.'

'Then...there's a chance we're on the same side, man,' he said.

'What side is that?' asked Geary.

'I don't know,' said Walt. 'But there's people who want me dead, and I don't think you guys are them.'

He stared carefully at us.

'Look, I'll tell you what I know,' he said. 'It ain't much, but...come on, easy with the guns.'

I glanced uncomfortably at Ella and Geary.

We kept the cuffs on them, but freed them from the chain. Ella and Geary stood holding the shotguns as Walt and Miko sat at the table. Walt poured a little tequila into a tin cup and held it to Miko's lips.

'There you go, baby,' he said.

'Tell me about the disk,' I said.

'I don't know what's on it,' said Walt. 'Fisher came to me, said he had some data he needed to secure. He was paranoid about it. There's plenty of encryption software he could have used, but he wanted something written especially for him...something that he knew wouldn't have any kind of secret backdoor.'

Ella stared at him. 'The data's encrypted?' she asked.

Walt nodded. 'You need to enter a passcode.'

'What passcode?' I asked.

He looked at me like I was an idiot. 'You think he told me?'

‘And Miranda?’ said Ella. ‘The name means nothing to you?’

He shrugged. ‘It could be the passcode…some anagram maybe. I doubt it though, Fisher was smarter than that.’

‘It’s not the passcode,’ I said. ‘People know what the inscription reads. They’d have figured it out already. The necklace means something else.’

I thought to myself a moment. ‘When did this happen, when did he give you the data?’

‘About fifteen years ago.’

Ella eyed him curiously. ‘How long have you been out here?’

‘Eight years.’

‘Fisher’s dead, you know that?’ she said.

Walt glanced uneasily at her, then nodded. ‘Swan sent a guy down here a few months back. Told me about the robbery...Fisher…said that I should be careful. Not that Swan gives a shit about me. He just wanted to know what I knew.’

‘Does he know what’s on the disk?’ I said.

‘Swan don’t know shit! The guy’s a fucking pussy,’ replied Walt.

‘Fisher never told him?’

Walt shook his head. ‘The disk might have made them rich, but Swan don’t have a fucking clue why.’

‘What do you mean it made them rich?’ asked Ella.

‘Are you kidding?’ said Walt. ‘When I worked for them, they were running a shitty little security company out of Chicago, on the verge of going under. Then Fisher turns up with this data. Within three months, banks are throwing money at them, government contracts left, right and fucking center. A couple of years later, they're pretty much a bank on their own. Now, that might not have anything to do with what's on the disk, but I wouldn't bet on it, honey.'

He stroked Miko's hair. 'You alright, baby?'

Miko nodded. She stared at me, then smiled bitterly at Ella.

'I like your boyfriend,' she said. 'He cum on my face when this is done.'

Ella stared at Walt. 'I'll put a bullet in her, do you understand?'

Walt nodded. 'Quiet, baby,' he said.

'This guy that Swan sent down,' I said. 'What else did he say?'

Walt smiled. 'Swan's shitting himself. Now Fisher's gone, he don't know what the fuck's going on. He mentioned some name…I don't know, some woman…'

'Lizzie Brager,' said Geary.

Walt stared at him. 'Brager. Yeah. They think she was behind the robbery.'

Geary shot me a look.

'And there's no other copies of the disk?' asked Ella.

Walt shook his head. He then went quiet like he was trying to remember something. He gazed down at the table.

'What?' I said.

He stood up – Geary pointed the shotgun at him.

'Sit down!' said Geary.

Walt ignored him and walked over to the door.

'Baby?' said Miko.

Walt opened the door and stepped outside. As Ella kept her gun on Miko, Geary and I followed him out. He headed over to the generator humming away by the side of the cabin. He switched it off.

'What are you doing?' Geary asked him.

Walt turned and gazed above the mountains. Geary and I looked up. Two stars in the sky were moving. Heading toward us.

'We need to get out of here,' said Geary.

I could hear them now. Their blades cutting through the air. Two helicopters.

'We're moving!' Geary yelled to Ella.

As Ella appeared at the cabin door, Walt stared up at a mountain ridge just north of the cabin.

'We need to get up into the mountains,' he said. 'Miko!'

She ran out of the cabin and into Walt's arms.

'Let us out of these cuffs,' said Walt. 'Come on, you can't leave us like this!'

Geary eyed him a moment, then tossed him the keys.

We started sprinting through the trees. As I followed Geary's lead, I gazed up at the helicopters – they were dropping in altitude fast. Black, military looking – personnel carriers. Their doors slid open as they descended toward the pines, the treetops twisting in the down-wash. Ropes dropped from the helicopter doors. Soldiers then began sliding down toward the cabin, maybe a dozen of them. Black uniforms. Heavy guns. The moment they were clear, the helicopters thudded back up into the sky.

I looked behind me as we kept running. No flashlights anywhere. These guys would have night vision – we wouldn't be able to spot them. Walt stopped and pointed at a sheer rock face a few hundred feet up the mountain.

'There's a small cave just above the rock face, they'll never find us,' he said.

Geary stared up at the mountain, then checked his shotgun. Only two cartridges in the magazine. There was a faint zipping sound – the leaves beside us shook. Geary dragged us down into the undergrowth.

'Sniper,' he whispered.

We went quiet. Geary listened carefully for a moment, then slowly raised his head and stared back through the trees. As Ella aimed her shotgun, Miko looked around for Walt. Miko pulled away at the undergrowth, then went still.

Walt was lying on the forest floor, struggling for breath.

Miko dropped to her knees. She lifted his head, her hands shaking as blood spilled from his mouth.

'Baby?' he said.

She looked terrified as she gazed at the single black bullet wound in his chest. He stared up at her, the life already draining from his heavy eyes.

He took a weak, rasping breath. 'You've got to run now, baby,' he said.

Miko shook her head in panic. Walt raised a hand and tried to touch her mouth. It dropped to the earth as his body went limp.

I heard noises in the trees behind us. 'Miko!' I whispered. 'Miko!'

She buried her head in Walt's chest. Ella tried to pull her away – and the rage erupted in Miko.

'Don't touch me!' she screamed. She pulled the shotgun away from Ella and turned it on her. 'It's your fault!'

Miko fired. We dived for cover – she pumped the shotgun slide and took aim again. As Geary swung round to take aim, a shower of bullets tore through the trees – they cut into Miko, her chest rupturing as she fell to the ground.

The bullets kept coming. Geary scrambled across the ground and pulled me and Ella deeper into the undergrowth.

The gunfire then stopped. We waited a moment, listening for any movement in the trees. Geary nodded at us, leaped to his feet and sprinted for the rock face. As Ella and I ran after him, I peered into the darkness, looking for the cave entrance. I ducked as a silenced bullet splintered the branches beside us – we skidded back down into the undergrowth.

Geary hushed us as he scanned the forest. He listened for a moment, then glanced at Ella, and gestured for us to stay put. I kept my eyes on him as he crept back through the trees. A second later he disappeared into the darkness. I stared at Ella, my heart beating like a hummingbird. I heard the faint sound of movement behind us – brushes and snaps, whispers and footsteps. A stream of bullets then tore over our heads. As Ella and I ducked down, footsteps rushed toward us. Geary grabbed my jacket – he pulled me and Ella back to our feet and hauled us toward the cliff. He had a machine gun with him now as well as the shotgun – he threw it to Ella. She immediately dived behind a pine and started firing – shapes moving all around us now. Geary pushed me back down, swung around and with two deafening booms emptied the shotgun into a soldier behind us. He turned – another soldier was hurtling toward him. Geary's shotgun clicked empty. The soldier took aim – I leaped out of the undergrowth and crashed into the guy. As we tumbled across the forest floor, I freed myself from his grip and smashed him in the jaw. I looked around for his machine gun – it was gone. He went for his pistol, took aim, then fell backward with Geary's arm around his neck. The two of them struggled and twisted across the ground. Geary hammered the guy's arm against the earth until the pistol fell away. The soldier whipped out a blade.

'Kill him!' Geary yelled.

I felt around on the forest floor for the pistol.

'Kill him!' repeated Geary, dodging the soldier's blade.

My hand brushed against a large rock. I heaved it above my head. The soldier kicked his legs trying to stop me – and I froze.

'Do it!' Geary yelled.

I'd never killed before. I gazed at the soldier's skull – at the knife in his hand. The rock thudded as I brought it down on his arm – the knife fell away. Geary freed one of his hands and felt around for the blade. He grabbed it and forced it toward the soldier's neck. The soldier struggled to keep the blade away, but the strength in Geary was too much. Geary stuck the knife deep into the soldier's neck, then pushed the body off him.

Geary jumped to his feet and grabbed me. 'I told you! You follow every fucking word I say!'

I nodded – and tried to still my shaking hands. Ella hurtled toward us, tossed her empty machine gun, then gestured in the direction of the cliff ledge. She ducked low and pointed through the trees. In the rock face just above the ledge was a small triangular fissure – the cave entrance. About four feet high, it was draped in roots and branches. As Geary searched the undergrowth for the soldier's gun, we heard more movement down the slope.

'Go!' he said to us.

Ella and I darted through the trees, then ducked into the cramped darkness of the cave. We scrambled deep inside – no light, no room to stand. I crouched low, steadying myself against the jagged rock – the cave roof just above my head. As a burst of machine gun fire snapped through in the forest, I picked up a shard of loose rock from the ground, and stared back at the entrance.

The gunfire echoed to a stop. Silence. I listened for any sign of movement outside, then glanced at Ella – she kept her eyes fixed on the entrance. The sound of rocks skittering down the hill just beyond the cave – I gripped the rock firmly in my hand. Geary then tumbled into the cave and scrambled across the rock toward us. He shook his head at Ella – no gun – but he was carrying something else. He unwound a ragged wire and draped it toward the cave entrance. I could see it now – the wire was linked to a headset mic and a battery pack. He'd ripped the tactical radio from the soldier. He gestured for Ella and me to stay silent, then switched on the headset.

I could just about make out the sound of voices on the tiny headphone – military speak. Geary listened intently, then glanced at the cave entrance. He switched off the headset, quickly wound up the wire and gestured for us to edge further into the cave. We crawled deeper inside, feeling our way blindly across the damp rock. It was pitch black this far in – we could have hit a ravine and not seen it. We reached a few outcrops in the wall, ducked behind them and stared back at the entrance in the distance.

We kept absolutely still. I could feel Ella's body right beside me. She held her breath as we heard a rustling sound outside. I pressed myself flat against the rock as a soldier crept past the mouth of the cave. My blood pounded as I listened to him continue on down the cliff edge. His footsteps stopped for a moment. I closed my eyes and prayed that he'd continue on. I heard him move again, the skitter of stones – his footsteps growing clearer as they headed back toward the cave. He reappeared at the entrance and stopped. He crouched down and peered inside. Flashlight then shone down the cave, flickering across the rocks in front of me. I heard the soldier crawl inside. In the glistening light I could see Geary pressed up against the cave wall opposite me. I kept my eyes on Geary as the soldier crept deeper in. The hollow scrape of body armor against the rock – he couldn't have been more than ten feet from us now. I raised the rock in my hand. Geary gestured for me not to move – not to make a sound. I stopped breathing. A clatter of loose stones then came from somewhere in the cave. Fuck. A red laser cut through the air between Geary and me as the soldier aimed his gun deep into the cave. The clatter of more stones, then the sound of running. A strobe of gunshot flashes lit the cave walls. I froze as blood sprayed across my face – gun smoke filling the air around me. The soldier ceased fire, then turned his flashlight to the cave floor. A dead animal lay on the rock in front of him – a mountain fox. As the soldier scanned the depths once again with his laser sight, I stared at Geary – Ella motionless beside me. Silence. Geary's face then went dark as the flashlight clicked off. The laser disappeared. I held my breath as the soldier slowly edged back out of the cave.

We didn't move for minutes. We waited until every sound outside had completely disappeared. Geary then carefully crawled back up toward the mouth of the cave and switched the headset back on. He listened.

'They've split up,' he whispered to us. 'One team heading over the mountain. The other, north along the river.'

His eyes flickered intensely as he continued to listen.

'We'll head east to the highway,' he said. 'The Jeep's going to be too risky. Hang on…'

He listened carefully, then pressed the headset hard against his ear.

'Fuck,' he said. He threw Ella a look. 'They've gone radio silent. They must know we have the headset. They must have found the soldier's body. Shit.'

He put down the headset and thought a moment.

'They'll change position, but east is still our best bet,' he said. 'We need to get to the highway.'

Ella nodded.

Geary stared out at the terrain beyond the cave. As I wiped the blood from my face, I went still. I could hear my name being whispered – a faint echo in the cave. I glanced at Ella and Geary – they heard it too. I stared at the headset. It was coming from the headphone.

'Michael?' came a man's voice. 'Can you hear me?'

I recognized the voice. Marcus.

'How are you?' he said. 'Hmmm?'

Geary covered the headset mic with his hand and turned the volume up.

'You've done very well, Michael,' said Marcus. 'Then again, I wouldn't have expected anything less. Are Ella and Geary with you? Can they hear me?'

He paused a moment.

'We have your friend,' said Marcus. 'We have Tully.'

Ella looked frozen as she stared at Geary.

'I understand that Tully saved your brother's life, Michael,' said Marcus. 'That awful business in Mexico, it sounded terrible. I'm going to give you a chance to return the favor. A straight exchange…Tully for the necklace. There's a small port on the north-eastern coast of Norway…Port Vardo. I'll expect you there in twenty-four hours. That's eleven a.m., local time. At one minute past, I'm going to shoot him, so try not be late. Port Vardo. We'll find you.'

The radio went silent.

Geary kept his eyes fixed on Ella as he switched off the headset.

This was a game changer for them.

I glanced back at the headset. 'He can't be sure that we heard him.'

'He suspects it,' said Geary. 'They'll kill him if we don't show.'

'We need to get hold of Cooper,' said Ella. 'Get a team in the air as soon as possible.'

Geary eyed her hesitantly. 'Twenty-four hours, shit.'

'We got Rutherford out of Egypt in less than that,' she said.

'Those guys weren't expecting us,' he replied.

Even I knew that our chances would be slim. I owed Tully, sure enough, but walking into an ambush wasn't going to help him nor me. Then again, leaving him behind didn't feel like an option either.

'Forget the port,' I said.

'We've got no choice,' said Ella.

'Norway's home territory for them,' I said.

'I don't care.'

'I care.'

'Yeah, about you, and that's it!'

'He's right,' said Geary. 'They'll have every angle covered. We won't get out of there alive and neither will Tully.'

'We're just going to leave him?' she said.

I thought carefully to myself.

'No,' I replied. 'But we're not going to Port Vardo either.'

My mind raced as a move started to come together in my head. Lizzie and Marcus may have come into the city when they thought they were just dealing with me, but things were very different now.

'Why the north coast?' I said. 'Why a port?'

'Cos that fucking boat of theirs is up there somewhere,' said Geary.

I gazed intently at him.

'They'll be expecting you to put an army together, right?' I said.

Geary nodded. 'Tully's got a lot of friends.'

'It's unlikely Lizzie and Marcus will come in then. Why risk it? They'll stay on the boat while their guys wait in port for us.'

Geary eyed me warily. 'The boat,' he said.

'It's going to be relatively empty. If they're expecting a war, all their men are going to be on shore, right?'

'What about Tully?' asked Ella.

'I don't know, but at least this way there's a chance,' I said.

'You just want to get your hands on Lizzie and Marcus!' she said.

'That's right!' I replied. 'But it just so happens that the best way of doing that might also be the best way to save Tully. If we can get our hands on either of them, then we've got some bargaining power.'

'And if we can't?' said Ella.

'There's still going to be a crew on board,' Geary said to me.

'A crew that won't be expecting us,' I replied.

'Any of them raise the alarm and we're done,' he said.

'All we need is time enough to grab one of them,' I said. 'A few minutes and a little luck.'

Geary thought to himself a moment.

'The boat ain't going to be anchored anywhere nearby, you can be sure of that,' he said. 'How the hell are we going to get on it?'

I shook my head. 'I don't know.'

'We know a lot of good soldiers,' said Ella. 'I say we go to the port.'

But Geary didn't look convinced. 'We've got a day to put an operation together, Ella. We don't know the territory...what numbers we're up against. We might just be getting a lot of good soldiers killed.'

Ella stared at him a moment.

The yacht was our best bet, and she knew it.

'Alright,' said Geary. 'We keep low, we keep quiet. We need to get to a phone, fast.'

10

Sunrise. We moved as quickly and silently as we could back through the mountains, but with no idea where Marcus' men might be, it was like walking a blade. Every noise in the trees cut through us. I tried to stay focused, but my mind was a mess – scrambled thoughts about Lizzie and Marcus. They'd stay aboard the yacht, I felt sure of that, but something else was worrying me. They'd been in the back of that Mercedes on Market Street, and I couldn't understand why. Tully was right – they seemed too remote and powerful to have come into the city just for the necklace. No matter how important it was to them, their men could have dealt with it – their men seemed to be doing everything else. I couldn't help thinking that they'd come into the city for some other reason. A meeting maybe – a conversation that couldn't be risked over the phone. I wasn't sure, but the more I thought about it, the more it troubled me.

The trees began to thin as we reached the eastern hills of Bitterroot. The distant hush of the highway way below us. We stayed within the tree line as we followed the road south for about a mile – toward a small hotel that Ella had remembered from the map. It sat in a clearing on the other side of the road – a wooden lodge with a diner stretching out to its right. I could see maybe twenty guests. Families. A few cars parked in the front lot.

'You got this?' said Ella.

I glanced frostily at her. 'A car and a phone, yeah, I've got it.'

I took another careful look at the diner, then headed out from the trees, and crossed the road.

I eyed the exits as I strolled into the diner, but it was more out of habit than necessity. Parents looking after young kids were the easiest lifts on the planet. All you needed to say was, *'Excuse me, but I think your son just put a coin in his mouth,'* and you had two minutes of blind panic to play with. Normally I wouldn't do it, but this was an emergency. Two minutes later and I walked out with a Samsung and a set of car keys. I hit the beeper – a silver Toyota Corolla lit up in the parking lot. Geary and Ella emerged from the trees on the other side of the road and jumped into the back of the car. I tossed the phone to Geary and hit the accelerator.

'We can't use Missoula,' said Geary. 'They'll be covering it.'

'There's Ravalli County,' said Ella.

'You know it?'

'Just what I saw on the map.'

'Big enough for a jet?'

'I think so,' she replied. 'You're going to call Dillon?'

'He's the nearest to us.'

'He's not going to be happy.'

'I couldn't give a shit. He owes us.'

Geary stared at the no-signal icon on the phone. 'For fuck's sake, come on!'

We sped north, back toward Hamilton and cell phone territory. As Geary willed the phone to pick up a signal, I caught Ella staring at me in the rear view mirror. I felt the anger in me rise again – things could have been so different with Jon if she'd just stayed out of it. She shouldn't have told him. At the very least, she should have confronted me, and given me the chance to speak to him myself. I froze her out and returned my attention to the road.

The phone picked up a signal. Geary punched in a number.

'Cooper, it's Geary,' he said into the phone. 'Yeah, Tully, I know…I fucking know! Where are you? I need you to put me through to Dillon. Just put me through to Dillon! Stay on the line!'

Geary waited to be connected.

'Dillon, Geary, where are you?' he said. 'I need you at Ravalli Airport, Montana, now. No, fuck that. Ravalli, now, fully loaded. I'll brief you on the plane. We're going to be there in an hour, I don't want to be waiting around for you, do you understand? Ravalli…say it back to me. Yeah, fine, we're even, just get going!'

Geary waited for Cooper to pick up the call again.

'Alright, Cooper, tell me what happened,' he said. He listened for a moment. 'You know how many?'

He shook his head to himself, then glanced at Ella. 'They got Tully on the 101, he was driving to see Max.'

He returned to Cooper. 'OK, listen to me. The Bragers have got him, they want this necklace. Yeah. Yeah, Port Vardo. I need you to put an eight-man team together and get airborne...no calls from DND, they could be bugging the lines. I'm going for the yacht.' He listened a moment. 'I don't have time, they've given us an eleven a.m. deadline, I need to move east now! Get your team airborne, and call Sam Bradley, we need everything he's got on the Brager yacht. Okay, go.'

Geary hung up and shot me a look.

'You know, for a guy who steals cars for living, you drive like my fucking grandmother!'

I floored the pedal.

An old McDonnell Douglas DC-9 was waiting for us on the strip at Ravalli. Its faceless gray fuselage loomed over us as we ran toward the stairs beneath its tail. It was covered in dents and patch-worked riveted panels. I'd seen planes like this for sale on the net – forty million dollars when they were new, but you could pick one up now for about four hundred thousand. Some of the cars I stole were worth more than that.

We climbed into a completely stripped-out cabin. Sheet metal flooring, and bucket seats bolted unceremoniously to the bare ribbed walls. This was a workhorse – a freighter. Dillon appeared at the cockpit door. In his thirties – jeans, flip-flops and a Captain America T-shirt. He sighed and pushed his sunglasses up into his hair.

'So where're we going?' he asked.

‘East,’ replied Geary. ‘Norway.’

‘Norway!’

‘Just get us in the air!’

‘Who’s paying for this?’

‘Are you fucking kidding me, Dillon!’

Dillon held Geary’s look for a moment, then rolled his eyes. ‘Fine,’ he said.

‘How soon can you get us up to the northern coast?’

‘We’ll need to make a fuel stop,’ Dillon replied. ‘Baffin Island. Reykjavik. I don’t know, ten hours maybe.’

Geary checked his watch. ‘That ain’t going to leave us much more than seven hours to get onto the boat, wherever it is.’

He shot Dillon a look. ‘OK, let’s move,’ he said. ‘And get me patched through to the satellite.’

‘You’re already up,’ replied Dillon.

He nodded toward a pile of military-style laptops and satellite phones on the rear seats. As Dillon headed back into the cockpit, Geary grabbed a laptop and logged into a site – government, by the look of it. Two passwords later and the screen was full of diagrams and photographs of a large yacht – The Warren Gate. Sleek edges and black glass, it looked like someone had taken a luxury hotel and carved it into a warhead. Geary picked up one of the phones and dialed a number.

‘Sam, Geary,’ he said. ‘Yeah, I got it. What am I looking at? Uh-huh. Hang on, I’m going to put you on speaker. Ella Ferrez and Michael Violet. Jon’s brother.’

Geary hit the speaker button on the phone. Sam’s voice sounded out in gentle Ivy League tones.

'According to MRC, the yacht isn't transmitting any location data at the moment,' he said. 'But we know its position as a result. Four days ago a Russian trawler radioed in a complaint to the Norwegian authorities. Apparently, during bad weather, the trawler nearly ran into a yacht that wasn't transmitting any ID. The Warren Gate.'

'Where?' asked Geary.

'Twenty-eight miles north of Svalbard. It's an island in the Arctic Ocean, about five hundred miles off the Norwegian mainland. There's a supply station on the island that we know they use.'

'Four days ago?' said Geary.

'Yeah, but I spoke to Frank Collins at Langley, he keeps tabs on the Bragers as a matter of course. If you look at the bottom of the page, he sent me a satellite photograph.'

Geary scrolled down the page to a grainy satellite photograph of the ocean at night. Between the clouds I could make out lights that formed the distinctive shark-nosed outline of the yacht.

'Yeah,' said Geary.

'This was taken seven hours ago,' said Sam. 'Twenty-eight miles north of the island…they've hardly moved. That said, I've been monitoring radio transmissions since you called…there's been helicopter movement between the yacht and the mainland.'

'Port Vardo?' said Geary.

'Yeah,' replied Sam.

Geary glanced at Ella and me. They were flying men out to the port – it was what we were hoping for.

'Listen, I heard about Tully,' said Sam. 'I'm sorry.'

'We're going to get him back, don't worry.'

'There's no one you can go to? What about MacKenzie?'

Geary laughed. 'The Bragers are in business with him and half of Washington. Forget it.'

'But you're talking about the kidnapping of a US citizen.'

'Hopefully,' said Geary, 'if we go official, it won't be a kidnapping for long. Tully will just evaporate into the air. No one's going to ask any questions, believe me.'

Sam paused for a moment at the other end of the line.

'Then be careful,' he said.

'We're going for the yacht,' said Geary. 'What do we need to know?'

Sam sighed heavily. 'Well, they run it with a skeleton crew of about twenty.'

'That's good.'

'It is, but knowing the Bragers, they're likely to be weapons-trained.'

Geary nodded.

'Getting off the boat isn't going to be a problem,' said Sam. 'We have the schematics from the company who built it. It has three escape boats housed in bays just above the water line…two at the stern, one at the bow. But getting on it? They've got surface-to-air missiles, RAMs, MK-49s…'

'Hang on,' said Geary. 'It's a civilian boat. They can't have ordnance, they'd have been picked up for it.'

'The Warren Gate isn't a civilian boat,' replied Sam. 'It may be the Bragers' private yacht, but they had it registered as a government vessel. Officially, it's part of the Norwegian navy. We can't touch them.'

'Fuck,' said Geary. He stared at the satellite image of the yacht. 'Twenty-eight miles off the island...if they're flying men out from this position, the boat's not going to move now. Coming in by sea's our only option.'

'Whatever craft you use is going to need to be very small and very quiet,' replied Sam. 'You'll have polar night on your side, but if they see you in the water, you won't last a second.'

'Yeah,' said Geary. He sighed. 'Alright, thanks, Sam.'

'Anything else you need, let me know. Good luck.'

Geary ended the call and dialed another number.

'Cooper, how soon are you guys in the air?' he said. He took a deep breath. 'Three hours, fuck.' He checked his watch, then thought to himself for a moment. 'You guys ain't going to get there in time. Alright, listen to me, I'm going to go in first…you prep your team to get us out. No, just get us out! It ain't going to happen, the fucking thing's armed…RAMs. Just get us out!'

He hung up. 'Fucking missiles,' he said. He threw me a look. 'Still want to be a good guy, do you?'

I stared nervously at the yacht. I might have been shot at a few times, but missiles were something else. But I'd come way too far to back out now. I steadied myself as the plane leaned back and took to the air.

'Alright, we need to pull up everything we can find on Svalbard,' said Geary. 'We're looking for a boat, an RIB, something small. As close to the northern coast as possible. Let's get to it.'

Ella nodded. She grabbed the laptop and started pulling up information about coastal research facilities and fuel stations on the island.

As she and Geary studied photographs and inventories, I trawled through pictures of The Warren Gate. Five hundred and eighty feet of sleek white decks and black windows. A helicopter hunched on a pad near the bow. It was impressive sure enough. A palace in the sea, and well defended. Two faceless white towers rose thirty feet above the main deck – steel housings that I guessed held the missiles. I studied the housings, but found that they didn't trouble me as much as the photographs did themselves.

Aside from a couple of images of the yacht undergoing maintenance, every other picture was taken way out at sea. Arctic Ocean, 2011. Norwegian Sea, 2011. North Atlantic, 2015. The Bragers weren't the kind who docked at Cannes for the film festival. By the look of it they didn't want anything to do with anybody. And again I found myself wondering why the hell they'd been in San Francisco in the first place. 'Who's important enough in San Francisco to bring the Bragers inland?' I said.

Geary glanced at me.

'It doesn't strike you as odd that they were there?' I said. 'Tully said they rarely come inland. How rarely?'

'Marcus comes in. But Lizzie? She's only ever been seen a few times.'

‘They wanted the necklace,’ said Ella.

‘They wanted it,’ I replied. ‘But that’s not why they came in.’

She stared at me for a moment. ‘You’re over-thinking it.’

‘I’m telling you, they were there for another reason. A meeting.’

She shook her head.

Geary continued studying the map, then paused.

He glanced uneasily at me. ‘Vice President Howard was in the city three days ago,’ he said. ‘It was an unofficial visit. A friend of mine’s on his security detail. He called me.’ Geary then thought better of it. ‘But he’d never meet with them.’

‘Why?’ I said. ‘You said yourself, the Bragers are in business with half of Washington.’

‘At an arm’s length,’ Geary replied. ‘They’re killers for Christ’s sake. The Vice President would never meet with them.’

‘Not officially,’ I said.

He kept his eyes on me for a moment, then turned to Ella. ‘Do a search,’ he said. ‘Find out if anyone near the President or Vice President is called Miranda.’

Ella sighed, then typed in the names and hit the enter key. She studied the page, then hit the ‘show more results’ button. She kept reading.

‘There’s a Miranda Copeland,’ she said. ‘Head of some animal welfare program, but…’

‘Is she still alive?’ I asked.

‘We’re wasting time here,’ she said.

‘Is she!’

Ella typed in Miranda Copeland's details, then scanned the results.

'According to her Twitter page, she bought a puppy yesterday,' said Ella. 'I don't know its name. I can probably find out if you want.'

'You know what, fuck you,' I said.

Geary grabbed me. 'We're all tired, OK!'

Ella got up from her seat, then shot me a look. 'You're an asshole, you know that?'

I smiled. 'It took you three days to figure that out, did it?'

'I'm going to find us a boat,' she said. She grabbed the laptop and headed up the cabin as far from me as possible.

Geary stared harshly at me. 'You need to stow this shit between you, you got me!'

'They came in for a meeting with the Vice President,' I said.

'Even if they did,' he replied. 'It ain't gonna save Tully now. Nor you.'

He pushed past me and joined Ella at the front to the cabin.

11

As the Atlantic darkened below us, I sat alone at the rear of the plane and studied a map of the island. I tried to absorb as much detail as I could, but my thoughts kept returning to the Vice President. His involvement itching away at me. I spun a coin between my fingers and tried to keep my attention on the task at hand.

Ahead of me Geary got up from his seat beside Ella, then headed down the cabin toward me. He grabbed the laptop and enlarged a location on the map.

'Salvesen Point,' he said. 'It's a fuel station on the northern coast of the island, serves Norwegian and Russian trawlers. According to its inventory it has two rigid-hulled dinghies.'

I stared at the location – the tip of an icy headland that stretched out into the Arctic Ocean. I scrolled the map south to the island's only airport.

'It's a hundred and twenty miles from the airport,' he said. 'I figure we can reach the station by eight a.m…that'll leave us three hours to grab one of the boats and head the twenty-eight miles out to the yacht.'

I eyed him a second, then reached into my jacket and produced the necklace. It was going to be too risky to take with us.

‘What about this?’ I said.

‘We’ll leave it here with Dillon,’ he said.

‘You trust him?’

‘He’s a pain, but he won’t fuck us over.’

I felt uncomfortable leaving the necklace with anybody, but Dillon was probably our best bet. I handed the necklace to Geary. As he wound it around his fist, he continued to stare at me.

‘What?’ I said.

He gestured toward Ella. ‘We can’t afford this shit now. I mean it. Get your head together.’

He turned and headed back up the cabin.

As he disappeared into the cockpit, I gazed thoughtfully at Ella. I watched as she studied the schematics of the yacht – images of missile towers and helicopters scrolling across the screen in front of her. I sighed – Geary was right. We didn’t need any more trouble than we already had.

I took a deep breath, then headed up the cabin and sat down beside her. She kept her eyes on the laptop screen.

I glanced uneasily at her. ‘You did what you thought was right, I know that,’ I said. ‘I just...I wish you’d spoken to me. Given me a chance to tell him myself.’

She looked at me, but said nothing.

I shrugged. ‘I guess the truth was always coming though, one way or another. I can’t blame you for that.’

She stayed silent.

I waited a moment, but she returned her attention to the laptop screen.

‘Alright,’ I said.

I got to my feet and turned to head back to my seat.

‘He called you a couple of times,’ she said.

I glanced at her.

‘Jon,’ she said. ‘He called you, but didn’t leave a message.’

I nodded. The hollowness opening up in me again.

‘I didn’t mean to hurt him, Ella.’

I rubbed some life into my face, then stared at the Bragers’ yacht on the laptop screen.

‘I’m trying to do what’s right here, OK?’

‘Are you?’ she said. ‘He wouldn’t have wanted you to kill them. Not in his name.’

She kept her eyes on me. She nodded thoughtfully to herself for a moment, then ran her hand across her stomach.

‘The guys who did this to me,’ she said. ‘There were three of them. It took me eight months to find them. Whatever you’re hoping to feel by killing the Bragers…justice, relief, escape. You won’t feel it.’

‘I’m going to kill those fuckers, and I’m going to feel good about it, believe me.’

‘Michael...’

‘You really see them standing in court, answering for what they did? I don’t.’

‘Then you’re no better than they are.’

‘Good. We’ll be on an even playing field.’

She slowly leaned back in her seat – a bemused expression on her face as she gazed at me.

‘You’re so far from anything Jon stood for,’ she said. ‘Why is that?’

I eyed her carefully. But it wasn't something that I was going to get into with her.

I shrugged. 'It happens.'

'And your parents?' she said. 'What would they have wanted you to do?'

'My parents?'

'Is this the path they'd have chosen?'

I may have wanted to smooth things out with her, but she was pissing me off again.

'You don't know anything about my parents,' I said.

'Jon told me a lot.'

I laughed. 'Is that right?'

'They stood for something.'

I closed my eyes. I was done with this.

I turned, headed back down the cabin and slumped into my seat. I grabbed the coin and spun it. Watched it dance across my fingertips – its spinning faces. Their whirling silver light calming the anger flowing through me now.

I loved my parents more than anything. I'd never have done anything to let them down. Growing up, most of my friends hated their parents, and I used to think there was something wrong with me because of how I felt about mine.

But my mom and dad were just cool – there's no other word for it. They owned this little book-store in Noe Valley called 'The Brilliant Tree' – all whale diaries and guides to solar-powered living. It was never going to make them rich, but they didn't care about that. Family, freedom and the environment, that was it for them.

My mom, Angie, was this suburban flower child – politically minded, but relentlessly positive with it. She might have missed Haight-Ashbury by about twenty years, but she was all Ginsberg, poetry and silver linings. My dad, Richard, adored her, and vice versa. The only problem there ever was between them was that mom was a strict vegetarian, and dad wasn't. She used to get really pissed whenever he'd sneak me and Jon out to McDonald's for our birthdays. But he'd just laugh it off. He used to joke that the country had spent so long looking for the commies under the bed, they'd forgotten to look for the hippies in the refrigerator.

But that was my dad all over. Happy-go-lucky. He wanted to be an actor when he was younger – he was a good-looking guy – but it didn't really happen for him. He did a couple of commercials, but that was about it. He was never fixated by the way he looked though – he dressed like a slob most of the time. His shirt buttons never seemed to be tied in the right holes, and no matter what he did with his hair, it always looked like he'd just gotten out of bed. His only concession to conservatism was a brown briefcase that he'd occasionally take to the book-store with him. Beyond that he looked like a homeless guy. But he didn't give a crap – he had the smile, and it carried him.

As free-thinking as he and mom might have been, they lived a pretty run-of-the-mill suburban life in San Rafael, on the western side of San Francisco Bay. They had a Spanish style bungalow on this leafy block in the north of the city. A lot of open space. It was a good place to raise kids – dull, but pretty. One of those neighborhoods where every street you turned down seemed to have the sun setting at the end of it.

Then when I was twelve, Nick Parry was shot dead in his parents' garage, two streets from our house. He was seventeen. He'd been selling smack – some deal that had gone wrong. I remember how shocked I was to hear it, but more than that, how freaked mom and dad were by it. Mom had always wanted to move to somewhere more rural, but dad wasn't so keen. After the shooting, he agreed to move.

A few months later they bought the farmhouse in Sonoma. It needed a lot of work, and would be an hour-and-a-half's drive to the book-store each way, but it was country living and there was a good school nearby.

Jon and I didn't want to move. We had a life in San Rafael. Friends. Plus I had Jarrod Hayes to think about. Jarrod was this awkward kid at school – a freckled rake with the largest teeth you'd ever seen. He'd talk and it looked like he was trying to swallow an ice tray. But he was a talented kid, and he and I had big dreams.

Jarrod had started the magic club at school. It wasn't a huge success – I was the only other member. But we both loved it, and had plans to put a stage act together. Violet and Hayes. I'd handle the close-up, sleight of hand stuff, and he'd do the big prop magic. We were convinced we were going to make it big. We used to watch Penn and Teller, and dream how they'd come to see us and be so impressed that they'd offer us a spot in their show. Me moving to Sonoma was going to be a big bump in our plans, and I explained this carefully to mom and dad.

Still, gunshots rule the world, and mom and dad took ownership of the farmhouse that November. We weren't going to move until the house was ready, but we spent Christmas there anyhow, painting and fixing the place up.

And I have to say it was the best time that I can remember.

The four of us worked on the house that Christmas, and it was like an adventure. Jon and I knocking down walls and stripping floors. Mom and dad up in the attic, fixing the roof. The hills around us dark and empty, but the kitchen burning bright downstairs. Our new neighbors visited with their daughter, Laurie, and it was like a revelation. Laurie was my age and about as cute as anything I'd ever seen – brown bobbed hair and flushed pink lips. I'd just turned thirteen, and her arrival was like the starting pistol for my hormones – they were racing around me like idiots, it was fantastic. I showed her my best coin tricks. I still remember the touch of her hand as she tried to figure out how I'd done it – her tiny, perspiring fingertips cool against my skin.

She might have been my first taste of budding romance, but everything about that trip felt special to me. I'd work with Jon on the house during the day, then at night I'd lock myself away and finish the Christmas present I was going to give dad that year.

It was a framed picture of a knight – a brass rubbing that I'd taken from a cathedral in England that summer. It was a clean image – finely detailed armor, sword and shield – but it made me smile. I don't know whether the paper had moved while I'd taken the rubbing, but the knight was leaning slightly to one side. He looked kind of casual, like he was just hanging out. He reminded me of dad – this effortlessly cool hero. And so instead of filling in the background with my usual mix of dragons, maidens and castles, I filled it with things that reminded me of him. Briefcase. Frank Zappa CDs. These furry Tibetan hats that he'd wear. All this stuff was just floating around in the background – but it was him. And he loved it when he opened it. Jon and mom too.

We spent two weeks at the farmhouse that Christmas, and it flew by. I didn't want to leave, but the school semester was starting and we returned to San Rafael in the new year. The farmhouse wasn't finished, but I felt better now about the idea of moving. Jarrod was still a worry, but mom and dad had said that it was cool for him to come and spend weekends with us once we'd settled.

It was a Saturday night when I went to see Jarrod. I told him about the weekends and he'd sounded excited by it – like traveling out to Sonoma meant there was a real plan and direction to this.

He showed me a new trick that he'd built over the holidays – a black wooden box that was going to hide a dove. Perfectly dark with hidden mirrors, it was beautiful. He'd taken the plans for it from Joe Golden's *Atlas of the Other* – this book on magic that he loved. It was written like a comic book – all dramatic frames and speech bubbles as the hero, Pico, tried to save the day with nothing but illusions. As the story unfolded, these complex illustrations explained the mechanics of the tricks. Jarrod gave me a copy soon after I joined the club. I remember him saying that I could have been the 'Other' of the book's title. That I had a gift beyond my years that separated me from everyone, including him.

We spent that evening thinking about what else we could hide in the box. We toyed with a few ideas, then wondered if we could fit a radio-controlled car inside that could just drive out. It would be a fresher idea than a dove, plus we wouldn't have to feed it. I had a radio-controlled car at home, and we decided to go and get it.

It was nearly ten at night when we walked to my place. I didn't live far from Jarrod, maybe half a dozen blocks. As we strolled toward my street, we heard the sound of dance music thumping out of a house on the corner ahead of us. A party at Pete Renner's place. We didn't know him that well – he was older. Sixteen. Prior to Nick Parry getting shot, Pete was considered the blight of the neighborhood – a rough kid with rough friends.

As we neared his house, I heard yelling. A kid then sprinted out of the front yard, tailed by this truck of a guy who was pounding after him. Jarrod and I decided to avoid the house – we might look like an easy target to a bunch of drunk assholes. We hung a right toward the park and took the back route toward my place – an extra ten minutes. We neared the corner by the park, and I looked back – four guys were standing outside Pete's house, staring at us. As Jarrod and I cleared the corner, the guys climbed into a navy Toyota.

Jarrod and I scurried along the sidewalk – no people anywhere. The Toyota then pulled into the street behind us. It slowed to a crawl about ten feet behind Jarrod and me, and just followed us. I was scared as hell, Jarrod too. The car crept steadily behind us, headlights blazing – these guys needed to be sure that we didn't live in one of the nearby houses before they did anything. But home was three streets from here. I pretended to look for my keys, like my house was the next one along.

Jarrod kept his eyes fixed ahead of him. 'Let's just knock on one of the doors,' he said.

But the houses looked dark. I didn't know what these guys would do if we rang on a door and no one answered. As the car purred behind us, I stared at the street corner about a hundred feet ahead.

'A friend of my dad lives in the first house around the corner,' I said. 'We stay cool until we reach the corner, then we run.'

I didn't know if my dad's friend, Tony Sullivan, was in, but there was a hedge on his front lawn that we could hide behind – a yard door by the house that we could scale if we needed. Patio windows at the rear. If the guys followed us over the yard door, I'd smash the windows. Sullivan had an alarm – these guys were looking for a fight, not the police.

The car kept creeping behind us. Jarrod and I reached the corner and calmly turned left. The second we were out of view, we sprinted – I heard the car screeching behind us as it tore for the corner. We tumbled over the hedge at the front of Sullivan's house, and laid low in the dirt. We listened as the

Toyota sped past us. It then ground to a halt and its doors clunked open – these guys weren't buying that we lived in any of these houses. I stared at Sullivan's house – no lights. I listened to the guys checking the yards just up the street, my heart racing as I heard one of them heading toward the hedge. I glanced at Jarrod – he had tears in his eyes. The yard door behind us was seven feet tall. Fuck it – I grabbed Jarrod and we ran for the door. The guy behind us yelled at the others. Jarrod and I leaped at the door, all four guys tearing after us. We clambered over the top, tumbled onto the garbage cans on other side, then scrambled into the back yard. A light from the patio windows lit the lawn – the sound of Tony Sullivan's voice. I ran out in front of the patio windows, and Sullivan stared at me from the living room sofa. I slowed to stop. Sitting opposite him was my dad – his briefcase lying open on the coffee table in front of him.

'Michael!' he said.

Dad flipped the briefcase shut and stood up. Jarrod skidded out onto the patio and stood beside me – but all thoughts of being chased had disappeared from me. I kept my eyes on dad's briefcase. I couldn't believe what I'd seen inside. Tiny plastic bags full of grass, like the ones he and mom tried to hide from us. Other ones, larger, and full of gray and white power. But sticking out from underneath some kind of notepad was what I swear looked like the barrel of a gun.

Dad slid open the patio doors. 'Michael, what are you doing here?' he said.

Jarrod panted. 'These guys were chasing us.'

'What guys?'

I gazed at dad for a moment.

'What are you doing here?' I asked him.

'Watching the game,' he replied. 'What guys?'

I heard the Toyota pull away down the street, but I didn't care now.

'Are you OK?' Dad asked me.

I nodded.

Jarrod caught his breath. 'These guys from Pete Renner's house.'

'Alright,' said dad. 'Alright, it's fine. Relax.'

Tony stepped out onto the patio.

'You want me to drive them home?' he asked my dad.

'Yeah,' said dad. 'Tony will take you back. It's fine now.'

As Tony headed inside to grab his car keys, dad strolled through the yard door to see who was out there. I watched him for a moment, then stared back at his briefcase lying closed on the table.

For days later all I could think about was what I'd actually seen. I kept replaying the moment in my head, trying to grab a clearer picture. I knew he and mom smoked grass. I didn't know if they took anything stronger, but the thought that they might didn't scare me nearly as much as the gun. The thought that dad might be selling drugs. That he was the local dealer. The distant fear that it might have been him who shot Nick Parry.

I didn't believe for a moment that he could ever kill anyone, but the thought wouldn't leave me. He'd never do it in anger, I knew that. But if he was scared, if Nick Parry had pulled a gun first, tried to rob him or something. I couldn't shake it from my head. As sick as the thought made me, there was something about it that kept drawing me toward it. A live wire that I just had to touch.

The days rolled on, and dad didn't mention anything about that night at Sullivan's house – he just carried on as if nothing had happened. But I was quiet, and he and mom could see it. They kept asking me if I was OK, and I said that I was.

I wanted to talk to dad about it more than anything. I wanted to breathe again as he explained away every little doubt and trouble in my head. But I was scared that I might think he was lying – or worse, that he'd tell me the truth.

I couldn't mention it to Jon. He idolized dad as much as I did, and I wasn't about to pollute that with suspicions that I couldn't even be sure of myself. I kept reading the local paper, trying to see if there was anything in it that would put my mind at ease – a lead, or description of the guy who'd killed Nick. A story then appeared that mentioned a witness who'd come forward – who'd seen a guy running out of Nick's house toward the park. The witness hadn't seen much, but the guy running had been carrying some kind of briefcase. My heart faded as I read the word. I tried to rationalize it – plenty of people carried briefcases. But the guy had been running – and I couldn't help wondering who turned up to a drug deal by foot. Some addict with no car. Or someone local.

I couldn't sleep. Thoughts about the house in Sonoma began turning over in my head. Mom and dad had closed on the house and we hadn't even sold our bungalow yet. We owned two properties, and on the back of what? It was a small hippy book-store – even I knew it didn't pay that much. At best my dad was a drug dealer – at worst he'd killed a kid. I was terrified. It was like I'd lifted the curtain on an illusion and seen its frightful mechanism.

It was a Thursday evening when dad sat me down and insisted that I tell him what was going on with me. I wanted to tell him, but the words wouldn't come. Instead, I told him that it was just the guys from Pete Renner's house, that they'd shaken me up. He said that he'd speak to Pete's parents, and find out who the guys were. And I regret telling him that more than anything. I wish that I'd spoken to him openly then, because I didn't get another chance. That weekend he took mom to Santa Cruz for her birthday.

They never came back.

I don't know whether my dad killed Nick Parry or not. But two months after we moved to Uncle Harry's, I found the picture of the knight that I'd given him, and I tore it to pieces. Jon was watching, but I couldn't stop myself.

I didn't tell Jon why I did it. I didn't tell him about any of it. He'd never have been able to think about dad again without wondering. It would have ruined every memory he had. And what would have been the point to that?

The search for magic in life is not a search for truth. If anything, it's the opposite. You don't want to see behind the curtain. You don't want explanations. As profound as the truth may be, odds are it's going to break your heart. You learn how they pull a rabbit out of a hat, and you'll never see it the same way again.

The magic is gone forever.

12

The Northern Lights shivered across the sky as we landed at Svalbard. Ghostly green ribbons that twisted high above the mountains. Ella, Geary and I stayed seated as the plane ground to a halt on the strip – its hydraulics buzzing and clicking as the rear staircase descended.

An airport official in his thirties climbed aboard. A gaunt-looking shadow wearing a padded Gore-Tex coat, he looked like a bubble-wrapped vampire. A sharp set of eyes on him though as he picked off his gloves.

'Good morning,' he said.

We nodded and handed him our passports. He looked at each of us in turn as he checked the documents.

'The satellite station?' he said.

Ella nodded. Our cover story was that we were staff heading for the US facility at Svalbard Station. Sam had already cleared it with the Norwegian authorities.

As the guy took a cursory look around the cabin, I kept my demeanor casual, like I made these kinds of trips regularly.

'How long are you here for?' he asked.

'Two months,' Ella replied.

He continued checking the passports, then strolled down the cabin. He glanced around, then stared at the steel panels that lined the floor. Geary glanced nervously at Ella.

'We rented three snowmobiles,' Geary said to him.

The official kept his eyes on the steel panels. 'Yes, they're here,' he replied. 'And the clothes you ordered.' He turned and looked at Geary. 'You didn't bring clothes with you?'

'Some,' said Geary. 'But we've never been stationed this far north before. We thought it might be an idea to get in some extra things.'

'You thought well,' the official replied. 'It's minus sixteen.'

He wasn't kidding. I could already feel the temperature in the cabin plummeting – my breath turning into clouds in front of me. He took another quick look at Ella and me, then nodded. He stamped the passports.

'Enjoy your stay,' he said.

'Thanks,' said Ella.

As the guy stepped back down the stairs, Dillon appeared at the cockpit door. He waited until he was sure that the guy was gone, then quietly unbolted one of the cabin seats from the floor. He put it to one side, unlocked the steel panel beneath it, then reached his arm into a shallow cavity. He began pulling out lengths of rope and grappling hooks. Binoculars. Pistols. Ammunition.

He glanced at Geary. 'I'm staying?' he said.

Geary nodded. 'If you haven't heard from us by noon, get out.'

'And the necklace goes to this Simon Faro guy.'

'The World Review,' said Geary. 'You tell him everything.'

Dillon continued piling equipment on the cabin floor. He then produced a small steel case. Geary opened it – inside was a plastic remote, detonators and soft gray bars of explosive.

Geary eyed me carefully. 'Cooper's team are coming in behind us,' he said. 'We go in first, we take out the missile launchers with this. We've all got to know how to use it.'

He handed me the remote – a plastic trigger the size of a cell-phone. As I gazed at it, the reality of what we were trying to do sank into me like a brick in water. Geary was the only one here who actually knew what he was doing. Ella might have had some moves, but she was only one step up from me – a petty thief playing soldier. The three of us storming an armed yacht in the middle of the sea? It was a huge gamble at best.

The aurora lit the snow plains beyond the airport – soft drifts glowing like they were lit from within. Icy air and blue silence.

Our snowmobiles hummed across the landscape as we rode north. We bounced and carved our way across hills stained with coal dust, the cold scraping into my lungs like grains of sand. I pulled the scarf tighter across my face and twisted the throttle. The fewer people who saw us the better, and we kept our distance as we skirted round Longyearbyen, the only town on the island. It might have been a remote settlement –

one of the most northerly on the planet – but nearly two thousand people lived here. I kept my eyes on its streets as we sped past. The town looked quiet – a sodium-lit pool of red and green wooden chalets. Abandoned mining buildings and cable car stations in the hills above them. It looked like a post-apocalyptic Christmas card – and in the middle of it all was a Radisson. This was polar bear country, but you could still get room service. It reminded me of a documentary I'd seen. Anthropologists trying to locate a lost tribe in New Guinea, only to find the kids running around in Nike T-shirts. It really was a lost world.

The town lights faded behind us, and soon the last outpost of civilization was gone. The snowmobiles' tracks spun plumes into the air as we sped on. A dark and alien world now ahead of us.

We rode across a ghostly terrain – a shadowy realm that brought back the taste of dreams. Pitch black peaks that loomed under an emerald sky. White valleys that dropped away in front of us, dizzying in their suddenness and depth. And all the while the icy air tearing through me. This was the world at its most brutal and honest. Unforgiving and cold.

The frozen land drifted by, hour after hour. The dark serrated peaks then fell away, and we emerged onto the rolling white plains of the northern coast. Ahead of me, Geary slowed his snowmobile to a quiet crawl. Ella and I followed suit as he led the way up a glistening snow-covered hill. We ground to a halt about fifty feet from its crest. Geary gestured for us to stay silent as we left the snowmobiles and crept by foot up to the hilltop.

The Arctic Ocean stretched out black and still ahead of us. Ice floes creaking against the shore. In the bay way below us sat Salvesen Point. A dirty oil soaked stain on the landscape, it was little more than a pyramid of fuel drums and a couple of fiberglass cabins. Beyond the drums, a wooden jetty stretched a hundred feet out to sea – its far end, broken and hanging limp in the water. No signs of life anywhere. We carefully searched the station with our binoculars. There were no boats in the water, but we could see the bow of one of the dinghies sitting in the snow just behind the cabins. Geary checked the station one more time, then nodded.

'OK, let's move.' he said.

We grabbed our gear from the snowmobiles, then carefully headed down toward the station. Geary kept his pistol ready as he arced around the cabins. The fiberglass dinghy appeared in the snow in front of us, a large outboard hanging from its stern.

Geary lowered his pistol and ran for it.

'Fuck,' he said.

I caught up to him – then I saw it. An ugly tear running down the length of the hull. A ragged hole like the dinghy had hit the ice at speed. Geary studied the damage – but it was useless. Even I knew that no makeshift repair was going to fix it.

Ella scanned the rest of the desolate station. 'There were two boats on the inventory,' she said.

She ran to the larger of the two cabins – Geary and I checked the other. The doors were padlocked. Geary switched on his flashlight and shone it through the barred plastic windows. Inside was a bare office – a few supply cabinets, a desk and a radio set.

Geary glanced at Ella.

'Nothing in this one,' she said.

'Shit,' he said. 'There's nothing else along the coast?'

'There's a research station,' Ella replied. 'But it's got to be forty miles south of here.'

Geary checked his watch. 'That's going to be cutting it too fine. Fuck.'

'There could be life rafts in the cabins,' I said.

He shook his head. 'Twenty-eight miles. It might get us out to the yacht, but not in time to save Tully.' He grabbed the satellite phone and dialed a number.

'Cooper, where are you?' he said into the phone. 'We're at Salvesen Point, there's no transport. The boat's trashed.' He listened a moment. 'Yeah, anything. Fast.'

He glanced at Ella. 'He's going to check what else is up here.'

As Geary hung on the line, I clambered back up the hill to get a better view of the coast. I searched the sea for the second dinghy – for any transport, trawlers, anything that might be coming in to refuel. I scanned the horizon, but the sea was lifeless. Just scattered ice floes glowing under the aurora like empty dance floors.

I heard Geary talking to Cooper again, then headed back down. As I trudged toward the cabins, I could see the footprints we'd left on our way down to the station. I glanced at them for a moment, then slowed. Cutting across them was another set of prints – they weren't ours. I shone the flashlight at them. Heavy boot prints heading east, away from the cabins toward an icy ridge about a quarter of a mile away. The prints looked crisp. Fresh.

Geary hung up the phone. 'OK, there's nothing else up here,' he said. 'I'm going to head for the research station, you stay-'

I hushed him and pointed at the ground.

He and Ella stepped toward me, then saw the prints. They stopped, and followed the prints east with their eyes. Geary raised his binoculars toward the ridge – a crest of jagged white peaks, maybe a hundred and fifty feet high.

'The tracks head right over it,' he said.

He lowered the binoculars, then thought carefully to himself.

'Both cabins are locked,' he said.

I nodded. 'This guy's gone for a while. Where?'

If there was anything on the other side of the ridge, it wasn't on any map – but I doubted our mystery man had just gone sightseeing.

Geary glanced at his watch – a little under two-and-a-half hours to go. He glanced down at the tracks, then nodded approvingly at me, like I was more than just baggage here.

With the coast too quiet for snowmobiles, we dumped our gear on the jetty and followed the tracks by foot. We plowed knee-deep through the drifts, listening for any signs of life on the other side of the ridge. Everything was still – just the sky dancing silently. Geary then slowed and gestured at the drifts near the water. I raised my binoculars and scanned the snow. A second set of prints led in from the sea and joined the first. Both sets then continued over the ridge together. Geary produced a pistol.

The ridge rose above us like a frozen wave. We followed the tracks up the slope, kicking our boots into the ice as the incline steepened. With the air beyond the ridge silent, we quietened to a crawl as we reached the crest.

On the other side was a frozen bay – a solid ice sheet that broke into floes as it met the sea. We saw it immediately – a small gray dinghy with an outboard, dragged up onto the ice. We grabbed our binoculars and studied where the footprints were leading now. In the glow of the aurora, I could see a white-washed wooden cabin at the far end of the bay, maybe five hundred feet from the boat. Three guys in white snow gear were moving around in the dark. One was working on the engine of a snowmobile that was lying dismantled beside a pile of steel fuel cylinders. The other two were carrying stacks of small plastic packages into the cabin. Two rifles resting against the cabin wall.

'Looks like the trawlers around here don't just carry fish,' said Ella.

Geary nodded. 'Fucking smugglers. Shit.'

We'd brought cash with us in case buying a boat turned out to be the safest option, but it didn't look like these guys were the types who were going to sell. We were going to have to take it.

Geary studied the ridge – it arced around the bay like a ragged white horseshoe. He pointed to a small double-pointed peak just behind the cabin.

'You think you can hit the fuel cylinders from there?' he asked me.

I stared at the peak. It was maybe a two-hundred foot shot. But the target was large – four cylinders, each one, five feet high. I nodded.

'When it goes up, I'll grab the boat,' said Geary. 'Ella, you stay here and keep us covered.'

'You're a better shot,' she said. 'I'll take the boat.'

He stared carefully at her for moment.

'You're a better shot,' she said.

He nodded. 'We meet back at Salvesen Point.'

I took out my handgun. As I screwed a silencer onto the barrel, Geary stopped me.

'Nine millimeter won't do it,' he said.

He reached into his jacket and handed me a huge silver pistol.

'One bullet, dead center,' he said. 'Don't give them time to figure out where you are.'

I nodded and tucked the pistol into my jacket.

'Good luck,' said Ella.

I took another cautious look at the guys by the cabin – their demeanor seemed relaxed. That was good. They weren't expecting any trouble way out here. I stepped down the slope a few feet, then started making my way around the inland side of the ridge.

The icy peaks rose and dipped beside me as I arced around the bay. I kept my pace slow – my footsteps gentle in the snow. I cleared the apex of the bay, the nerves in me rising as I began to hear the guys' voices in the air. I listened carefully. They sounded Russian. I didn't understand the language, but their tone seemed calm.

The double-pointed peak rose just ahead of me – its icy tips, forty feet apart, connected by a gentle trough. I took the pistol from my jacket, hunkered down against the ice, then edged my way up.

I reached the trough and carefully raised my head above its crest. I could see the guys clearly now – all three were standing by the cabin, smoking and sharing a bottle. I checked to see if there was any one else we might have missed, then took off my padded glove. I grabbed the pistol in my bare hand and eyed the cylinders – gray steel, frosted with ice. I aimed at the dead center of the nearest cylinder, kept it steady in my sights for a second, then squeezed the trigger. The cylinder rang as the bullet ricocheted off its side – a puff of ice crystals filling the air around it. All three guys glanced at the cylinders. I fired again. Another ricochet sparked as it caught the snowmobile. The guys stared up at the ridge, then ran for cover – one of them grabbed a rifle. Fuck. As I tried to stop my freezing hand from shaking, a red laser sight flickered across my jacket. I ducked down – a bullet tearing into the ice just beside me. I scrambled for another vantage point along the trough. As I did, I went still. The guy with the rifle was shouting at the others – I heard him say the name 'Brager'. I couldn't believe it – they knew them. We couldn't afford these guys radioing anything in. I kept low as a stream of rifle-shots splintered into the ice above me – but I couldn't just wait – they'd have a radio in the cabin for sure. I raised my head through the hail of bullets and aimed the pistol. The laser flashed across my face. I squeezed the trigger, then fell back as an explosion hammered against the slopes of the bay.

The crackling of burning wood in the air. The dull crunch of ice breaking. I picked myself up out of the snow, crawled back up to the crest and stared at the bay. The cabin was gone – what scraps were left were in flames. One of the smugglers was lying still by the snowmobile. A second was lying on the ice. Both looked like they were still breathing – struggling to move. I kept my gun on them as I looked around for the third. I couldn't see him.

I stared down at the frozen bay – the ice was separating. I could see a shadow moving in the distance – Ella scrambling down the ridge toward the boat. She sprinted out onto the ice sheet, then slid to a halt. The sheet beneath her was breaking – black veins spreading though the ice around her. As she turned to find another path, gunshots echoed across the bay. My blood jumped a gear, the pistol shaking in my hand as I searched the darkness. Machine guns flashing on the eastern crest of the ridge. Two new figures – army fatigues, heavy weapons. I took a shot at them, but it was useless, they were way too far out. As their machine guns tore into the ice around Ella, Geary returned fire. One of the figures went still – the other dived for cover, blazing bullets at the peak where Geary was perched. The guy then turned his gun back on Ella – and the panic gripped me. I didn't know whether she'd lost her pistol, but she wasn't shooting back – she was just lying low, a target on the ice.

Movement in the corner of my eye as Geary tumbled down the ridge toward her. I followed suit. I cleared the crest and clambered down toward the bay. As I did, I caught sight of the dinghy in the distance – the ice was separating around it – it was drifting out to sea. Bullets thudded into the floes beside Geary as he ran for Ella, the ice erupting into clouds around him. I scrambled down into the bay, trying to get close enough to give him some cover. I took a shot at the machine gun, but the fucker kept shooting. Not that the bullets seemed to matter to Geary – he just kept running – making himself the target, drawing the fire away from Ella.

'Go!' he yelled at her.

Ella got to her feet and leaped across the teetering ice toward the dinghy. As the guy swept his machine gun fire toward her, Geary raised his pistol and squeezed a single shot. The machine gun went quiet. Ella jumped into the dinghy and fired it up. As she swung it round and headed out of the bay, more gunshots cracked through air – pistol fire. I couldn't tell where it was coming from. I sprinted toward Geary.

He looked around for the shooter. 'You see him?' he shouted at me.

I searched the ghostly shadows for any movement. The two guys from the cabin were still lying on the ice. The third guy must have survived too.

'They know the Bragers!' I said.

Geary stared at me for a second. Bullets then splintered into the ice beside me. Geary swung round and fired at a figure clambering up the ridge just behind me – white snow gear – the third guy from the cabin. As Geary ran for the ridge, the ice around him began to shatter. He ground to a halt.

'He's heading for the radio at the fuel station!' Geary shouted. 'If they know we're coming, it's over!'

I turned and ran across the creaking ice behind me – could see the guy nearing the peak of the ridge. I aimed the pistol squarely at him, held him in my sights, then paused for a split-second – shooting a guy in the back – fuck!

'Do it!' yelled Geary.

I squeezed the trigger, but too late – the guy disappeared over the ridge. I bounded up the slope, pulling myself through the clinging snow as fast as I could. I cleared the peak, and saw him sprinting for the cabins at Salvesen Point. I tumbled down the inland side of the ridge and fired again – the bullet plowed into the drifts ahead of him. He kept running, harder now. He turned and took a shot back at me – I dived to one side. As I aimed at him, I heard a crunch in the snow behind me. I glanced back – Geary had collapsed to the ground. The guy took another shot – I swung my pistol round and fired. A mist filled the air around his head as he crumpled into the snow – a single, fleeting moment that stretched right through me.

I'd killed.

I struggled for breath, then stared back at Geary. I picked myself up out of the snow and scrambled over to him.

'Geary!' I yelled. 'Geary!'

The bullet had hit him in the neck – a thick stream of blood pumping into the snow beneath him. I pressed my hand against the wound to stem the flow.

He stared up at me as he fought for breath.

'Hold on!' I said. 'We'll find some help!'

I could already feel the wound soaking through my glove.

'Just hold on!'

Fuck, I didn't know what to do – his eyes were closing. A black stain spreading around him.

'Geary!' I said. 'Stay with me! We'll find Cooper, we'll get some help!'

His blood poured through my fingers as he tried to speak – his voice nothing but whispers and breath.

'Tell Ella…,' he said. 'I'm sorry.'

'No, no, come on, Geary.'

'Tell her,' he whispered. 'I loved her. Tell her.'

The fear in me as he stared weakly into my eyes. A vague smile crept across his blood-soaked lips.

'You did good,' he said.

'Geary.'

I pressed harder against the wound. 'Geary!'

His eyes went still. I pressed my palm against his chest and pushed. I grabbed his mouth, breathed into his lungs, then pushed again against his chest.

'Geary, please.'

I kept going – kept pushing. But the blood just poured out of him, black as oil in the polar night. It drenched the snow around his body, draining the life from him, and any hope I had of saving him.

I slowed, then took my hands off his chest. I gazed down at him. His eyes were empty.

As the cold spun around me, I heard footsteps tearing through the drifts by the sea. I turned to see Ella heading for the ridge. She raced up the slope, then slowed as she saw Geary's body lying in front of me. She ground to a halt and just stood there, a frightened shadow in the snow. I stared emptily at her, then shook my head.

High above us, the aurora shivered across the sky.

The misery in Ella as I laid Geary's body on the cabin floor at Salvesen Point. I closed his eyes – the hurt at having to do so, more than I'd ever have guessed. I glanced at Ella standing silently at the cabin door.

'I'm sorry,' I said. 'It was my fault. I had a shot. I didn't take it. I'm sorry.'

I meant it. I pictured him running into that gunfire as he tried to save Ella. The courage in him to do what was needed. He'd deserved better than this. Better than me.

I gazed at this body, and felt weak. Scared.

I was all Ella had to rely on now. Jesus. All my talk and anger, it was just noise. A fucking car thief playing soldier.

But the fact was I'd killed someone now – that seal was broken. As sick as it had made me feel, I wouldn't hesitate next time. I needed to be as strong for Ella as Geary had been. I stared dejectedly at Geary's body, then glanced at the scar on my hand. If he'd had left a mark on me, I prayed it went deeper than that.

Ella wiped the tears from her face, then stepped toward his body. I waited a moment – but there was nothing more I could say.

I left her to say her goodbyes.

I headed down to the water's edge and stared at the black haze of the horizon, the Bragers hidden deep within it. I tried to keep the heart in me alive – that we could do this. But there was a truth here as cold as anything. The chances of Ella and me getting out of this alive were next to nothing now. Geary had been the best weapon we'd had.

I glanced at the dinghy rocking gently in the water by the jetty, our bags and ropes resting on the wooden slats beside it. I stared carefully at the equipment for a moment – and there was no question in my mind. The yacht was my idea. Geary was my failing. If there was more blood to be spilled, it should be mine, not Ella's.

I glanced at the cabin door, then stepped aboard the dinghy. I quietly dragged our gear onto the seats, then sat down at the wheel, the Arctic air marching right through me. I pushed the ignition switch. The engine didn't so much as stir. I stared at the console – the ignition key was gone. I scanned the seats, the floor – my heart then sinking as I heard Ella's voice behind me on the jetty.

'What are you doing?' she said.

I eyed her carefully – the ignition key hanging from her fingers.

'I don't want you dying for this,' I said.

She nodded.

'And you?' she said.

'You've got family? Friends?' I said. 'I've got no one. It's not going to matter.' I held out my hand. 'Give me the key, Ella.'

She stared out at the horizon, then leaned her head back and bathed in the glow of the aurora.

She took a deep breath. 'We're going together,' she said, and she stepped aboard the dinghy.

I shook my head. 'I don't want this.'

She handed me the key.

'Ella…'

She sat down on the rear seats, unzipped the bags, then started checking the pistols.

'We need to move, Michael.'

'Ella...'

'Now.'

I stared intently at her. But there was no fight here that I was going to win. This meant as much to her as it did to me.

I nodded. So be it.

I slipped the key into the console, then pressed the ignition switch. The engine sparked into life.

As I took hold of the wheel, I paused a moment. 'He said that he was sorry. That he loved you.'

She went still and just stared at the gun in her hand.

'Let's go,' she said.

I eased down the throttle, and took us out to sea. A dark horizon ahead of us.

13

It didn't feel like bravery any more. It didn't even feel like stupidity. As the dinghy carved its way through the freezing black water, it was as if gravity was pulling me forward. Like the forces of nature had grown weary of me, and were dragging me toward honor against my own will.

I glanced down at the GPS locator – its numbers silently ticking away. We were getting close now, less than two miles to go.

Behind me, Ella hung up the satellite phone.

'Cooper's team are sixty-four miles south of us,' she said. 'They're heading for a marine station on the eastern coast.'

'They know about Geary?' I said.

She nodded. 'They think we should wait for them.'

I eyed her carefully. We had a little over forty minutes until Marcus' deadline. We wouldn't make it in time if we waited.

'You think they'll kill Tully just like that?' I said.

She nodded.

'Then we don't wait,' I said.

'Are you sure?'

'Yeah.'

She kept her eyes on me for a moment, then unzipped a bag and laid out two heavy silenced pistols on the seat. As she reached for the spare clips, she paused. She turned and stared at the sea behind us – gazing into the darkness.

'Turn off the engine,' she said.

I shut down the outboard, and the dinghy slowed to a drift.

I could hear it – a faint roar in the air behind us. Ella turned the GPS locator's glowing screen face down on the seat, and we ducked low in the dinghy.

A helicopter thudded over us. A spinning silhouette against the aurora. Maybe two thousand feet up, its altitude began to drop as it turned and headed into the distance. We grabbed our binoculars, and watched as it descended into the haze beneath the aurora – dropping toward the horizon – and a vague shadow that was now visible in the sea.

The Warren Gate.

I turned the dial on the binoculars and brought the yacht into focus. It sat in the night like a ghost ship. Not a single light anywhere. Dark, lifeless decks. Its sweeping black windows revealing nothing but reflections of the sky. The helicopter descended toward it, then came to rest on the pad near the bow. I studied it carefully. Beyond the pad, two huge armored towers rose above the deck. The missile silos. Their steel housings were now gone, exposing rectangular blocks of launch tubes secured in U-shaped mounts. I could almost feel their electronic eyes searching the sea.

I lowered the binoculars, then glanced uneasily at Ella. She nodded. I started the engine and gently eased the throttle – keeping it at a low purr as I took us forward.

No signs of life anywhere on board the yacht. The sky twisting above it, but the ocean around it as still as steel. I listened nervously to the dinghy engine as we edged closer. The yacht's malignant shadow slowly growing ahead of us.

A thousand feet out and Ella signaled for me to cut the outboard. We grabbed a couple of paddles from the dinghy floor and began arcing them in long strokes through the water. Silence – just the sea lapping against the dinghy's hull. The Arctic air motionless around us.

An alarm then rang out across the sea – a siren from the yacht. I froze. The sound of gears grinding – the muffled boom of metal hitting metal. I gazed at the deck. The missile silos were turning. Fuck.

I leaped for the ignition switch, my heart pounding like it was trying to break free. The engine spluttered, but didn't fire up. I looked back – the launch tubes were facing out toward us. I hit the switch again – my eyes fixed on the silos as I waited for the star-like brilliance of a rocket engine to tear through the darkness. The outboard roared into life. I went for the throttle, but Ella grabbed my hand. She shook her head for me to wait.

The alarm had stopped. I stayed deathly still, my fingers gripped around the throttle. Ready to accelerate. Ready to dive headlong into the ocean if I had to.

But no star-like brilliance. No roar that filled the sky. The silos remained lifeless.

The yacht was still again.

Ella leaned across me and switched off the engine. She scanned the decks. If they'd seen us, there'd be people, lookouts, guns. But there was no movement anywhere. I don't know what had happened – a system test maybe – but the quiet had returned.

Ella eyed me for a moment, then lowered the paddle back into the water.

'Slowly,' I whispered. And I meant it – really fucking slowly.

I took a deep breath, my gaze glued to the launch tubes as I grabbed the other paddle.

We gently pushed ourselves forward. The speed of driftwood. The silence from the yacht like a tease – like we were ants in the shadow of some bored teenager with a hammer.

We pulled our way through the water. Ever more slowly – ever more delicately. An icy stillness all around us as The Warren Gate loomed just ahead of the dinghy.

The missile silos disappeared from view as the yacht's colossal bow rose above us. I brought the dinghy to a stop and listened for any movement up on deck. They may not have known we were here, but that was little comfort. They'd know soon enough.

As I kept the dinghy steady, Ella unwound a coil of rope. One end of it was secured to a grappling hook – its tips covered in rubber to deaden the sound. She swung the rope and launched the hook toward the rails fifty feet above us. The hook caught instantly – silently. As she tugged the rope to make sure it was secure, I tied the rope's free end to the dinghy.

Ella picked up the case of explosives, hung it from her shoulder, then nodded at me. I stared up at the yacht – its bow cutting a huge shadow against the glowing sky. I gripped the rope tightly in my hands, then started to climb.

We rose through the freezing air, the dinghy shrinking away below us. A fifty-foot climb, but in less than twenty my fingers started to seize in the cold. However talented my hands may have been, they weren't built for this. They ached as I kept pulling myself higher – the pain searing through me as the lip of the deck neared. I shot out a hand, and clung desperately to one of the deck railings. I caught my breath for a second, then glanced down – Ella was right behind me. No time to recuperate. I slowly pulled my head above the deck line and searched the yacht for any movement.

The main deck was a mess of shadows cast by the silos and the helicopter rotors. Beyond the helicopter, the upper decks rose like an apartment block. Black glass and empty balconies. I listened for any voices, any signs of life at all. I tried to pick out any CCTV cameras watching the deck, but the murky polar night wasn't giving anything away. That worked both ways though – I doubted they'd spot us that easily either.

The missile silos sat twenty feet to my left. This was the point of no return – the realm of the commando. I might have been little more than a pickpocket, but hatred is a powerful ally. I grabbed my pistol, slid over the rail, then ducked across to the starboard silo. I kept my sights set on the upper decks as Ella cleared the rail and followed after me.

She crouched low behind the silo, then opened the case. She took out two bars of C-4 and a detonator the size of a golf tee. She handed them to me, then nodded at the two axles that connected the silo to the mount. If we took out either one of the axles, the giant armored structure would crash to the deck.

Ella stuck the detonation trigger deep in her pocket, grabbed the rest of the C-4, then started climbing the starboard silo. I checked the coast was clear, then crept across to the port side silo.

I stared up at the silo's heavy armored plating. I found a finger-hold and began scaling the riveted panels and cable housings. I stayed on the ocean side of the mount, hiding myself from any prying eyes on the upper decks. Twenty feet up, I secured my foot against the launch tubes, then started packing the soft explosive into one of the axles – deep into the thick cogs in the mount. I sunk a detonator into the C-4 just like Geary had shown me, then gently twisted its head until a green light blinked once. It was armed.

Ella darted over to the base of the silo below me. As I crept back down, I kept my eyes on the main entrance to the upper decks – a black glass door, maybe fifteen feet tall. It was a good bet that Lizzie and Marcus were somewhere just beyond it. But it was the main door – it was going to be safer to head down into the hull and work our way up.

I scanned the deck as I stepped off the silo. Beside the helicopter pad was a stairwell that headed down into the hull. I knelt down beside Ella and signaled in the direction of the stairwell. She nodded. We'd take out the silos once we'd grabbed the Bragers, but until then, stealth was going to be our best ally.

We kept low, darted through the shadow of the helicopter, then down the stairwell. A white metal hatch stood at the bottom. As Ella grabbed the handle, I aimed my pistol – the nerves buzzing in me. I glanced at Ella, then signaled that I was ready. She gently turned the handle and pulled the hatch open.

A gently lit corridor on the other side. Black marble walls that opened up into an Art Deco styled room just ahead of us. Sleek chrome trim and curved black sofas – chandeliers of glowing ellipsoids hanging from the ceiling. Quiet – just a distant electrical hum. As Ella closed the hatch, I swung inside the room, my finger fixed to the trigger as I checked the corners.

On the far side lay another passageway – the dark marble walls leading to a T-junction maybe twenty feet from the room. Ella kept her gun aimed behind us as we crept over to it. I slowly leaned my head around the junction corner. To our right, was a smoked-glass staircase heading down. At the bottom I could just about make out rows of black, chrome-trimmed doors – each one numbered. Crew quarters, maybe. To our left, a narrow corridor led to another corner maybe thirty feet away. I raised my gun and darted over to it. I peered around the corner and down a main passageway that disappeared into the distance. Too little light to see what lay at the other end, but it was a good bet that it would take us below the upper decks. I glanced at Ella – she nodded.

We crept down the passageway, edging silently past rows of photographs hanging from walls – all of them depicting the same event. Eclipses of the sun. Norway, June 30th 1954. Indian Ocean, October 23rd 1976. Images of brilliant rings and black skies. We crept further along, scanning the perpetual twilight ahead of us for any CCTV cameras. I then stopped. I could hear muffled voices. Footsteps approaching one of the doors further down the passageway. Ella nodded toward a narrow corridor branching off to the right just ahead of us. As we ducked into the corridor, I heard a door open out in the passageway. The crisp rap of shoes on the marble floor – heading toward us. I stared around the narrow corridor – it was a dead end – just a single door in the wall beside us. I stared at a plaque beside the door, trying to gain some sense of what was on the other side – it was written in Norwegian. I gazed at the words, but they shed about as much light as birthday candles on a black hole. The footsteps were getting closer – fuck it. I glanced at Ella, readied my gun, then pushed the door open.

We slipped inside a long, empty room. A Moroccan lantern hanging from the ceiling cast a web of shadows across a deep red carpet. No furniture, no desks, nothing. We closed the door and waited for the footsteps outside to pass. As Ella listened at the door, I glanced nervously around the murkily lit room – its black walls polished to a high sheen. A shuffling sound then came from somewhere inside. Ella spun round and took aim. Within the maze of shadows, something moved – a ripple in the darkness at the far end of the room. My gun trembled as a shape stepped forward. I felt like I was dreaming. It was a deer. A fawn – its huge black eyes staring at us. As it took an anxious step away from us, Ella headed further into the room, and stared into the shadows at the far end. She beckoned me over, then gestured to another door in the far wall. It would be a safer route than the passageway.

We darted across the room, the startled fawn cowering against the black walls. Ella reached the door and listened. Silence on the other side. She readied her pistol, then slowly opened the door. A spiral staircase appeared on the other side. Ornate silver steps and handrails. Roses carved into the winding metal balustrade.

We cautiously stepped out and took a look up. The staircase twisted around the walls of the large atrium, maybe eighty feet high. A huge black sphere, twenty feet in diameter, hung from the atrium roof – back-lit by the lights of the uppermost deck. Distant voices high above us. I listened carefully. The murmur of conversations. Radio static. Four or five decks up.

We crept up the staircase, my blood pounding in my ears as I scanned the deck entrances above us. As we climbed, the marble passageways that had surrounded us below, gave way to black wood – ebony walls and patterned mosaic floors. Golden statues of animals lining the passageways – gleaming tigers and deer.

Ella ground to a halt – footsteps above us heading for the atrium. We ducked low behind the balustrade and waited. A guy dressed in a neatly pressed white uniform appeared two decks above us. In his thirties, Asian-looking, Japanese maybe. He strolled down the staircase, a gun holstered at his side. I peered through the gaps in the balustrade as he wound round the atrium. Ella got herself ready – aiming her pistol at the apex of the spiral just beyond us. The guy then slowed to a stop. He glanced around the atrium for a moment – then reached down toward his gun. Fuck. I leaned back on the steps and aimed my pistol through the gaps in the balustrade. I held my breath as he raised his hand back into view – he was holding a phone. He studied it a moment. He then stepped off the spiral and headed down the deck just above us. As the guy's footsteps disappeared down the corridor, I lowered my gun and breathed again. Ella carefully eyed the entrance to the upper levels of the atrium.

We climbed further up the spiral, slowing as we approached the deck that the Asian guy had taken. We waited for his footsteps to completely disappear. I listened as he opened a door way down the corridor and entered one of the rooms. As the door closed behind him, I shot Ella a look – the sound of a woman's voice from inside the room.

There might have been any number of women on board, but the only one we knew for sure was Lizzie. We gazed down the softly lit corridor. The doors here had names etched into their surfaces. Kobi. Atheneus. Azra. These definitely weren't crew quarters. Ella kept her eyes on the door at the far end marked Azra. An amber glow around its edges.

We stepped off the staircase and edged down the corridor. Behind us, the murmur of voices drifted down through the atrium. We stopped beside the door. No sound from the other side. But it had definitely been a woman's voice we'd heard – this door was a good enough bet to run the risk. Ella nodded at me. I got my gun ready. She carefully grabbed the steel door handle, then swung the door open.

We darted inside a large, ornate study – twisting bronze ivy creeping across rows of book cases and ebony-paneled walls. I swung around the book cases as Ella weaved across the room. We checked the corners and annexes – but the room seemed empty. No movement anywhere – just sunlight sparkling on water. I gazed at the walls – in place of windows, the drapes opened onto huge LED screens displaying the view from a lakeside house at sunset. Beside one of the screens sat a black, circular table – four chairs surrounding it. I paused a second and stared at the table. A glass of green tea resting on it. I stepped over to it and touched the glass. It was hot. Faint lipstick traces on the rim. I nervously scanned the walls – this was definitely the right room – there had to be another door here somewhere.

I glanced at Ella as she stepped toward one of the annexes. She lowered her gun, then just stood there, gazing beyond the corner. I ran over to her, and the annex came into view – a computer screen sitting on a desk at the far end. Not that Ella was staring at the computer – her eyes were fixed on the near side wall.

The entire wall was covered in photographs. I couldn't believe it. Pictures of Jon. Of me. Ella. The necklace. My apartment. Beneath them were pages of addresses and phone numbers. Bars that I visited. People that I knew. Jesus, they must have been watching us for months.

Ella approached the computer screen – it was scrolling through long lists of words and phrases.

Airman Ford. Marina Ford. A Dinar Form. Beside each phrase, the computer was listing possible definitions and meanings. As Ella studied the phrases, I glanced at my watch. We were running out of time – less than ten minutes left. We needed to find the Bragers.

'We've got to move, Ella.'

I headed back toward the main door, but she reached out an arm and stopped me. She kept her eyes on the computer screen – on the random phrases that kept appearing.

Her eyes then widened.

'Airman Ford,' she said. 'Anagrams of For Miranda. They're trying to figure it out.'

She stared down at the desk beneath the computer screen, then pulled open its drawer. Inside was a velvet-lined tray with nine gold necklaces laid out in it. Nine of the two hundred that had been made – each with the same diamond-studded sun pendant. She picked up a couple of the necklaces and held them to the light – carefully studying them, comparing the patterns of the sun rays in the pendants.

'They're identical,' she said. 'No inscription, but…'

I shot her a look.

I grabbed another couple of necklaces from the tray and gazed at them. Identical. The word spun around my head as a moment of clarity crystallized in me. A distant memory that now appeared as sharp as the diamonds in the necklaces.

The greatest pickpocket I ever knew was my old friend, Patrick. He had the touch, the psychology, the charm, he could take anything from anybody. He made a small fortune over the years – cash, cars, watches. But his real passion was jewelry. He loved it. Loved it to the point that he rarely sold a single item that he lifted. In the weeks before he died, I stayed with him at his house in LA – the place was like Aladdin's cave. Diamond rings, brooches, bracelets, he'd kept them all. I remember asking him why, and he launched into this romantic speech about how diamonds were eternal. How each one was a frozen moment in time.

And how each one was unique.

That was the key. The sun pendants were identical – almost. The diamonds in all of them were roughly half a carat, but 'roughly' was the trick. The exact weight of each of the diamonds in micrograms wouldn't be the same – the numbers wouldn't match. It had to be that – it was the only characteristic of Fisher's necklace that was unique and unchanging. The gold could be scratched and damaged over time, but the diamond would always remain the same.

'It's the passcode to the disk,' I said. 'The exact weight of the diamond in Fisher's necklace.'

Ella stared at me – the truth of it sinking into her.

'We need to find the disk,' she said.

She went quiet – the sound of a door opening. From the annex I could see that the main study door was still closed. It had to be another door that we'd missed. We pressed ourselves up against the annex wall, listening as a single set of footsteps crossed the room toward us.

The Asian guy cleared the corner of the annex, his eyed fixed on an iPad. He froze as Ella pointed her gun at his head.

'Not a sound,' she said.

He eyed us nervously, then glanced at the photos on the wall. His expression turned cold. 'You,' he said. He reached inside his shirt. 'They're here! They're – '

Ella struck him in the face with the butt of her gun – he collapsed to the floor. As he tried to yell again, I covered his mouth with my hand and pushed the barrel of my gun against his forehead. He went silent. Ella listened for any signs of alarm outside, then took the guy's pistol from its holster.

I kept my gun aimed squarely at him as I slowly removed my hand from his mouth.

'Where are the Bragers?' I said.

He stayed quiet.

'Where are they?' I said.

'Private deck,' he replied. 'You won't reach them.'

'Yeah?'

He nodded. 'You need a passkey.'

'You got one?' I said.

As he shook his head, I caught sight of a chain hanging around his neck. I tore open his shirt. Hanging from the chain was a tiny silver disk with a black button at its center. I ripped it from his neck, and held it in front of him.

'What's this?' I said.

'It's no use to you,' he replied.

'Oh yeah?' I said.

I put my thumb on the button.

'No!' said Ella.

I pressed it. Alarms rang everywhere – sirens spinning in the room, the LED screens turning red. Motherfucker. I pointed my gun at the guy's head, but Ella stopped me. She aimed her pistol at his leg and pulled the trigger – the guy screamed as the bullet shattered his knee. We ran out of the annex and across the study. I opened the door – sirens spinning out in the corridor. The clamor of people hurtling down the spiral staircase to our right. Ella grabbed the remote detonator – there was no waiting any more. She flipped open the safety guard and squeezed the trigger.

Two huge explosions shook the yacht – the floor shuddering beneath my feet. We darted left, cleared a corner, then hurtled down a red-lit corridor. Another guy dressed in a white uniform emerged from a room ahead of us. He reached for his pistol. No fucking hesitation now – I shot him to the deck. Ella then buckled forward as a bullet tore into her arm. She swung round and fired back down the corridor – the shooter behind us spun and fell against the wall. He raised his gun – I emptied my pistol into his chest.

More people approaching, front and back. No choice – I grabbed Ella, dragged her into one of rooms and locked the door behind us.

'Ella!' I said.

She gritted her teeth against the pain, her upper right arm pouring with blood. I glanced around the room. Cabinets stacked full of computers lined the walls – dizzying streams of numbers flickering across their screens. To our right, a second door – I could already hear people hurtling toward it. Fuck. I ran over to it and locked it.

A couple of screens crashed to the floor behind me as Ella ripped a cable from them. She held one end of the cable in her teeth, then tightened the length around her arm to stop the bleeding. Bullets tore into the lock of the main door. I barged one of the cabinets in front of it, then pushed another over onto the floor. It hit the marble in a shower of glass and electrical sparks – I dragged Ella behind it. As she grabbed a clip from her pocket and reloaded, gunfire hammered into the second door – I took aim at it. It slammed open as the lock gave out. Ella and I fired at two figures standing in the crimson glow outside. One fell to the deck.

The second figure ducked back, then shouted, 'Geary!'

I threw Ella a look. I couldn't believe it – it sounded like Tully.

'Tully?' said Ella.

She look stunned as he appeared in the doorway.

He ran over to us. 'Ella!'

She threw her arms round him. He caught his breath, then looked her up and down. 'You're hurt,' he said.

The cabinet blocking the main door started to slide as the crew on the other side barged at it.

'We've got to move!' I said.

Tully dragged her to her feet. 'This way,' he said.

He headed for the second doorway. He grabbed a passkey and gun from the body lying on the floor, then ran down the passageway. I kept my gun aimed behind us as he led the way round a maze of tight corners, then down a deserted corridor. We reached another heavy wooden door at the end – the sound of crew members running along the passageway on the other side.

Ella stared at Tully as we waited. 'Thank God you're OK,' she said.

'Good you came here,' he replied. 'There was never going to be any exchange. They were going to shoot you on sight. The moment they got the necklace, me too.' He eyed her carefully. 'Where's Geary?'

She eyed him a moment, then shook her head.

He went quiet – his eyes turning cold.

'Cooper's team are on their way,' she said.

'How far out?'

'I don't know, fifty minutes, maybe. We've got a boat by the stern.'

More voices ran past the other side of the door. Tully thought carefully to himself.

'We're going to need to go through the upper decks,' he said. 'Too many crew on the lower ones.'

'Where are the Bragers?' I asked.

'Fuck them,' he said. He then shot me a look. 'Tell me you didn't bring the necklace.'

I shook my head.

'You're sure it's safe?' he said.

'It's on Dillon's plane.'

'We can't let them get hold of it. It's all they give a fuck about.'

'Yeah, I think I know why.'

He eyed me intently. Ella listened at the door – the clamor on the other side had faded.

'It's clear,' she said.

She carefully opened the door out into a black wooden corridor. Tully nodded toward a glass staircase rising just ahead of us. We checked the coast was clear, then darted up the stairs – toward a brilliant white glow at the very top. I kept my gun aimed ahead of us as we reached a small landing – a white glass floor lit from beneath. A single ebony door in front of us.

Tully paused a moment and checked his gun. He shook his head. 'Fucking thing's jammed.'

He placed it on the glass floor, then gestured for Ella's pistol – she handed it to him. He checked the clip, then ushered her behind us. He nodded for me to get ready. As I took aim, he brushed the passkey against an access panel by the door – the lock clicked softly. He raised the pistol, then cautiously pushed the door open.

On the other side, the glowing glass floor stretched down a narrow wood-paneled hallway. A plush reception room at the other end. Gray silk sofas and velvet drapes. Rose patterned cornices and glistening chandeliers. We crept down the hallway, glancing nervously around the reception room as we stepped inside. No windows here either. The drapes hanging from the walls opened onto oil paintings – landscapes with black skies. Above a cream stone fireplace hung a huge canvas – a painting of a solid black circle against a dark gray background, delicate filaments emanating from its edges. A permanent eclipse that filled the room. This was definitely Lizzie's deck.

I went still as I heard a man's voice in the distance. I glanced at Tully. He gestured for me to stay silent, then nodded toward an open set of double doors at the far end of the reception. They led into a main hallway, maybe sixty feet long. Open doorways all the way down – a sleek white kitchen at the very end. The voice was coming from one of the doors along the hallway. We crept through the double doors, then edged silently forward, Tully leading the way across the white glass floor. We passed a bedroom – a sea of soft gray furnishings, a black ellipsoid hanging from the ceiling. In a glass cabinet opposite the bed sat three china dolls in delicately embroidered gold dresses.

Tully slowed to a halt ahead of me. The man's voice was coming from the doorway just before the kitchen. I listened carefully.

'I don't care,' came the voice. 'Raiden says it's just the two of them. I want them found now.'

I stared at Ella. It sounded like the French guy from the hotel. Ella nodded at me.

I crept up to the open door and peered inside a brightly lit study. French had his back to me as he studied a bank of video monitors on the desk in front of him. They were displaying live footage – soldiers in the port. Teams waiting in cars. Snipers on warehouse roofs. I gazed at the monitors, and felt the rush of it. That this might actually work. That we might get out of this alive.

As French dialed another number on the phone, Tully and I stepped into the room, Ella behind us. French glanced back, then spun around and reached for his sidearm. I aimed my gun at him.

'Don't,' I said.

He went still.

'Put down the phone,' I said.

He eyed me for a moment – his nose bruised and broken from our encounter at the hotel. He carefully placed the phone beside the monitors.

'Where are the Bragers?' I asked him.

He said nothing.

'You think I won't shoot you?' I said.

'I think you won't,' he replied.

As French smiled at me, Tully raised his gun and pointed it at the side of my head.

'Give me the gun, Michael,' said Tully.

I gazed at him.

'The gun,' he repeated. 'Now.'

'What are you doing?' said Ella.

He held his gun at my temple, then grabbed the pistol from my hand.

'Tully?' said Ella.

He eyed her uneasily. 'I'm sorry,' he said.

Ella's expression went cold – the light disappearing from her eyes as she stared at him. French took out his pistol and held it on us. He touched a keypad by the monitors, and the distant sirens across the yacht went quiet.

French glanced at a closed door behind him – a steel-riveted panel painted white. He stepped over to it and pressed an intercom button.

'They're here,' he said. 'It's secure.'

He stepped away from the door, then smiled. As he raised his gun at us again, Tully shook his head at Ella.

'I'm sorry,' he said. 'No one was meant to get hurt, Jon included. They wouldn't listen to me.'

But she wasn't listening. She looked empty – lost – like the world had dissolved beneath her.

Tully glanced at the gun in his hand, then sighed heavily. 'Thirty years I've been fighting for the country, Ella. I've got nothing to show for it. It's time you woke up to the reality of what we do. The world don't give a shit.'

He paused a moment as the locks in the white steel door began to grind open. Tiny red lights in its frame turning green.

'They won't hurt you,' he said to her. 'I've made sure of that.'

He glanced uncomfortably at me for a moment. Whatever deal he'd made, it didn't sound like I was included. Not that it made any difference to me now either way.

The sickness in me as the door then opened. As Lizzie and Marcus stepped into the room.

It felt like they were moving in slow motion. Marcus studying me – his dark, wide-set eyes, alien-like against his pale skin and swept-back hair. He calmly strolled around me – detached, like I was some exhibit at a gallery. I kept my eyes on him – tried to get some measure of him. Gray, tailor-made silk suit. Crisp white shirt, open at the collar. He might have carried himself with conservative elegance, but he was wearing a Hublot Black Caviar wristwatch. A million dollars worth of white gold and black diamonds, you don't wear something like that unless you wanted to make an impact. As calm as he liked to appear, he was a showman. Vain motherfucker.

The same couldn't be said of Lizzie though. Still the pretty brown-eyed girl of her youth – petite nose and porcelain skin. But her hair was cut short like a boy's now – shaved at the back, unevenly so. White cap-sleeved blouse. Tight, knee-length skirt. An air of functionality about her. The only real indication of any thought to her appearance were the heels that matched her black nail polish. She looked a graduate from Nazi secretarial college. And she was nervous. Not that we were here – just naturally so. Gently patting at her neck and jaw with the pads of her fingertips.

Marcus smiled.

'This...this is bold of you, Michael,' he said. He shook his head to himself. 'Hiding from a pickpocket. Unbelievable.'

Lizzie perched herself on the corner of the desk and brushed the creases from her skirt.

She sighed wearily at Tully. 'You said they'd go to the port.'

'We have them now,' Tully replied. 'That's all that matters.'

'Perhaps you don't know them as well as you think,' she said. 'Where's the necklace?'

'You're looking for an old DC-9. It'll be at the island airport. A guy named Dillon.'

I laughed bitterly at Tully. 'Fuck you!'

Marcus nodded to French, who then picked up the phone and started passing on the orders.

'This Dillon, is he armed?' asked Marcus.

'He will be, but he's no fighter,' said Tully. 'You won't have any trouble with him.'

Lizzie closed her eyes and gently rolled her head around her shoulders.

'No more surprises,' she said.

Tully nodded. 'There's a back-up team on its way. They don't need to get hurt, I'll deal with them.'

She threw him a look. 'Back-up?' she said. 'Here?'

'It didn't need to be this way,' he replied. 'I told you, just leave them to it. I had it under control.'

Marcus laughed to himself. 'This must be some definition of control that I was previously unaware of.'

I glanced upward as a soft thudding sound filled the room – the helicopter leaving for the island. As the sound swelled and disappeared above us, a clamor of rapid footsteps approached from down the hallway. Four heavily armed crew members entered the study – all white uniforms and black machine guns, like an Art Deco hit squad. As they stood behind Ella and me, Tully eyed me intently.

'You said you figured out what the necklace means,' he said.

'Go to hell!' I replied.

Marcus took a step toward me. 'You know what it means?' he said. 'That's very good. Very good, Michael. Tell us. Why are we here?'

The venom in me as I stared back at him.

'We know it's the passcode to the disk,' he said. 'We'll figure it out soon enough, with or without you.'

He opened a desk drawer and produced a blank DVD in a clear plastic case. The disk glinted in the light as he twisted it around in his fingers.

'Do you know what's on this, Michael?' he said.

'The launch codes to your personality? You soulless fucking dirt-bag.'

He sighed to himself, then nodded to one of the crew behind me. Splitting pain as the butt of a gun caught the back of my head. I fell to the floor.

'You really should learn to be nicer to people with guns,' said Marcus.

As I picked myself up to one knee, Lizzie beckoned for French to give her his pistol. He handed it to her – my heart racing as she then stepped toward Ella.

Lizzie glanced at me. 'Strong, are you?'

She stopped in front of Ella, then gently brushed Ella's hair away from her face with the tip of the pistol. Ella didn't move – didn't even look at her.

'You care for her?' Lizzie asked me.

As she traced the tip of the gun across Ella's cheek, Tully eyed her uneasily. 'This wasn't the deal,' he said. 'Ella don't get hurt. I'll get it out of him, don't worry.'

'Are you sure about that?' said Lizzie.

'Don't worry,' he replied.

Lizzie kept her eyes on Ella for a moment, then stepped away.

She nodded. 'You've done well, Tully. I suppose we can forgive a few hiccups.'

'Like I said, it's under control.'

She raised the pistol and shot Tully in the head – his blood spraying the study wall behind him. He collapsed to the floor, a thick crimson pool spreading across the glass. Lizzie eyed him distastefully for a moment, then glanced at one of the crew behind me.

'Ask Riley to clean this up, please,' she said. 'Take the girl downstairs.'

Two of the crew grabbed Ella and cuffed her hands behind her back. She stared lifelessly at me – holding my look as they dragged her out of the room.

'Don't tell them,' she said. 'No matter what.'

She disappeared from view, and the dread gripped me cold.

I gazed down at the floor. At the blood creeping across the glass. And Lizzie's reflection in it.

14

It had been an hour since they'd taken Ella away. The longest hour I could remember. She wouldn't talk, I knew that – she'd rather die than let Jon and Geary's deaths have been for nothing. But I felt sick at the thought of what they might be doing to her. Knowing that the strength she'd need to stay quiet, I didn't have.

I knelt in a cabin in the lower decks, my hands tied behind my back. Plastic riot cuffs – no keys. The heat of my breath in the black sack that covered my head. I listened to the guards shuffling around behind me and tried to make out any sounds beyond them – conversations – anything.

I went still as I heard the distant thud of the helicopter returning to the yacht. They had the necklace. It was just a matter of time now before they'd break me – before Ella and I would be disposed of. Jesus. I closed my eyes and prayed that Cooper's team would get here. But whatever hope they offered felt hollow. The Bragers were expecting them now, and it was a sure bet that the yacht had enough weapons left to defend itself. Lizzie and Marcus certainly hadn't sounded too worried by it.

I held my breath as the door behind me clicked open. An indistinct conversation between two men. The door then closed, and I heard the sound of footsteps approaching me – two people. My heart raced as one of them stopped behind me – another one ahead. Silence for a moment, then the sack was lifted from my head.

I blinked the sweat from my eyes. Lizzie was standing in front of me, a pistol in her hand. I stared intently at her – her silk blouse now stained with faint traces of blood.

She eyed me curiously, then nodded to the crew member behind me. 'You can leave,' she said.

As the guy headed out, I quickly glanced around the stark steel cabin. A heating duct in the ceiling. CCTV camera in the corner. A metal console desk that stretched across the wall ahead of me. Lizzie placed the pistol on the desk, then leaned herself against it.

'Where's Ella?' I said.

Lizzie opened her left hand – the necklace dangling from her fingertips as she held it in front of me.

'What have you done to her?' I said.

She kept her eyes on the necklace.

'It's not pretty, is it?' she said. 'Sun pendant.'

'If you've hurt her...'

She glanced expectantly at me. 'Yes?'

I held her look. I've never so much as raised a hand to a woman in my life, but I'd have pushed her face first through a fucking cheese grater.

She toyed with the pendant for a moment, then put it to one side.

'Do you know anything about me?' she said.

I stayed quiet. Not that my silence meant anything – Lizzie's veiled life was no secret, and she knew it. She folded her arms and gazed emptily into the distance for a moment.

‘Do you know what the girls in Oslo used to sing?’ she said.

She laughed softly to herself. She then began to sing – a few lines of Norwegian. A childish tune like a nursery rhyme.

She finished the rhyme, then glanced at me. ‘It means...call for your mothers and your fathers, Lizzie’s in the shadows.’ She shrugged. ‘It doesn’t rhyme in English.’

‘Am I meant to feel sorry for you?’ I said. ‘I hope you fry on a tropical beach, you creepy fucking bitch. Shit, that nearly did rhyme, didn’t it?’

She smiled – but she had to dig deep for it. An icy glint in her eyes.

‘I’m not telling you a thing,’ I said. ‘We’re dead anyhow. I couldn’t give a fuck.’

‘Not about you, maybe,’ she replied. ‘But Ella?’

‘Going to let her go, are you?’

‘No,’ she said. ‘But there’s no pain in death. Only in life. It’s life that you should be scared of.’ She brushed her fingertips back and forth across her neck. ‘It’ll be much easier for her if you tell us.’

‘You killed my brother,’ I said. ‘You really think she’s that important to me? Go fuck yourself.’

I eyed her intently and tried to keep the fire in me alive. But I was weakening – my words stronger than the heart behind them.

She shook her head to herself.

‘You’re making a mistake,’ she said.

‘Yeah, well I’m all about that.’

The door behind me swung open. Marcus strode across the cabin and stood in front of me. No jacket now – his shirt sleeves rolled up to his elbows. Beads of sweat on his brow. He stared bitterly at me for a moment, then leaned down and punched me in the stomach. I cramped over with the pain.

'You shouldn't talk to her like that,' he said.

I caught my breath, then stared back at him.

'Motherfucker,' I said. 'Or is it sisterfucker, I get confused.'

He stood bolt upright and kicked me in the face. I toppled to my side, the blood dripping from my mouth. I eyed him again and laughed.

'How did your meeting with the Vice President go?' I said.

He glanced at me. There it was – the vaguest hint of concern in his eyes.

I nodded. 'A lot of people know what's going on,' I said. 'Whatever happens, they're going to come after you. Don't think this is over.'

He took a deep breath, then straightened out is hair. 'I doubt that,' he replied.

'You met with the Vice President in San Francisco three days ago,' I said. I recalled what Walt Travers had said and took a guess. 'You discussed Fisher's security company. The Vice President turned it into one of the largest in the country.'

'He did,' replied Marcus. 'But that's no secret. The question is why? Are you going to tell me that?'

He eyed me a moment, then smiled at Lizzie.

'No,' he said. 'But you know what the necklace means. And you're going to tell us now.' He gestured to one of the guards by the door. 'Bring him.'

A guard stepped forward – a bald guy in his forties with the thick-armed charisma of a butcher. He hauled me to my feet and dragged me out of the cabin. Lizzie and Marcus followed as the guy led me down a dark, steel corridor in the depths of the yacht. I heard voices coming from a room at the far end of the corridor. A man, yelling. The fear rising in me as I gazed at the room's faceless black door.

'You know, your brother called out for you?' Marcus said to me. 'At the very end, he called out your name. I wonder who you'll call out for.'

Motherfucker. I turned and spat at him.

He smiled, then plucked a handkerchief from his pocket and wiped his face.

I gazed back at the door. The man yelling on the other side – I recognized the voice. It was Dillon.

The butcher opened the door and pulled me inside a large steel room lit by stained glass lanterns. Two metal gurneys sat in the middle of the floor. Each had arm rests that rose from the sides like laid down crucifixes. Dillon was lying on one of them, his wrists and ankles secured with leather straps. French was standing beside the gurney – an oxyacetylene torch and gas cylinder on a wheeled frame beside him. I froze as I stared at Ella lying on the floor by the far wall. Her hands were tied behind her back, the wound in her arm bleeding across the floor. A red-haired guy in a white boiler suit pulled her up to her knees. She gazed at me, ashen faced – weak.

Dillon yelled out. ‘Michael, tell them! I don’t know anything, tell them!’

As Dillon struggled against the gurney’s straps, Marcus shook his head.

‘I gave you a chance, Michael,’ he said. ‘You’ll talk now whether you want to or not.’

Lizzie kept her eyes on me as she strolled over to the gurney.

‘Please!’ yelled Dillon.

She gently stroked Dillon’s hair, hushing him.

She then glanced at me. ‘Would you like to see what the sun does to me?’ she said. ‘How it feels?’

She closed her eyes as she took a deep breath. She stepped back from the gurney, and nodded for French to begin. French grabbed the frame holding the oxyacetylene torch, and wheeled it toward the gurney. He switched on the gas and ignited the torch. A roaring blue flame, he held it above Dillon’s face.

Dillon gazed at me – tears in his eyes. ‘Please!’ he said.

I couldn’t believe they were going to do this. I stared at Ella. She shook her head for me to stay silent.

Dillon screamed again. ‘Please!’

I closed my eyes. Fuck.

‘It’s in your power to stop this, Michael,’ said Marcus.

As French lowered the torch toward Dillon’s eyes, Marcus stepped beside me. I tried to summon up what strength I had left, but it wasn’t enough. This was no way for anyone to die.

Marcus studied me. Could see me fading – buckling in the glow of the flame, and the knowledge that they were going to do exactly the same thing to Ella.

He raised his hand for French to wait.

'Michael?' he said.

'No!' Ella shouted.

The red-haired guy clamped a hand around around Ella's throat. As she struggled against the guy's grip, Marcus stepped in front of me. He held up the necklace.

'What does it mean?' he said.

I gazed at Ella, the strength in me dissolving.

'I know,' said Marcus. 'She's beautiful. Do you really want to experience her this way?'

It was no use. I couldn't bear the thought of it. Jon wouldn't have let them do this to her – not to Ella. They'd figure it out with or without us. There was no point to this suffering.

The steel in me finally turned to sand and washed away.

'It's the weight of the diamond,' I said. 'The passcode to the disk, it's the exact weight of the diamond.'

I stared back at Ella. She closed her eyes like we'd just lost everything.

Marcus stared at the pendant – the diamond glinting at its center. And he laughed to himself.

'All the anagrams,' he said. 'All the languages. Historical references. The diamond. Yes. Of course.' He flashed his eyes at Lizzie. 'There. Simple.'

He wrapped the necklace around his palm. 'I'm going to find out what this is all about.'

He headed for the door, then paused and glanced back at Lizzie. He spoke to her briefly in Norwegian. He waited for her to reply, but she stayed silent – didn't even look at him. She just kept eyes fixed on the torch roaring above Dillon's face. As Marcus opened the door, I gazed in horror at Lizzie. She wasn't going to stop.

I turned to Marcus. 'Wait! I told you what you wanted!'

'And I'm grateful,' he replied. And he left the room.

I gazed back at Lizzie, my blood pounding. I shook my head at her. 'No...,' I said.

She eyed me for a moment, then shrugged plaintively. 'It helps me,' she said.

As the red-haired guy took hold of Ella, the butcher grabbed me and held me to the spot. Lizzie stared back down at Dillon, then nodded for French to continue.

Dillon shut his eyes. 'Please! Don't do this!'

French lowered the torch toward Dillon's eyes.

I couldn't watch.

I closed my eyes, but my other senses weren't so forgiving. Dillon's cries tore through the air. The gurney rattling as he struggled against the straps. The smell of burning flesh drifting into my lungs. The sickness of it. The flame tearing through it all.

I wanted it over. I wanted Dillon to die.

His screams then faded into gasps. His fight against the gurney's straps growing weaker until all I could hear was the thunder of the torch. The gentle sound of fluid dripping to the floor.

Then silence as French turned off the flame.

I gazed at Lizzie. There were no words for the hatred in her – for the darkness that had twisted her.

She gestured for the butcher to strap Ella in. My skin tore as I tried in vain to squeeze my hands out of the cuffs. As the redhead took hold of me, the butcher picked up Ella like she was nothing and dragged her toward the second gurney. She struggled against him, her eyes fixed on mine as he hauled her onto the gurney's base. He placed a thick arm around her neck and pulled her down to one side.

As the butcher kept hold of her, French tugged her cuffed hands toward a leather wrist strap hanging from the end of one of the armrests. He tied the strap around one of her wrists, then cut the plastic cuffs from her hands with a pair of cable cutters. He forced her other wrist onto the second armrest, strapped her in, then secured her ankles with a leather belt.

He threw me a look as he grabbed the torch and ignited it again. I couldn't just stand here – any death was going to be better than this. I barged the red-head back against the wall, then ran at Lizzie. The red-head chased after me and wrestled me to the ground. As we writhed around, I head-butted him in the face – he crumpled to the floor. I tried to get back to my feet, but the butcher descended on me and closed his arm around my neck. I twisted and kicked – but he was too powerful.

'Strap him in,' said Lizzie.

The butcher dragged me toward the gurney. I stared at Dillon's body – his face nothing more than charred bone. French unstrapped the body from the gurney and rolled it onto the floor like it was garbage. The butcher then hauled me over to the gurney and pushed me down onto the damp base.

French dragged my cuffed hands toward one of the arm rests. I stared at Ella – the desperation in her eyes.

As French tied the leather strap around my left wrist, I glanced at his pistol. I kept my eyes on it, and tried to remember the fight we'd had at the hotel. As the butcher kept a firm hold around my neck, French cut the plastic cuffs from my hands. My left arm was strapped to the gurney, but for a moment my right arm was free. I reached weakly for French's pistol – clumsily. He saw it coming and knocked my hand to one side.

He smiled. 'You want this, do you?' he said.

He grabbed the pistol, tossed it to the floor, then shook his head at me.

'It's fine,' I replied.

He eyed me for a second, then glanced down at his belt. He looked for the crescent shaped blade that he'd cut my neck with at the hotel. He didn't have it. I jabbed the blade deep into the butcher's throat, his blood pouring over me as he collapsed backward.

'Kill him!' said Lizzie.

French ran for his gun. I sliced open the leather strap that held me to the gurney and raced after him. He grabbed the gun, turned and fired – the bullet zipping past me as I dived at him. I plunged the blade deep into his chest. The fucker went still. I leaped off him and looked for Lizzie – she was gone. Just the red-head still reeling on the floor. As he scrambled for his holstered gun, I grabbed French's pistol and shot him in the chest.

I ran over to Ella and cut her free from the gurney. She sat up and threw her arms around me – holding on to me like I was all that there was in the world. I ran my hands across her hair and listened to her breathing. As I checked the wound in her arm, the sound of heavy gun-fire erupted from high above us. We glanced upward as an explosion rocked the upper decks – the lanterns in the ceiling shaking and crashing to the floor.

Cooper's team were here.

Ella leaped from the gurney, the strength flooding back into her – her eyes alive as she grabbed the butcher's gun.

We ran out into the passageway. Machine gun fire from the upper decks. We scaled a winding staircase, then tore down a torn, smoke-filled passageway. We cleared a corner, then ground to a halt – two crew members were at an open window, firing Uzis out toward the sea. One swung his gun toward us. I ducked back behind the corner – but Ella was in no mood to be patient. She dived headlong onto the floor and emptied her pistol into them – both guys collapsed. We sprinted over to them, grabbed their weapons, then slowed as we caught sight of the view from the window.

It was nothing short of war outside. A dozen members of the crew were on deck, firing heavy machine guns at a large trawler about three hundred feet away. Two rocket trails flew out from the trawler and exploded against the yacht's bow. A bone-jarring impact – the deck shook beneath us.

A hatch in the yacht's main deck then slid open. A gantry rose out of the depths – a colossal anti-aircraft gun. Its barrel swung round and fired a glowing beam of lead at the trawler. The beam tore effortlessly through the trawler's wooden cabins.

Ella ran for a staircase at the end of the passageway.

'They won't last against that,' she said. 'You find the necklace!'

'Ella!'

She slowed, then glanced back at me. I held her look for a moment – the longing in me for her to stay safe.

She nodded.

I watched as she disappeared down toward the main deck, the yacht shuddering as another rocket hit the bow.

I turned and scanned the passageway, looking for the quickest route up to the Bragers' private deck. Tully had used a passkey to get in. I stared at the crew members' bodies lying at my feet, then rolled them over and searched for one. Their pockets were empty. Nothing hanging around their necks. I checked the deck around their bodies – then paused. I gazed at the floor for a second. Something wasn't right. A couple of empty shell casings lying on the floor beside me. They were beginning to roll to one side.

The yacht was listing.

Lizzie and Marcus wouldn't stay now – they'd head for the escape boats. I tried to remember. Sam had said that there were three escape boats – one in the bow, two in the stern. But the bow had been hit – they'd be heading for the stern.

I scrambled toward the staircase, the marble passageways shaking around me as I headed back down into the depths of the yacht. The escape bays would be just above the water line, maybe three decks beneath me. I gripped the Uzi tightly as I hurtled further down.

The marble walls then gave way to steel and aluminum – thick pipes running the lengths of the corridors. The engineering decks. The bays would be here somewhere. I scurried down the winding corridors, searching every corner, every cryptic shadow – the heat growing thick around me. As I cleared another junction, the yacht juddered violently – an explosion on the decks way above me – I toppled against a corridor wall.

The lights in the corridors then flickered and went out.

Pitch black. Not even the faintest glow to guide me.

I placed a palm against the wall and cautiously felt my way forward. The deck shuddering beneath me – the wall trembling against my palm like some fairground horror-house. I felt my way through the dark, my fingertips brushing against door frames and intercom panels, conduits and cable boxes. Every noise ahead ringing alarms in me. My fingers traced their way along a riveted steel panel, and I slowed – I could feel a corner just ahead of me. I stopped and listened.

No sound beyond the corner – just distant gunfire echoing way above me. But there was something else. The temperature was dropping. Icy air streaming past my fingertips. I carefully glanced around the corner. In the darkness ahead of me, a faint green glow emerged from a half-open hatch at the end of the passageway.

I eyed it intently, then began edging my way down toward it. I could hear voices on the other side. The crystal clear sound of lapping water. I crept further, steadying myself against the wall until I could see through the gap in the hatchway. I went still. On the other side was a steel bay the size of a large garage. A small white powerboat sat on a hydraulic platform. Just beyond it, a thick steel door in the hull was wide open – the aurora-lit sea beyond it. In the ghostly light I could see three people moving as they loaded the boat.

I gripped the Uzi tightly, then pushed the hatch wide open. Lizzie and Marcus's silhouettes turned to face me. The crew member who was with them reached for a weapon – I squeezed the trigger and cut him to the ground.

Silence as I stepped into the bay. The Bragers standing motionless in front of me. I gazed at them, and the rage rose in me like a wave. This was the moment I'd prayed for – just the four of us – them, me and a big fucking gun.

'The necklace,' I said. 'The disk.'

Marcus eyed me for a moment, then nodded toward the powerboat.

'Step back,' I said.

He and Lizzie moved away from the boat and stood by the door in the hull. I carefully approached the powerboat, keeping the Uzi aimed squarely at them as I stepped up onto the hydraulic mount. I reached an arm inside the boat. A metal briefcase lay on the seat –

I snapped it open. Inside were the disk and the necklace.

I grabbed the case and stepped back down off the mount.

Gun-fire in the distance as Lizzie and Marcus kept their eyes on me.

'What now?' said Marcus.

A simple question with a simple answer.

'You killed my brother,' I said.

The words sunk into me like a blade. I aimed the Uzi at them – my finger quivering against the trigger. The hurt coursed through me as their silhouettes stood in the line of the gun sight. I wanted to watch their bodies fall to the ground. I wanted it more than anything.

But I just stood there.

I stayed absolutely still.

All I could think about was Jon. If he'd seen me standing here. Those thief's hands that had hurt him so much, were now those of an executioner. It would have been the greatest hurt I could have inflicted on him.

My brother. He wouldn't have wanted this.

I picked up a rope from the bay floor and threw it at Marcus.

'Tie her hands,' I said.

He stared down at the rope.

'Now!' I said. 'Do it!'

As he reached down for the rope, a huge explosion shook the stern – I fell against the powerboat and lost hold of the Uzi. Lizzie ran for a metal case beside her. She swung it open, pistols and grenades spilling out across the floor. She grabbed a pistol and fired at me. I dived to the deck. She fired again – the bullets shearing an electrical cable attached to the hydraulic mount. It sparked as it slithered across the floor among the grenades – a blinding flash then throwing me across the bay.

I was dazed. A harsh ringing in my ears. Blood dripping from my face. I dragged myself back to my feet and looked around for the Bragers. As I peered through the dense clouds of smoke, I heard footsteps running toward me. I frantically reached around, trying to find the gun. I froze as a figure hurtled toward me.

'Michael!' said Ella.

She took hold of me and wiped the blood from my face.

'Michael! Cooper's taken the yacht! Where are the Bragers?'

I just stared at her for a moment.

'Where are they?' she said.

I glanced around the bay, then peered through the drifting smoke at where they'd been standing – at the open door in the hull. I stumbled over to it and stared at the icy waves outside. In the spectral glow of the aurora I could see Marcus lying in the sea. He was struggling to breathe – a gaping black wound down the side of his face. Lizzie was in the water just below me, scraping her hands against the hull. She gazed up at me as she breathlessly tried to pull herself out of the freezing sea.

Ella watched them for a moment, then reached for a length of rope lying on the floor. As she approached the hull door, I held out a hand and stopped her.

She eyed me intently.

'This isn't what Jon would have wanted,' she said.

I shook my head. I may not have killed them when I had the chance, but I certainly wasn't going to save them.

'They have to answer for this, Michael.'

As I stared back down at Lizzie, Ella stepped forward with the rope. I stopped her again.

'You can't do this,' she said.

I stayed silent.

'You'll be no better than they are,' she said.

I nodded.

I took the rope from her and let it fall to the floor. It may not have been right or just, but I didn't care. I could have had the Ten Commandments tattooed on the inside of my eyelids, I wouldn't have known what was right or wrong any more. I gently sat myself down on the edge of the hull door, and gazed at Lizzie and Marcus in the sea.

It didn't take more than a few minutes. Marcus' exhausted attempts to stay afloat faded to nothingness. Lizzie's struggle against the side of the hull became ever more weak – ever more silent – until she finally went still. Her frozen eyes fixed skyward.

And I just sat there and watched. Cool as the air around me. And content with it.

Their bodies drifted out to sea – and soon they were little more than shadows lost in the waves. I nodded to myself, then glanced at Ella.

She couldn't look at me.

15

It felt as if I wasn't really there. As if everything was being projected onto a screen that I was watching from way back in an auditorium. The images just drifted across me. The bow of The Warren Gate disappearing under the sea. The island appearing beneath the glowing Arctic sky. The silent silhouettes of Cooper's team as they picked up Geary's body from Salvesen Point.

I stood alone on the trawler deck as we continued south. I hadn't seen Ella since we'd boarded the trawler, and wasn't sure that I wanted to. The disappointment in her eyes. I didn't want to see it.

As I stared at the sea, the cabin door behind me opened and Cooper stepped out onto the deck. The rings on his fingers gleamed in the light as he offered me a cigarette. I shook my head.

'How is she?' I asked.

'I sedated her,' he said. 'She'll be fine. The wound's clean.'

'She say anything?'

'Just Tully.' He shook his head and lit a cigarette. 'The motherfucker.'

He toyed broodily with the rings on his fingers for a moment, then stared at the island. He gestured toward the coast.

'There's security at the airport,' he said. 'We can't risk landing the trawler. A guy's going to come out by boat and pick you up. There's a plane waiting, it'll take you back to San Francisco.'

'Me?'

'We're splitting the team up,' he said. 'The Bragers...too much fallout. We're going to stay low for a while.'

'Where?'

'I don't know. Just until the heat dies down. A few months maybe.'

'But Ella's coming back to the US?'

He eyed me carefully as he took a deep pull on his cigarette.

'You need to take the disk back home, Michael. That's what you came here for, right?'

I couldn't believe it – they were edging me out already.

'I need to see her,' I said.

'She's out.'

I turned and headed for the cabin door.

'Michael, forget it,' he said.

I headed down into the trawler's cramped lower decks – the hull torn and burnt all around me. The smell of gun-smoke still heavy in the air. Four of Cooper's team were packing away weapons, talking on satellite phones. Another was sitting by a small blue cabin door – a black guy in full body armor. He got to his feet as I approached. He glanced at Cooper standing just behind me.

Cooper nodded at him. 'It's OK.'

The guy stood away.

I stepped into a cramped wooden cabin – its bullet strewn walls overlooking a tiny oak cot. Ella was lying asleep under a heavy blanket, her head resting gently to one side.

'She's fine,' said Cooper.

I nodded.

I watched her breathing for a moment, then sat down on the cot beside her. She didn't stir. But I don't know what I'd have said to her even if she had. I knew that I'd let her down – a small-time thief, turned killer. Jon probably wouldn't have been proud of what I did either – but Ella was here, and it felt like I'd done at least one thing right.

I took hold of her hand. The narcotic warmth of her skin. I brushed my fingertips against her palm – the delicate ridges and lines. Her sleeping fingers curled against mine. I don't think I've ever been in love, but as I held her hand, the pain of it felt real to me. I couldn't shake the feeling that this would be the last time that I'd see her. If I knew her at all, she'd disappear back into the shadows. I wouldn't find her even if I looked.

One of the team stepped toward the cabin. 'The boat's approaching,' he said.

'That's your ride,' said Cooper.

I glanced at him. As I did, the other guys in the team slowly drifted into view and stood behind him. No aggression – but they were closing ranks. Whatever I was, I wasn't one of their kind.

'Time to go,' he said.

I nodded. And I let go of Ella's hand.

I zipped the necklace and the disk into my jacket pocket, and headed up onto deck. Back into the night. And out in the cold again.

It was probably going to be the story of the year. The coded disk, and the video footage that it contained.

The footage starts with a boy in a smart, New England-style hotel suite. Fresh-faced, he's seventeen or eighteen years old. He's immaculate – dressed in a crisp blue shirt. Expensive shoes. Perfect black hair combed in a neat side parting.

He may look like a parent's dream, but he can't focus his eyes. He's stoned out of his skull, laughing to himself as he hides a small video camera between the paperbacks on a bookshelf in the bedroom. He adjusts the camera's aspect slightly, then steps toward the bed. He tries to restrain his laughter as he peers toward the bathroom door.

'Are you ready?' he asks.

There's no answer.

'Miranda?' he says.

'In a minute,' comes a woman's voice from the bathroom.

He sits on the bed, places his hands on his cheeks, and playfully rocks his head from side to side as he waits. He jumps to his feet as the bathroom door then opens. A woman in her late thirties strides into the room. Long black hair, she's wearing white stockings and underwear. She's attractive, but in a tired, weather-worn way. Shadows beneath her deep brown eyes. The boy giggles excitedly, and the woman smiles to herself.

'The money?' she says.

The boy reaches over to the bedside table. Beside a tiny jar of pills and a large bottle of vodka lies a white envelope. He hands it to her, and she starts counting the bills inside.

'It's all there,' says the boy.

She nods. 'If I can't trust you, who can I trust, huh?'

As she places the envelope in her bag, the boy hunches his shoulders and tries not to laugh. She steps toward him, kisses him on the mouth, then takes off his clothes. He pushes her onto the bed, and she smiles. The boy pulls off her underwear and immediately climbs on top of her. He pushes himself deep into her, grinding his hips against hers. As he writhes around, he strokes her hair for a moment, then places his hand around her neck.

The woman shakes her head. 'No,' she says.

As he takes hold of her throat, she winces and turns her head to one side.

'I don't like that,' she says.

'Quiet,' says the boy.

'I don't like it!'

'Shutup!'

His demeanor turns violent as he places his other hand around her throat. She tries to wriggle out from underneath him, but he holds on even harder – squeezing her neck as he fucks her.

'No!' she says.

'Shutup! Shutup! Shutup!'

She struggles and manages to free one of the boy's hands from her throat. He reaches to the bedside table and picks up the bottle of vodka. He keeps her held down as he takes a huge mouthful. The woman fights to throw him off her and slaps him. He swings the bottle down at her head. It doesn't break. The woman goes limp. The boy drinks some more, puts the bottle back down on the table and carries on fucking her.

By the time he rolls off her, the pillow beneath the woman's head is soaked a full red. The boy doesn't even seem to notice. He just sways on the bed for a moment, then lies down on his side. His eyes begin to close. He laughs quietly to himself, then falls asleep.

For the next two hours of footage nothing in the room moves. Just the boy breathing heavily as a red stain seeps across the sheets.

At two hours-forty-three minutes into the footage, there's a knock at the door.

'Lance?' comes a man's voice from outside. 'Lance, did you get back OK?'

Silence for a moment. The door then slowly opens and Senator Robert Howard – the current Vice President – steps into the room. He stops in the doorway, horrified by the scene that confronts him.

'Lance!'

He runs to the bed and tries to wake his son. Lance groans but doesn't get up. The senator runs toward the woman on the bed. He goes to revive her, but instead reels back from her.

'Oh God, Lance, what have you done?'

He stares around the room, then covers Lance with a blanket and drags him off the bed.

'Lance!' he yells.

The boy groans as he rolls around on the floor. The senator realizes the room door is still open. He closes it, then takes out his phone. He stands just out of shot as he makes a call.

His voice is shaking. 'Chris,' he says. 'You need to get to the hotel now, something bad has happened. No. Lance. The Barker Suite, make sure...'

The screen then goes black. The footage stops.

Silence. I took a deep breath, then closed the laptop screen. I couldn't believe what I'd just seen. I don't know what I'd expected to find on the disk – government data, technology – I don't know. But this felt like the worst. I hoped they fried them both, the worthless motherfuckers.

I sat in the shredded remnants of my apartment, and gazed again at the necklace – its diamond now resting separately beside it. I'd been back in San Francisco for less than six hours. The moment I got off the plane, I went straight to SF State and paid some student fifty bucks to weigh the diamond for me. The nine-digit code had unlocked the disk.

I grabbed a mouthful of whiskey, and tried to make some sense of it all. Whatever job the senator did covering it up, it was a good bet that his son's hidden camera had remained hidden. Probably found by a maid. I remember Ella saying something about Fisher's wife divorcing him because he'd had an affair with a housekeeper. Any money, she worked at the same hotel.

Fisher must have been blackmailing the senator for years. Receiving government contracts in return for a guarantee that the footage remained hidden. How the Bragers found out about it, I don't know. Fisher died during routine surgery – maybe the doctors behind the masks weren't who he thought they were.

Not that it mattered now. All that was important to me was that the footage was made public and that Jon got the credit for it. I thought about the best way of breaking the story. Going to the *World Review* was out – it would mean too many questions. Ella and Cooper wouldn't want any link to this, and there was no way I was going to be able to explain my involvement without dragging them into it.

Better if I didn't explain anything at all. I stared back at the laptop. Amelia507. It was the name of the first girl that Jon ever fell in love with, and her address on Cumberland. It was also the password to Jon's web page.

One final post from Jonathan Violet.

The laptop's hard disk gently crackled as it uploaded the footage – an uneven murmur that was going to turn into a full-blown storm in a few hours. As the laptop whirred away, I headed over to the balcony window and gazed out at the bay.

It was all done now. But I felt no sense of relief. No escape. Jon was gone and the pain of that wasn't going away any time soon. I watched the cars coasting down the Embarcadero. A Porsche Cayenne heading for the financial district. An Audi R8 turning into Green Street. I watched them and waited for some familiar bell to ring within me – some semblance of my old life to invite me back. But nothing sounded. The cars just coasted by. I was back on my home turf, but it felt as alien to me as the island had.

I gazed at my hands, and felt more lost than I'd ever been.

As a child I used to believe that magic was real – that it was a genuine force in the world that brought hope and wonder into peoples' lives.

It's a cold day when you realize that all you've ever believed in were tricks and illusions. Beautifully crafted and elegantly played maybe – but tricks nonetheless. The priest might point to heaven, but it's what's going on in his other hand that you should be concerned about. And I was no better. Painting my little pictures to Jon. Making him believe in the something that wasn't there.

I'd have done anything to put that right.

I climbed the shallow hill toward Jon's grave. The air cold and gray. The sky like ash above the trees.

I reached the grave – the broken earth still soft around the wooden plaque that bore his name.

I sat down in the grass and closed my eyes.

Quiet. Just the hush of the city in the distance.

'I'm sorry,' I said. 'I should have been a better brother to you. I should have told you. I messed it all up, Jon. I'm sorry.'

I wiped my eyes, then stared at his name – the delicate letters carved into the wood. I waited for some memory of his voice to echo in me. Some forgotten moment of forgiveness that I could hang on to.

But the silence continued to pour though me. The earth remained cold beneath me. And the sky drifted on.

I was alone.

I picked myself off the ground, then headed over to an empty bench on the cemetery path just behind me. I grabbed the whiskey bottle from my jacket and took a sip.

I didn't know what I was going to do now. I just sat there and gazed emptily at the handful of visitors in the cemetery. A young woman adjusting flowers by a headstone way down the hill. Another reading a book as she sat in the rose garden. As she turned a page, she nodded politely to a guy in his late sixties strolling through the garden. The guy smiled back, then headed up the path toward me.

He stopped beside me and gestured at the free end of the bench.

'You mind?' he said.

I shook my head.

He sat down, then reached into his tweed jacket. He produced a small plastic container and peeled off the lid. Inside was a slice of cake, a plastic fork and a napkin. He grabbed the fork, then scooped up a mouthful of cake.

He eyed me sheepishly. 'My wife,' he said. 'She doesn't let me eat this stuff any more.'

I said nothing.

He took another mouthful, then glanced down at the container. He held it out to me. 'You want?'

I shook my head again. I stared at what was left of the whiskey bottle, then offered it to him.

'No,' he said. 'But thank you.'

He smiled warmly. He looked like a grandfather. Gray hair and matching mustache. Gentle, bespectacled eyes, and a portly build that spoke volumes about his love for desserts.

He took another mouthful of cake, then wiped his mustache clean with his fingers.

'That was an interesting video you posted,' he said.

I shot him a look.

'I've got a question for you,' he said. 'You killed the Bragers. Some others too, I hear. You enjoy it?'

My heart jumped a gear as I got to me feet. 'Who are you?'

'Did you?'

Only Ella knew what had happened with the Bragers. I scanned the cemetery. A pearl black BMW 7 was parked near the gates. Like the one that pulled up that night at DND Storage.

I eyed the old man carefully. 'You're the guy Tully worked for,' I said.

'Apparently not,' he replied.

'You're government.'

He shrugged. 'I have friends who are.'

He took another mouthful of cake, then glanced back at me.

'You enjoy killing, Michael?'

I held his look. I wouldn't have answered if I hadn't been in the shadow of Jon's grave.

I shook my head

'Good,' he said. 'Good, that's what I wanted to hear.'

He put away the fork, then wiped his mouth with the napkin.

'I believe in the law, Michael. That said, I'm not averse to employing people who haven't always shared that perspective. I often find these people can be very effective at protecting the same laws that once defined them as unsavory.'

'Unsavory, am I?'

'Yeah. I'd like to offer you a job.'

I laughed. 'Forget it.'

'A man of your talents? A whole world of trouble you could put right.'

I noticed a couple of mean-looking suits on the hill. The old man's bodyguards. I eyed them uneasily.

'There's no threat here, Michael,' said the old man. 'No one's going to force you to do this.'

'Good.'

'You want to return to stealing cars, be my guest, it's of no real interest to me.'

'I'm done with that.'

'Then what?' he said. He leaned back on the bench. 'I understand you had a love for magic as a child. Perhaps you could return to that. Earn yourself a spot entertaining tourists on cruise ships.'

I shot him a bitter look, then started walking toward the main gates.

'I'm offering you a chance to join the fight, Michael,' he said. 'To honor your brother. Keep some part of him alive.'

I slowed to a halt – the words clinging to me like iron.

As I stared back at Jon's grave, the old man got up from the bench. He strolled over and stood beside me.

He nodded toward Jon's plaque. 'I knew him,' he said. 'Not well, but we talked on a number of occasions. A man of good taste, I think. A fan of Mark Twain.'

He smiled to himself.

'But it's interesting,' he said. 'You know who wrote his favorite quote?'

I glanced at him for a moment, then nodded.

'Oscar Wilde,' he said. "Every saint has a past, and every sinner has a future." He laughed. 'Damn right.'

He placed a comforting hand on my shoulder, then beckoned me to follow him.

'Come on,' he said. 'We've got a lot to discuss. Maggie's do a great peach cobbler, I'll buy you one.'

He headed down the hill toward his car. As he did, I gazed at Jon's grave.

I didn't know what it was that I'd hoped for. A sense of forgiveness? A glowing break in the clouds? Some fleeting moment of worldly magic that I could read something into?

It may not have been the moment that I'd wanted – but if this is what it was going to take to put things right, then fair enough, Jon.

I took a final look at his plaque, then turned and followed the old man down the hill.

The End

About The Author

Born in London, Alex pursued a writing career that took him to Los Angeles where he created shows for Disney, Universal and NBC.

After five years in LA, and the constant request for him to come up with a vampire show that was 'kind of like The Office', Alex decided to write something purely for his own pleasure.

The result is his first novel 'Black Violet'. He is currently writing the second novel in the series

Proudly published by Accent Press

www.accentpress.co.uk